North Of Fifty-Four

A Crime Must Be Committed To Prevent A War

by

Nigel Seed

The Seventh Book In The Jim Wilson Series

www.nigelseedauthor.com

Copyright © 2018 Nigel Seed

The right of Nigel Seed to be identified as the author of this work has been asserted.

All rights reserved. No part of this publication may be reproduced, stored in a retrieval system, or transmitted, in any form, or by any means (electronic, mechanical, photocopying, recording, or otherwise), without the prior permission of the publisher. Any person who does any unauthorised act in relation to this publication may be liable to criminal prosecution and civil claims for damages.

This is a fictional work and all characters are drawn from the author's imagination. Any resemblance or similarities to persons either living or dead are entirely coincidental except where they are detailed in the factual chapter.

ISBN-13: 978-1721875948

ISBN-10: 1721875948

For Dr Henk Landa of Clinica San Carlos in Denia and the staff of Hospital Clinica Benidorm. Without their skill and care I would probably nothave been here to complete this book

Acknowledgments

We are all travellers in the wilderness of this world and the best that we can find in our travels is an honest friend.
-Robert Louis Stevenson

I have been blessed with a number of honest friends who have helped me by reading my book at the embryonic stages and giving me useful criticism. They know who they are, but they deserve a mention for putting up with me. My grateful thanks to Pam and John Fine, Glenn Wood, Brian Luckham and Peter Durant.

I have been privileged to work with an exceptional editor, Hilary Johnson, who has improved my work considerably. Any errors that are still there are all mine.

The biggest debt though is to my wife who has lived this project with me and been supportive throughout, especially when I was struggling

May 2nd 1982 in the South Atlantic

South of the Falkland Islands, in poor visibility, the Commander of the Royal Navy Churchill class attack submarine, HMS Conqueror, watched the Argentine Light Cruiser *General Belgrano* through his periscope. Sensors revealed that, somewhere close by, two destroyers were escorting the cruiser, though they were not visible at the moment.

Although the cruiser was outside the declared exclusion zone around the islands, a signal intercept the day before had revealed that the Argentine warships had been ordered to execute a pincer attack on the approaching British Task Force. The other half of the pincer was a second task group, led by the Argentine Carrier, ARA *Veinticinco de Mayo,* that was somewhere to the north of the islands.

Because of the order that the Argentine Naval Command had given, Prime Minister Margaret Thatcher had given orders that any enemy ships near the islands were to be attacked to protect the Task Force heading south to liberate the Falklands after the Argentine invasion. This order had been passed on to the Conqueror through Naval Headquarters at Northwood.

At 15:57, HMS Conqueror fired three Mark 8 torpedoes. Two of these struck the *Belgrano* fore and aft of her side armor. The first blew off the bow and the second struck in the aft machine room. Despite being at action stations, watertight doors throughout the ship were still open and the water rushed in, far too fast to be controlled. The ship went down by the bow and listed to port. Twenty minutes later the Captain ordered the crew to abandon ship and inflatable rafts were launched. Because of a total electrical failure caused by the explosions, the *Belgrano* was unable to send a distress call and her escorting destroyers were unaware of the attack. By the time they realised what had happened night had fallen and the weather had deteriorated.

Over the next two days 772 men were rescued by Argentine and Chilean ships, but 323 had died. Most had been killed by the explosion in the aft machine room. Conqueror dived and continued her patrol.

Following the loss of the *Belgrano*, the Argentine navy returned to base and played little part in the rest of the short war. Carrier-borne aircraft from the *Veinticinco de Mayo* were obliged to operate from land bases at the extreme end of their range, reducing their effectiveness considerably.

Chapter 1

Jim looked up from his newspaper as the café door slammed shut in the wind. He had expected it to be his wife arriving from her usual expedition to the dress shop, but instead he was looking at a stranger. The man looked completely out of place in this backwoods Canadian village with his well pressed suit and shiny black shoes.

As the man stood by the door his eyes slowly swept around the room before his gaze passed across Jim. The slight lift of his eyebrows did not escape Jim's notice and the way he walked across the room, directly towards him, confirmed that he was the one the stranger was looking for.

The man in the sharp pale grey suit stopped by Jim's table and bowed slightly. "You are Mr Wilson, perhaps?"

"I'm Jim Wilson. How can I help you?"

"May I sit? I have a business proposition for you."

"Really? Well sit yourself down. I've got time on my hands."

The well-dressed man pulled the chair out at the opposite side of the table and seated himself slowly. He waved the waitress away as she approached them, then turned and looked at Jim for a long moment.

"Made a mistake there," Jim said. "The coffee here is excellent, much better than that weak swill you'd get in one of those coffee chains."

"I have no taste for American-style food or coffee. I prefer more subtle tastes. Now, may I tell you my business?"

"Fire away. I'm all ears. Maybe we could start with your name?"

"Perhaps later, if we come to an agreement. I have a need for a pilot and an aircraft, both of which need to be capable of flying in and out of a difficult landing site on a lake."

"I see, but why come to me?"

"Mr Wilson, you have a remarkable reputation as a pilot in this area and I have seen the Beaver aircraft that is sitting on the waterway by your cabin. Together, I think that is a combination that would fit my needs."

"Well, it's very nice of you to say that, but I am going to have to decline. The aircraft belongs to the University of Vancouver and I am employed by them as well. I don't think they would look kindly on me using their aircraft for moonlighting. However, I don't want to disappoint you, so I can give you the names of a number of fine pilots who could help you out."

"Maybe you would reconsider when you hear the salary for this work. I think you will find it most attractive."

Jim smiled and shook his head slowly. "No doubt I would, but as I say, I have commitments that I can't break at present. Sorry, but the answer has to be no, I'm afraid."

The man sat very still gazing at Jim, who looked back calmly. Jim noticed that with his jet black hair and slightly almond-shaped eyes the man might possibly be of Asian descent, though his English was flawless. Eventually the man gave a small nod and stood up. As he slid the chair back under the table he looked down at Jim.

"I am disappointed that you feel unable to help me. I shall have to find another solution to my problem. We may meet again."

Jim watched the man leave the café and then waved his coffee cup at the waitress for a refill. She walked over with the coffee jug and filled his cup.

"Seems your friend didn't want my coffee. You tell him how good it is?"

Jim smiled up at her. "I certainly did, but he seems not to like strong tastes, or so he said. You seen him around here before?"

"Maybe. There's been a couple of Chinese guys staying at Tom's hotel for a day or so. He could be one of them."

Jim nodded and then smiled as Megan came through the door with packages wrapped in brown paper. "Looks like I'll need another cup of that coffee of yours, eh? Make it a strong one; Megan likes it thick enough to strip paint."

He stood up and pulled the chair out for his partner, who sat down with a sigh.

"Coffee's coming. Looks like you had a successful shopping expedition. Buy anything nice?"

Megan shook her long hair back off her face and smiled across the table at him. "Not for me this time. All this is for the baby. She's growing like a weed, so we need everything in the next size up."

Jim nodded and waited as the waitress brought the coffee for Megan. "Did you see the Chinese guy who just left? He offered me a job flying for him."

"The one in the pale suit? Yes, I saw him. He was staring at me as I came across the road. It felt a bit creepy."

"He seemed OK to me. A bit disappointed when I turned him down. You're probably imagining things."

Megan took a sip of the strong black brew. "And your memory needs a reminder."

"Really? How so?"

"Jim, the last time you sat in this coffee shop and told someone they were imagining things, some guy tried to shoot you an hour later. I'm telling you, there was something creepy about the way he looked at me."

"OK, OK. We'll keep an eye out for him, but now let's go home and relieve Mary from her babysitting. There are times when I envy her being deaf around our daughter. It must be a huge advantage."

"Daniela's not that bad. All babies cry when they're hungry or upset."

Jim smiled. "And our little princess is no different, but if she carries on at this volume she's going to be an opera singer. We'll have to get Mary to teach her that sign language that you two use. Maybe that will quiet her down a bit. Come on then, let's go."

They walked out to the parking lot and went towards the battered red pickup truck. Jim looked around as Megan loaded her packages into the vehicle, but he could see nobody watching them. He had a feeling Megan could well be right, though; with her part heritage from the original inhabitants of the west coast, she was more perceptive than most.

He climbed into the driver's seat and looked across the cab at her. "You may be right. You usually are, so we'll keep an eye out when we are in town, but for now let's go home and let Mary get back to her dad before nightfall."

They drove out of the village until they reached the start of the track through the forest down to their cabin by the waterside. Jim drove carefully down the bumpy surface and parked the pickup before helping Megan carry her purchases and the food they had collected earlier into the cabin. Once Megan's conversation with Mary, in sign language, was finished Mary waved to Jim and left for home. Since Daniela was quiet for the time being, they settled down by the massive log burning stove, Megan with another coffee and Jim with the newspaper he had bought in the village.

Megan looked across the top of her coffee mug and watched Jim for a moment or two. The light through the window behind her was picking out the flecks of grey hair that were appearing on his head, in addition to the two small patches of grey at the temples. His eyes were still that clear blue she loved and he didn't need glasses yet. He really was quite handsome, she decided.

He felt her watching him and looked up from the paper. "Regretting hooking up with me?"

She shook her head a little. "Not yet. I think I'll keep you a while longer."

They both looked round as the cabin door swung open to see two men standing in the entrance. One was the man in the sharp suit Jim had met earlier and the other could have been his twin. Jim was about to tell them to get the hell out when he saw the automatic pistol in the hand of the second man.

"Forgive the intrusion, Mr Wilson, but our conversation earlier did not reach a satisfactory conclusion, at least not for me. We need to correct that."

Chapter 2

Jim looked across at Megan. "Sorry. It looks like you were right all along."

Megan gave him a small smile and turned to face the two intruders. "So what can we do for you two gentlemen?"

The man in the sharp suit looked at Megan and bowed very slightly. "A reasonable approach. That will make things much easier all round. May I sit?"

Megan nodded. "Please do. The sooner you state your business, the sooner you can leave and take your friend and his ugly pistol with you."

The man smiled sadly. "Unfortunately I do not have that luxury. I am afraid that to avoid any unnecessary unpleasantness I must insist that Mr Wilson comes and works for me."

Jim shook his head. "I've already told you that no matter what the price you are offering is, I am just not available and the gun doesn't help."

"The price has changed and will persuade you, I am certain. If you cooperate and do just as you are told, this lovely lady and your daughter may stay alive. My companion here and some other colleagues will ensure that they stay safe while you are away and will keep them supplied with food and any other essentials. If you do not wish to join us or if you attempt to betray me they will be dead within minutes. A very simple arrangement, I think."

Jim started to get up, but stopped as the large pistol swung towards Megan. He sagged back into his chair and looked across at her.

"And what is to stop me calling the authorities the minute you leave?" asked Megan.

"Ah, a good question, madam. Intelligent as well as beautiful. If you contact anyone, then Mr Wilson here will be the one to die and then, of course, we will come for you and the baby. Plus, of course, we will remove your telephones and computer and the rifle you have mounted over the door will be put away safely as well." He smiled calmly at them both. "You see, you really do not have a choice. I need someone to fly into and out of a difficult location for a while. At the end of the operation I will vanish from your lives and everybody will be safe and happy."

"How do we know you will keep your word?" Jim asked.

"You don't, but then again what are your choices? I will give you ten minutes to pack what you need and then we are leaving. Just hand luggage will do for now; anything else you need will be provided."

Jim sat still and contemplated the man sitting opposite him. "You're bluffing. You simply cannot be serious."

The man in the chair sighed a little and then reached under his jacket to produce a pistol, which he aimed at Megan. "I was hoping to avoid the need for a demonstration of my sincerity, but if you insist. Chung, go and kill the child."

The second man swung round and started walking towards the bedroom where the baby slept. Megan surged to her feet.

"No! You can't!"

"Chung, wait a moment. We may have a solution."

"Jim, you have to do it. I'll be all right. Please."

Jim nodded slowly and turned his head towards the Chinese man sitting across from him. He contemplated the man, who looked back at him without expression.

"OK, it seems I have little choice. What do I call you?"

"Very sensible. You may call me Mr Han. Now it is time for you to pack and say your goodbyes."

"Not quite, Mr Han," Jim said quietly. "You are blackmailing me into working for you, so I assume this is something illegal. You need to know that if my family are hurt in any way, this world is not big enough for you to hide in."

Han smiled. "An empty threat, as you will come to understand, but you have my word that your family is safe, as long as you continue to do as you are told. Who knows, you may even enjoy the challenge."

Twenty minutes later Megan heard the engine of the Beaver floatplane cough into life and then settle down to a steady beat. She walked to the window that overlooked the waterway and watched as the yellow and white aircraft taxied into the right position for its take-off run along the waterway that ran past the front of the cabin. She heard the engine note change as the old plane surged forward, leaving white wakes behind the floats, then it leapt into the air and started a slow turn to the north. She watched as it grew smaller and then disappeared into the haze. She brushed a single tear from her cheek and walked through to check on the baby.

Chapter 3

The vibration in the fuselage eased as Jim throttled back into the cruise. He looked across at Mr Han, who sat calmly in the co-pilot's seat wearing a lightweight intercom headset. With the aircraft now settled on a northerly course and heading up the coast and across the jumble of islands and shining waterways that wended their way between them, Jim thumbed the button on his control column to allow him to speak to his passenger.

"So when are you thinking of telling me where we are going?"

"This seems like a good time. We will be flying to just north of the town of Prince Rupert, on the coast. We will then turn north-east towards the abandoned village of Kitsault, at which point we turn north again."

"And then?" Jim asked.

"Then we will come to a narrow lake, in a steep-sided valley that has a sharp bend in it. There you will land the aircraft, taking care not to let the wing strike the cliff face as we turn in."

"I take it that's what happened to your last pilot?"

"Indeed. Most regrettable. He was bringing my immediate superior to see me. Neither of them survived. The wreckage is still somewhere at the foot of the cliff or on the bottom of the lake. I suggest you do not examine it too closely on the way in, as that is the trickiest part of the approach."

"What happens once we get there?"

"Once you have landed the aircraft we will taxi it along the lake to where it is to be stored when not in use. A boat will meet us and take us to the cabin where you will be staying. You will be well treated, I assure you, and the cabin is quite comfortable and I will even provide some entertainment for you. I need my pilot in good condition. You are less expendable than some of my other guests."

"Other guests? What does that mean?"

Mr Han smiled slightly. "All will become clear to you once we arrive. I will conduct the guided tour myself, tomorrow. I need to see what progress has been made in my absence."

"Progress with what?"

"Enough," Han said testily. "I grow tired of this idle conversation. I have told you that you will learn all you need tomorrow."

Jim turned his head forward and checked the instruments. The old plane was singing along as sweet as a nut. His care over the winter months had corrected any minor issues and now his aircraft was in as good a shape as when she left the de Havilland factory. He checked the chart and compared it to the terrain they were flying over.

"Right, Mr Han, we're just coming alongside Prince Rupert, so it's time for our turn inland."

"Good, but not quite yet. Carry on past the town and then follow the large waterway between Wales Island and Somerville Island. Then, as I told you, turn due north just short of Kitsault village. From there I will direct you."

Jim swung the aircraft into a gentle turn to follow the waterway that Han had identified. With Wales Island to his left and Somerville Island to the right he lined the aircraft up to the north-east along the broad, shining inlet. As the village of Kitsault came in sight he turned due north so that they never crossed the US border into Alaskan airspace. Han sat up and peered through the windscreen.

He glanced across at the air speed indicator. "At this speed you should see a jagged peak directly in front of us in about ten minutes. That marks the bend in the lake we are to land on. The approach should be to the right of the pinnacle with a turn just by it."

"I'll need to fly over the lake to make an assessment before we attempt a landing if it's as tricky as you say."

"A wise precaution. I have no wish to join my old supervisor in the afterlife, at least not yet."

Jim stared ahead until the jagged peak appeared and then lined the aircraft up to pass to the right of it. As he flew past and banked left he looked down through the pilot's door window. The lake was narrow and the mountain rose up steeply from the water on both sides. The bend by the jagged rock was tight, but not impossible. He saw a building at the end of the left-hand arm of the lake and assumed that was his target. He made another circuit of the lake looking for options.

"This grows tiresome, Mr Wilson. I think it is time for you to land."

Jim levelled the aircraft and looked across at Han. "You know," he said, "when I did my basic flying training with the Army Air Corps they used to hammer a little maxim into us that's stayed with me."

"And what was that, pray?"

"Fail to plan and you plan to fail. I think maybe your original pilot was too cocky for his own good. Still, I'm ready now, so tighten your seat harness: this may be a little rough."

As the aircraft lined up on the right-hand arm of the bent lake Jim heaved his own harness tight to make sure he stayed firmly in his seat. He throttled back and allowed the old aircraft to sink towards the steep-sided valley. As they dropped in he glanced at the rock walls that flashed past them on either side. He swallowed and waited for his moment. As the turn point arrived he put the aircraft into a sharp left-hand bank that took them around the rock and slipped them down towards the water below. Once round the turn, he levelled the wings and looked ahead. The sideslip had put them down close to the water and seconds later the floats kissed the surface and twin plumes of snow white spray erupted behind them.

Jim eased the throttle back and allowed the aircraft to slow. He steered carefully towards the building that he could now see was a large wooden cabin set into the forest at the head of a shallow bay. A small boat with two men in it was already setting out from a low wooden dock and steering towards them.

"Cut your engine. The boat will tow the plane to its mooring."

Jim did as he was told and watched the boat slip below the aircraft nose and hook on a twin tow rope. The tow lines tensioned as the boat slowly and carefully pulled the Beaver to a small black buoy that floated near the dock. In moments the floats had been secured to the buoy and the boat moved alongside them. Jim had to admire the skill of the boat handler as he climbed down onto the float and stepped back along it to the cargo door. He reached in and grabbed his bag before climbing down into the boat.

As the boat puttered towards the dock Jim looked around. Apart from the cabin and the dock, the only sign of any unusual activity was a tumbled scree of rock and debris that flowed out of the forest and into the lake. What the devil was Han doing here? And how the hell was he going to get out of this?

Chapter 4

Megan sat in the rocking chair by the bay window that looked out onto the waterway beyond the thin screen of trees, holding Daniela in her arms. As she rocked, the baby drifted slowly to sleep, burbling gently as she did so. Megan's mind was racing, trying to find a way out of this before she or any of her small family were hurt. It seemed impossible, Han had both her and Jim over a barrel, but she had to make her child safe and she knew Jim would agree with that.

She stood up slowly and carefully, so as not to wake the little girl she cradled, and then walked quietly into the small room where the crib stood. Laying the baby down, she carefully covered her with the fluffy pink blanket. She straightened up and looked through the window as one of the Chinese men guarding her walked by.

She paused and then a small smile crossed her lips. She walked quickly to the front door and opened it. Walking down the short flight of steps, she turned and walked around to where the guard had been. As she turned the corner of the cabin she saw his head jerk up and he walked towards her.

"What you doing? You should be inside. Not walk around outside."

"I'm sorry, but I've just remembered, we have a problem."

"What problem? What has this to do with me?"

She paused and hoped this was going to work. "A friend of Jim's is due to visit us in about a week's time. I had forgotten in all the stress. I need to call him and tell him not to come."

The guard shook his head. "It is a trick. You are try to fool me."

She shook her head. "No, I'm really not. Listen, if I talk to him using the laptop computer you can sit out of sight and listen to everything I say. You will know I am not trying to be clever."

He paused and looked at her while he considered this. "I ask Mr Han. You go back inside. Go now."

Megan spun on her heel and walked back into the cabin. She was already working out the details of her plan.

Two hours later the guard walked into the cabin. He walked across the room and opened the padlocked cupboard, then returned, carrying her laptop computer. "Mr Han say is all right, but you be careful. He say I shoot the child if you say anything wrong."

Megan nodded as she took the laptop. "All right, I will sit at the table there and you can sit just around the corner where you can hear everything. Make sure you are out of sight or this won't work."

The guard looked to where she had pointed and nodded. He went and picked up a chair from one of the bunk rooms and placed it around the corner where he could not be seen by the laptop's camera. Megan checked the time and then went to the table and opened up the computer. She waited as the machine went through its short start-up routine and logged into the Internet. She called up the Skype program and then clicked on the icon to call Ivan, Jim's old Sergeant Major from his army days.

Just about 5000 miles away ex-Sergeant Major Ivan Thomas was working on the accounts for the church in rural Wiltshire, that he was now the custodian for. The old black Labrador was sitting beside him having his ears gently tickled by the large rough hands of a man who had served in some hard tours of duty. He heard the Skype signal for an incoming call and clicked on the icon. Megan's face appeared.

"Hi, Megan, what's up, or is this just a social call?"

"Hello, Ivan, nothing's up, but we need to change your travel plans."

Ivan, puzzled, was about to speak when he saw Megan's fingers signing. "*Play along.*"

"Oh really, what change do I need to make?" Ivan said.

"Jim has had to go into Vancouver for work, so it's not a good time for you to visit. We don't know how long he'll be away, so could you delay your flight?"

"*We're in trouble. Jim has been kidnapped and I am under guard. We need your help. If we contact the police, they'll kill us.*"

"That's a shame. I was looking forward to seeing you both. How is Jim, by the way? I haven't heard from him for a while."

"*I'll round Geordie up and we'll be there as fast as we can.*"

Megan smiled into the camera. "Oh, he's fine. He'll be disappointed not to have a couple of week's fishing with you. Maybe you can come later in the summer when he's back?"

"There's an armed guard on the cabin all the time. I think there are three or four of them taking turns."

Ivan nodded. "Yeah, that would be good. It should be a bit warmer then anyway."

"Hang in there. We'll get you out of this."

Megan sighed. "Sorry to mess you about like this, but it's only for a little while. Oh Lord, I'm sorry, Ivan I can hear the baby crying, I'll have to go. Bye."

"Hurry, please. This is scary and I'm worried about Jim."

"Not a problem. I'll see you later in the season."

"Be there before you know it."

The screen went black as Megan broke the connection and Ivan sat back in his chair. He had thought his days of adventure were over since he left the Army. Trust his old commander to get himself into trouble again. He reached for his mobile phone and called up the number for Geordie Peters. He placed the call and listened as it rang.

"Hello, Ivan. Nice to hear from you."

"You know, I miss the days when an incoming call was a mystery. Where are you?"

"I'm in Spain with Janet. Why?"

"Still with Jim's ex-wife? I take it that's working out for you both?"

Ivan heard the slight chuckle down the line. "It certainly is. She's still writing children's books and when I left the army, I got a job as a foreman with that construction company we used when we were over here last time. We get along really well, so life is good, if a bit quiet."

"Not so good in Canada. Jim's in trouble and he needs our help, or at least Megan does to start with and then Jim."

"Oh crap! What's he done this time?"

"No idea, but Megan is scared and she doesn't scare easily. Can you come?"

"Undomesticated equines could not keep me away."

"Let me guess, a *Star Trek* quote?"

"No, *Stargate* this time."

"Call me when you've booked and I'll meet you at Heathrow. And Geordie …"

"Yes?"

"Don't hang about, mate. I get the feeling this one is serious."

Chapter 5

The British Airways flight to Vancouver landed on time, so, with only hand luggage to carry, the two men were walking towards the car hire office by seven-thirty in the evening. The four-wheel drive pickup truck they had ordered was waiting for them and, having declined the offer of an upgrade to a luxury saloon, they started heading north. The remarkable ability of soldiers to sleep anywhere when the opportunity arises had stood them in good stead and they were rested after the flight. Even so, as they drove out of the Vancouver suburbs Geordie made himself comfortable in the cab of the truck and went to sleep.

After three hours of driving Ivan pulled into a truck stop, nudged Geordie awake, and they went in for a something to eat and a rest. They sat in the booth and sipped the strong brew before either of them spoke.

"So then, Ivan, you've had plenty of time to think on the way here. Do we have a cunning plan yet?"

Ivan put down his coffee mug carefully, and looked at Geordie. "Not really, mate. We still don't know enough to make any decisions. I've got as far as getting close to the cabin, then sneaking through the trees to see the lie of the land. After that we improvise and overcome."

A smile lit up Geordie's dark features. "No change there then. I wonder if that trap door in the cabin floor is still accessible. It might be an idea to sneak in and speak to Megan up front. She must know about the opposition. In any event, once we have Megan and the baby out of there, what next?"

"We get them somewhere safe and then we start to worry about the boss. I just wonder what the hell they are getting him to do for them that would justify all this. Anyway, I was going to take advice from Megan about where to take them, once we have them free."

Geordie nodded. "How about weapons? If these characters are armed, a little firepower might come in handy."

Ivan gave Geordie one of his rare smiles. "That one I had thought of. At the end of the last event we had at the cabin, the local First Nation people who helped us had collected all the bad guys' weapons."

"Yeah, but the RCMP took those away from the Heiltsuk folk when they turned up for the prisoners."

"They did, but the pile in the back of the Mounties' truck was smaller than the pile the local lads had collected. My guess is that a few choice pieces were slipped away before the authorities got there."

"So we go and see David Red Cloud before we start anything?"

"No, I don't think so. First, we see what we are up against, then we go and find David. You finished? It's your turn to drive."

Ivan went to the counter of the diner and paid for the coffee and food while Geordie went out and started the truck. Ivan joined him carrying a folded map and a small flashlight.

"Do we need that?"

Ivan grunted. "We might. The SatNav is hopeless out here and the map from the car hire place expects people to stay around the city and we ran off the top of their map about an hour ago."

With Geordie driving, they continued north turning onto smaller roads as they left the main highway. Another two hours brought them to places they started to recognise and after driving through the village nearest to the cabin, they came to the track into the forest that they were looking for. They drove past the turning and parked the truck in the trees where it would not be obvious to any passing vehicles.

"OK, Geordie, ready for a walk?"

"Always ready for a stroll in the moonlight with you, Ivan."

"Ha! Right we'll take the track to start with. I don't want to get turned around in the forest in the early hours of the morning. We'll go through the trees once we get closer."

"You really are making this up as you go along, aren't you?"

"Yep. Any problems with that?"

"Starting to feel like being back in the army. Lead on, MacDuff. I always enjoy the mystery tour."

Chapter 6

Ivan and Geordie walked slowly and carefully down the rough track, grateful for the silver light of an almost full moon. As they neared the cabin Ivan signalled to Geordie and they split up with Ivan heading for the front of the building and around to where the rocky beach was washed by the waters of the Pacific that filled the waterway. Geordie slipped into the trees and walked carefully on the silent pine needles until he could see the rough wooden walls of the cabin in front of him.

Sinking to his knees and then on to his belly, Geordie wormed his way into the crawl space beneath the large cabin. He was aiming to come up inside the main room through the trapdoor that he knew from previous visits was there. He could only hope that Megan had nor slid the bolt across and locked it. He found the hatch and gently pressed it upwards. He was in luck; the entry way was not locked. It creaked as he pushed against the rusty hinges. With the hatch raised just above floor level he peered into the dark room as much as he could. He saw nothing and decided to risk opening it all the way.

Pushing the door up, he stood up ready to hoist himself into the cabin, but froze when the cold steel touched his neck. Keeping very still, he swivelled his eyes as far as they would go, but couldn't see the assailant who stood beside him.

Drawing a quiet breath, he said, "I take it this isn't the back door to Woolworths then?"

He heard the quick intake of breath from behind him and then the knife was gone as Megan dropped to her knees and threw her arms around him. "Thank God you've come. I've been terrified."

"That's OK, bonny lass, the cavalry's here. Can I get out of this hole yet?"

Megan pulled back and watched him climb through the trapdoor then close it gently behind him. "Is Ivan not with you?"

Even in the darkened room Geordie's broad smile lit up his face. "Oh he's here, never fear. He's just having a skulk round outside, to see what's what. He'll be along soon for breakfast."

"Does he know about the guards they have watching me?"

"Yeah, we know. He's gone to have a look for the one on duty. Where is he?"

"They usually sit down on the big rock by the totem pole at night. I hear them talking when they hand over."

Geordie walked to the bay window at the front of the cabin and peered out to the water that he could see gleaming in the moonlight. Although he could see the totem that showed the location of the cabin to visitors who arrived by boat, he couldn't see the guard.

"How long ago did they change shift, do you know?"

"About an hour ago, I think. Why?"

"An hour is a good time for a sentry to get bored and sleepy, if he doesn't have the sergeant of the guard checking on him. Do they patrol round or just sit there?"

Megan stepped up behind him. "I don't know. Come away from the window, will you? I don't want him to see you or they might get nasty."

Geordie chuckled. "One advantage of this skin colour is I don't show up too well at night, and through a window he's not going to spot me. Now what about the patrolling?"

"I really don't know. During the day they walk around, but I'm not sure what they do at night. What are you going to do?"

"Do? Nothing right now, except go and make some tea, ready for when Ivan comes in."

"Shouldn't you be out there helping him?"

"The only person outside who needs help is your guard, if he runs into Ivan."

"But, Geordie, he has a gun."

"And Ivan has the two most powerful fists I know. Yon fellah with the gun will be no trouble and you can take that one to the bank."

Chapter 7

At the edge of the treeline Ivan lay perfectly still, watching the guard. He could see the moonlight reflected off the barrel of the weapon the man held across his lap as he sat by the totem pole. The rocky beach, with all the small pebbles, made a silent approach to take the sentry down impossible.

Ivan smiled to himself and picked up a handful of beach stones. He flicked one off to his right and was rewarded by a small sound. In the still night, the noise carried to the sentry, who stood up and looked towards where the sound had come from. The twig that Ivan snapped between his fingers put the guard on alert and he swung the rifle around to a ready position. The next two small stones landed together and gave a reasonable approximation of someone stumbling in the dark.

The man with the gun walked slowly towards where the sounds had come from. Ivan could see the whites of his eyes as he scanned the trees. He passed by the Welshman lying in the leaf litter and moved slowly into the forest.

Years of army training had given Ivan an uncanny ability to move silently despite his size. He rose up from his hiding place and walked up behind his quarry. The first the guard knew of his approach was when a massive hand gripped his shoulder at the base of his neck. The firm grip on the pressure point paralysed him and seconds later he passed out. Ivan caught his weapon as it fell and allowed the man to slump to the ground. He checked the pulse in his neck and then searched his pockets for spare ammunition and his phone.

Ivan turned and walked up to the cabin, tapping on the door before he opened it. The door swung open and Geordie smiled at him.

"Got yourself a trophy, I see. How's laughing boy?"

"Out for the count. He had some keys on him. Are they any of yours, Megan?"

Megan crossed the room and hugged the big man. "Thanks for coming, Ivan. I feel a lot safer with you two here. And yes, those are my keys. They locked my phone and my laptop away in the big cupboard after I spoke to you."

Ivan nodded. "Well then let's get them and then get the hell out of here before our boy wakes up or his relief arrives."

"How long will he be out, do you think?" Geordie asked.

"Usually about an hour and then he wakes up with a stinking headache. Can you pack what you need in that time, Megan?"

Megan turned round from the cupboard with the laptop and a phone in her hands. "I packed as soon as I knew you were coming. We just need to grab the bags, the baby and the dog and we can go. Where are we going, by the way?"

"No idea. We'll work that out when we're clear. Geordie, can you go and get the truck? Megan, better bring some food for the baby. We don't know how long this will take."

"All sorted out and ready. Be careful, Geordie. Do you want to take the Winchester with you? It's in the cupboard."

Geordie smiled, picked up the rifle and opened the front door. He checked around, then trotted down the short set of steps and began to jog along the track back to where the pickup truck was hidden. He was back in less than a quarter of an hour and helped Ivan load Megan's bags into the bed of the truck. They made a bed of rolled blankets in the rear seat for the baby and loaded Bracken, the collie dog, into the front footwell, where he settled down immediately. Megan climbed in, holding the baby, and settled her down. Ivan put the truck into gear, then set off for the highway.

As he pulled out onto the road Ivan looked over his shoulder. "Any ideas about where would be safe, Megan?"

"How about our apartment in Vancouver, near the university?"

Ivan shook his head. "Much too obvious. They could find you just by looking in the phone book."

"Here's a thought," said Geordie, turning round to look at Megan. "Where's that rather attractive photographer friend of yours? She was damned useful when we were on the run before."

"Kelly? I'm not sure. She's still doing work for the *National Geographic*, so she could be anywhere."

"Is it worth a call?"

Megan delved into the bag she had beside her and found the mobile phone. She switched it on and waited until it had completed its start-up sequence and had found a signal. She called up the directory and selected Kelly's number.

She heard it ring and then a sleepy voice. "What? Do you know what bloody time it is? Who is this?"

"Hi, Kelly, it's Megan. I'm in trouble and I need some help."

The voice from the other end of the call changed. "What do you need, babe?"

"First of all, where are you?"

"You remember the cabin I was in when you last needed help? Well, it's been rebuilt and I'm there again. I'm doing a photo assignment on bears and wolves for *National Geographic*."

"Any chance we can stay with you a while?"

"Who do you mean by we?"

"Me, the baby and I've also got Ivan and Geordie with me."

"Of course you can stay, but where's Jim?" Kelly asked.

"I'll tell you when we get there. We'll be a while, so go back to sleep. And Kelly, thanks."

Megan rested the phone in her lap and sighed. "You got all that? You remember the way?"

Ivan nodded. "No problem. You settle down and we'll have you there in no time."

Megan smiled and sat back in her seat. She looked down at the phone and saw there were text messages waiting for her. She opened up the application and gave a sharp intake of breath.

"Ivan, there's a message from Jim on here. He sent it two days ago."

"What does it say?"

Megan touched the message and it opened up. "It says 'North of fifty-four de …' That's all. It looks like the message isn't finished. What does that mean?"

Ivan shook his head. "No idea. We'll try and work it out when we get to Kelly's place."

Chapter 8

The room Jim had been taken to was a reasonable size, but sparsely furnished. It was set in the corner of the building, with one window looking out over the lake and the other facing the forest. Apart from the bed there were two wooden chairs and a table, nothing more. Through a second door Jim found there was a small bathroom. He had heard the main door being locked behind him as he came in, but he tried it anyway. With the door locked and the bars across the two windows, it looked like he was to stay here until needed.

More in hope than expectation he slipped the small mobile phone out of his pocket and flipped it open. Han had taken his usual phone, but had not known about the emergency back-up that was kept in the plane. Against the odds there was a weak signal. He listened at the door for a moment or two and then went to sit down in one of the wooden chairs.

He had hardly started his message when the door slammed open and an angry man stormed in, yelling at him in Chinese. Jim just had time to press the send key before the small phone was slapped out of his hand and spun away across the room to shatter against the wall. Jim waited while the angry man walked across the room and stamped on the electronic device to ensure there was no hope of repair.

Jim sat still and waited for the blow he was sure was coming. To his surprise, the man walked back to the doorway before turning around to look at him and spat on the floor before slamming the door closed and relocking it. Then Jim noticed the eyehole in the upper door panel. So much for privacy. He had no idea if the incomplete message would have gone before the phone disintegrated and the little he had managed to write would not be overly helpful.

    He stood up and went to the window. The lake ran along the steep-sided valley before it vanished around the sharp bend at the base of the jagged cliff. There was no sign of the aircraft wreckage that Han had spoken about. He guessed it must be somewhere at the bottom of those frigid waters. He sighed and went to lie down on the bed.

Chapter 9

Ivan drove the truck slowly and carefully up the steep, rough track towards Kelly's cabin so as not to upset the baby. He pulled into the rough parking area in front of the wooden building and climbed out. Geordie left the vehicle and opened the door for Megan.

"You need me to hold the baby for you?"

"Thanks, that would help. Here you are."

Geordie cradled the small child and stepped back to let Megan exit. As they turned around, the door of the cabin opened and Kelly stood there with her long brown hair cascading over her shoulders. To either side of her were her dogs, both were Welsh Border Collies. She gave them a quiet word of command and they sat down, still staring at the newcomers.

As Ivan walked forward Kelly held up a hand. "Hang on, Ivan – you remember the routine with my dogs?"

"I remember the dog whispering performance, *Cariad*. Go ahead."

Ivan stood still as Kelly walked to him and placed a hand on his arm. She turned to the dogs and spoke clearly.

"Friend, friend."

She walked to the other two visitors and went through the same routine. "It's OK, they won't bother you now. In fact, they will probably be delighted with the company."

Megan kissed Kelly on the cheek. "What about Bracken? He's in the truck."

"No problem. Paddy, Sam, come!"

The two dogs trotted down the short stairway from the cabin and sat in front of Kelly. "OK, Megan, bring him out."

Megan put her collie on a leash and brought him around the end of the truck. Kelly walked to him and placed a hand on the dog's back. She turned to her own dogs and spoke again.

"Friend, friend."

The two dogs wagged their tails immediately and came to sniff the new arrival. Kelly straightened up and looked at Megan.

"They'll be fine. Now how about introducing me to the little one?"

The two women walked across to where Geordie was standing with the baby in his arms. Kelly opened up the blankets around the child's face and smiled down at her.

"Hello, Daniela, I'm your Aunty Kelly and you're going to live with me for a while." She looked up. "Come on, then. I'm just ready to make a breakfast and then you can tell me the story. Hopefully this time it doesn't get my cabin burned down."

With the baby settled and breakfast done, Kelly sat and listened to the story of Jim's kidnapping and the blackmailing of Megan. "So you still can't call the Mounties in then?"

Ivan shook his head. "Much too risky. We are counting on them keeping Jim safe, if only because he is useful to them. If they just don't tell him that Megan has done a runner then he will keep doing whatever they need to keep her alive until we find him and tell him she's safe."

Kelly nodded slowly. "But what next? Megan and Daniela are safe here, but what about Jim?"

Ivan looked at Geordie and then back to Kelly. "Now we go find him."

"How? North of fifty-four is not much of a clue. What the hell does it mean anyway?"

Geordie shifted in his chair. "I've had a thought about that. If you've got a map of Canada we can see if it works."

Kelly said nothing, but went across to the big old desk pushed into the corner of the room and returned with a folded map. Geordie and Ivan spread the map across the table and bent over it.

"Here, Ivan," said Geordie, pointing at the northern end of British Columbia. "Latitude 54 runs across here, just around Prince Rupert and Graham Island. Could that be what Jim was trying to tell us?"

Ivan looked down, contemplating the map. "It makes sense, but look at the map; it's a bloody huge area to the north. Hell, the whole of Alaska is there."

Geordie nodded. "True, but he said 'North of Fifty Four', not fifty-five. So my thinking is that he is somewhere between the two."

"OK, I'll buy that, but it still leaves an enormous area. How the devil do we search that for one small aircraft and one retired army officer with just us two?"

Megan spoke quietly from behind them. "Use the First Nations."

Ivan turned. "What?"

"The First Nations. You remember, that's what we call the native peoples who were here way before the Europeans arrived."

"I know who the First Nation people are. I was asking how we use them."

Megan nodded and sat forward. "There's not just the Heiltsuk group who live near us. There's a lot of them all up the coast in different bands and tribes. If they keep an eye out, you've got a lot of people looking and they know this area better than anyone else."

Geordie and Ivan looked at each other and smiled. "David Red Cloud," they said in unison.

"Come on, then," Kelly said. "Who or what is David Red Cloud?"

Geordie turned to her and smiled. "David is a member of the Heiltsuk people who live along the coast by Megan's cabin. He's a superb wood carver and he uses that name for his clients who can't pronounce his native name."

"And his daughter, Mary, is our babysitter. She's deaf, which is why I learned to sign and could get the message to Ivan. He could sign because his younger sister was deaf."

Geordie smiled broadly. "So we have a starting point. When do we go and see David?"

Ivan folded the map. "First thing in the morning. We get Megan and the baby all organised properly here today and then we leave first thing. We need to see if he can set us up with some better weapons as well, since we don't know what we are walking into."

"I'll stay with Megan's Winchester," Geordie said. "With the scope on it, it makes a bonny target rifle."

"No, we'll leave that with Megan. She's used to it. David will have something for you no doubt and I don't like the idea of these two being here unarmed apart from that shotgun of Kelly's."

Chapter 10

With the truck parked at the back of the small village by the waterway, the two men walked across to the cabin that they knew belonged to David Red Cloud. They could hear the sounds of him working behind his cabin and saw his carving on the fallen tree trunk behind the house as they walked around to find him. The totem he was working on was a tall one with many exotic symbols that would be even more impressive once painted.

The dark-complexioned man with the almond eyes and the scarred hands straightened up as they came towards him. He waited silently until they reached him before nodding a greeting.

"Hi, David, where's this one going?"

"Ivan, Geordie, good to see you again. This will stand in front of one of the high schools in Vancouver. Some fool burned the last one down."

"That's a shame. Look, cutting to the chase, we've got trouble and we need your help again. It's serious."

David laid his chisel and mallet down on the carved tree trunk and gestured for them to follow him. "In the house to talk about problems. Mary will be pleased to see you again, Ivan, and you, too, Geordie. She often speaks of you."

Together they walked around to the front of the cabin and in through the door. As they walked in the girl by the stove turned from the pot she was stirring and her face lit up with a beautiful smile.

Her hands flew into a blur as she signed to Ivan, who returned her greeting in the same way.

"Hell, David," Geordie said, "your daughter gets more beautiful each time I see her. Living out here in the forests must agree with her."

He glanced at Mary and noticed her hands were still and she was blushing.

"You do know she can also lip read, don't you?" Ivan asked.

"I'd forgotten, but it never hurts to give a lovely young lady the praise she richly deserves."

David grunted. "Enough of the chatter. What do you need?"

Ivan sat in the carved wooden chair by the fireplace that David indicated and Geordie took the other.

"OK, straight to business it is. David, Jim's been kidnapped and is being forced to work for some Chinese guy. They were holding Megan and the baby in the cabin and had promised to kill them if Jim didn't play along."

"What do they need him to do?"

"We're not sure, but it's something to do with the Beaver floatplane. They forced him to fly that out of here and they were talking about what an accomplished pilot he is."

David looked from one to the other and, seeing no sign that this was a joke, he nodded slowly. "I was wondering where the aircraft was. I haven't seen it for days. All right, what can I do?"

"The only clue we have is a partial text message he managed to get out. It said 'North of

Fifty Four de..' and we are guessing that means north of fifty-four degrees latitude."

"Where is that?"

Geordie pulled out the map and spread it on the floor. "It seems to be somewhere around Prince Rupert or Digby Island. But apart from that, we don't know."

"I don't see what you want from me. That's a huge area. I can give you a boat to go there and I can come and help you search, but what else?"

"We were hoping you could contact people along the coast north of here and get them to watch for the plane," Ivan said. "If we can spot that we have a start point and then we might take you up on the offer of a boat."

David nodded. "I can do that, no problem."

Geordie looked up from the map. "How do you do that? Drums?"

"You've been watching too many cowboy movies. If I phone each of the tribal elders groups they will spread the word around their people. You'll have eyes watching from all along the coast by tonight."

Chapter 11

"Ah, good morning, Mr Wilson. Do sit down and join me for breakfast. I take it you slept well?"

Jim carried on walking towards the large table where Mr Han sat waiting for him. The guard who had summoned him remained by the door, watching. Jim pulled out one of the heavy high-backed chairs and sat down. Before he could speak, a servant in a white waiter's jacket had swooped from nowhere and placed cutlery and a snow-white napkin in front of him.

"Tell him what you want to eat and he will bring it to you."

"What are my choices?"

"You may order the customary breakfast of this country if you wish, or something more civilised."

Jim looked at the waiter who stood silently by him and ordered ham and eggs over easy. The man bowed and moved swiftly into the next room.

"Well, Mr Wilson, or should I call you Major Wilson? Your mention of the Army Air Corps on the way here intrigued me, so I had my people check into your background. You have had an interesting life. They even found a video of you online just after you had crash-landed an old aircraft on the runway at Gibraltar. I'm sure that will make a fascinating story one evening, when we have some time to spare."

Jim held his tongue and waited for his food to arrive. He sipped at the coffee that had been put in front of him without him noticing. He waited for Han to carry on.

"Today, as I promised, I will take you to see what this is all about. I think you will be surprised, but I think you will also see why we need such secrecy."

The door opened behind Jim and he turned to see a tall, ruddy-faced man with remarkably broad shoulders enter the room. He wore the flannel checked shirt customary in the area and heavy workboots with stout trousers tucked into them. He approached the table and, dragging out a chair, sat down. He looked at Jim before turning round to yell towards the kitchen.

"Chin, you idle bastard, get my breakfast out here!" He turned around to the table and held his hand out to Jim. "Martin van der Merwe, mining engineer. I guess you must be the new pilot?"

Jim shook the man's rough, calloused hand and said, "I guess I must be. Jim Wilson by the way. Where do you fit in around here?"

Han cleared his throat. "That will all become clear during our tour. For now your breakfast is arriving and both of you gentlemen need to keep your strength up, so there are no delays."

Jim started eating the ham and eggs that had appeared before him and tried to avoid looking at van der Merwe, who seemed to have considerable difficulty in closing his mouth as he chewed.

"Hope you're not going to kill yourself like the chink pilot did. Hell of a mess he made of the plane. He's still in the wreckage. Did you know that?"

"Yes, Mr Han did mention that on our way here."

"Indeed, Major Wilson. As you saw, most of the aircraft is in a difficult position at the base of the cliff and I felt no need to divert my workforce to recover the body of a failure."

With that Han stood up from the table and dabbed his lips delicately with his napkin. "I will send for you in an hour so that we may make our tour. I see Mr van der Merwe has finished his breakfast with his customary speed, so we will meet him later at his workplace."

Van der Merwe pushed back his chair noisily and stood up. He took a large swig of coffee and slammed down his mug before setting off for the door.

"See you later, pilot. You can tell me about this Major stuff later."

Chapter 12

"Any news, David?" Ivan said as he came out of the bunkroom where they had stayed the night before.

"Nothing. I will call around again later to see what they know."

Ivan eased his aching back. The bunk had been made for a much smaller man. He looked through the window to check the weather then turned back to David.

"I had a thought during the night. We've asked your people to look for a small aircraft in a damned big country. Maybe we could widen the search a bit."

David nodded. "Certainly. What are you thinking of?"

"Well, the people who are doing the looking know this country and the waterways far more than we do. Can we ask them to report anything that seems out of place, anything that seems unusual in any way?"

"We can. What are you hoping for?"

"To be honest with you, David, I don't know, but Jim has been taken up there to fly a plane. There has to be a reason for that. Something must be going on, though I have no idea what it might be. So, if we cast the net wide enough, your people might catch us a clue. Maybe we can even narrow down the search area."

"I will call them now. They are sensitive to things going on around them. Far more than most Europeans, I think. It's worth a try."

Ivan went back into the bunk room and kicked Geordie's bed. "Get up, mate. We've got some work to do. Where did you put the big map?"

Geordie struggled blearily awake and groaned. "I was having a lovely dream there and then the nightmare turned up. It's over there on that feed bin. What's up?"

"Get your boots on and come by the fire and I'll tell you."

Geordie rolled out of bed, still fully dressed from the night before, and pulled on his boots before following Ivan into the main room. By the time he reached the warm area around the fire Ivan had the map spread out on the table. He looked up as Geordie approached.

"I had an idea in the night, while you were snoring like a buzz saw. David is going to contact all the groups up the coast and ask them if they have seen anything odd, not just the aircraft. If we plot any strange things on here we might just be able to identify some kind of hot spot."

Geordie stifled a yawn. "Good idea, but speaking of hot spots, have we got any coffee on the go?"

"Why don't you make yourself useful and go and make some? See what we've got for breakfast while you're there."

Geordie grinned. "Now that's an even better idea."

Chapter 13

Geordie and Ivan walked along the shoreline towards Megan and Jim's cabin. As they got close they could see that the door stood wide open and at least one window had been smashed. Ivan glanced at Geordie and nodded before they walked up to the cabin and through the front door. It was clear that someone had vented considerable frustration on their friends' home. Furniture had been overturned, pictures ripped off the walls and slashed. The kitchen was littered with broken pots and glasses.

Geordie spun around slowly, taking it all in. "Looks like somebody has a major sense of humour failure about Megan leaving."

Ivan nodded sadly. "Nothing we can do right now. We've got other fish to fry. If we let David know, maybe his people can help, before Megan sees this."

Ivan closed the door carefully on their way out and then they walked back to David's cabin. As they approached they could see Mary on the front porch waving to them to come in. They quickened their pace and followed her into the main room.

David looked up from the map as they entered. "The elders have come back to me. Nothing much happening until you get just south of the Alaskan border. There's been a couple of things up there."

"Like what?" Ivan asked.

David pointed at the map. "Just around here, three brothers took their canoe across the water to go hunting. They haven't been seen since and they aren't answering their phones."

"Is that unusual?"

"Maybe not, it's rough country up there, but taken with other things it might be. A fishing boat went out a couple of weeks ago and that hasn't come back. They aren't answering radio calls. Then a trawler has been seen going up the waterway a few times with no flag flying and no registration letters on the hull."

"All in the same area?"

David nodded. "Pretty much. I'm waiting for another call from one of the elders up there – and there he is, I guess," he said as the phone started to ring.

David picked up the telephone and listened. He looked across at Ivan and Geordie with no expression on his face. He finished the call and walked back to where they stood by the map. He pointed to a small bay on a major inlet.

"They've just found the brothers' canoe here."

"And?"

"And somebody has smashed a hole in the bottom. Still no sign of the brothers, though."

"Has anybody seen Jim's aircraft?"

David shook his head. "Not yet. There are a few Beavers working up that way, but they haven't seen the one you want. At least, not up to now, but they will keep looking."

"OK, Ivan, what do we do now?"

Ivan contemplated the map for a moment, then looked up. "Now we go up there and start looking around. It's going to take a while to get that far north, but if we start now we should be there if anything else shows up." He turned to David. "Can any of your people loan us a boat when we get there?"

David smiled. "Not a problem, but if these things mean something, won't you need weapons?"

Ivan smiled back. "We were wondering if any of the ones those city thugs left behind after the attack on Megan's cabin might be suitable."

"The RCMP took those when they collected the prisoners."

Geordie stroked his ear as he looked at David. "Of course they did, but maybe a couple fell off the back of the truck as they were leaving?"

David turned and picked up his cap from the back of a chair. "Maybe a couple. Come, we will see what we can do."

They followed David around to the small store shed at the back of his cabin. As he opened the door they could see his heavy duty woodworking tools laid out on boards that were mounted on the walls. Every tool had its shape painted on the board behind it, so David would know instantly if one was missing.

Ivan looked around, admiring the tools. "Nice shadow boards there, David."

He nodded. "They taught me to do that when I was in the army. Just seemed the right thing to do when I moved back here. My father just used to keep the tools in heaps. He would stand in the middle of the shed and turn slowly until he saw the one he wanted. This is a lot better."

As he was speaking David walked to the back of the shed and reached into a corner. He flipped a catch and one of the big boards swung towards him. As it opened Ivan and Geordie could see a display of firearms mounted on another board behind it.

Geordie grinned. "Good job the Mounties didn't count the number of crooks and the number of weapons then."

"We thought of that," David said. "We made sure each of the attackers had a weapon to be charged for. Most of them carried more than one when the attack started. So now, what do you think you need?"

Ivan stepped forward and ran his fingers across the weapons. "That M4 Assault Rifle looks like it would suit me. Have you got the ammunition for it?"

David bent down and opened a stout wooden crate below the weapon rack. "Here you go. Magazines already loaded, slings and cleaning kits. We got those after the excitement."

"We?"

"That's right, these belong to the village. I just store them behind here in case any outsiders get too interested. Geordie, what do you like the look of?"

"What's that bolt action job with the scope and the bipod? That looks pretty useful."

"You have a good eye. That is a Remington Model 700 and the scope is a good one, too. The US Marines use a version of it as a sniper rifle. We'll take it out and try it if you like, but I thought you'd be more interested in something with automatic fire."

Ivan gave David one of his rare smiles. "No, mate. Our Geordie boy here is a craftsman with a rifle. He doesn't like 'spray and pray'. Bolt action will suit him just fine."

David looked at the smiling black man who was cradling the Remington and running his hands over its smooth lines. "Looks like you two are well suited for each other. Now you better take one of these each as well," he said, reaching across the board and detaching two automatic pistols. "Colt M1911 pistols. 45 caliber and a real stopper if you get into trouble. I've got two tactical leg holsters in the box."

"Why do you think we'd need them? Just extra weight and we've got the rifles."

"Weapon of last resort and you might not have the rifle with you all the time. This is bear country and these are good and noisy. They might not stop a bear once an attack has started, but the noise might persuade one to go away."

David handed the big pistols to the two men. They hefted them in their hands and Ivan looked back at David.

"Always take good advice from the experts, they say. So thank you, these will be fine."

David nodded. "Now let's go and zero these rifles in for you. I've got a wooden post across the inlet we can use as a target."

Chapter 14

"Major Wilson, it is time for the tour I promised you. I am combining it with my own inspection tour, so it may take a while."

"Thank you, Mr Han, I would be interested in seeing just what is going on around here."

Han led the way to the door and Jim followed him. As they exited the building, two armed guards fell in behind them.

Jim looked over his shoulder and then at Han. "Are you expecting me to make a run for it, through all that forest?"

Han chuckled. "No, Major. These men are here for our protection. You will understand why very shortly."

They walked across the narrow beach with Han leading the way. He paused and pointed out at the aircraft that sat on its reflection on the calm lake water.

"You see we have draped coloured sheets across your aircraft. They are designed to make sure it is not visible from the air. No doubt you saw that the mooring buoy was black for the same reason. Those sheets come off just before you fly my packages out of here and go back on as soon as you land."

Jim looked at the camouflage on his aircraft, then at Han. "And just what is in these packages?"

"Allow me to be a showman for a while. You will see when we get where we are going. I think you will be surprised."

They trudged on across the beach and then entered the forest edge, just by the side of the rock scree Jim had seen before. Steps had been cut into the ground to make the climb up the steep slope a little easier. As they climbed Jim saw a dark shape on the cliffside ahead. As they approached it became clear that what he was seeing was a large hole in the earth.

"A mine entrance?"

"Correct, Major. It is indeed a mine entrance. As an engineer I think you may find it interesting."

Jim swallowed and balled his fists. His claustrophobia was not going to make this pleasant. He could already feel the cold sweat starting on his back, but he was damned if he was going to show weakness to this man.

They entered the mine and Jim was handed a dented helmet with a battery pack and lamp. He fitted the battery to his belt and adjusted the helmet before following Han into the shaft that sloped downwards. The two guards remained close behind as he walked.

The four men walked for five minutes before they could see light coming from in front of them. As they rounded a bend in the tunnel they were confronted by a set of iron-barred gates with a guard sitting beside it with an AK47 rifle across his lap. He rose as Han approached and unlocked the gate before swinging it open. Han, Jim and the two guards passed through and then the iron gate swung closed behind them.

"Why the hell would you put gates in a mine? What happens if there is an accident and the miners need to get out quickly?"

Han gave him a thin smile. "An accident would be unfortunate, as you will realise when we see the miners."

The tunnel continued to slope downwards until it entered a wider gallery. All around were crude wooden scaffolding contraptions with men, stripped to the waist, working at various levels with picks and sweating in the heat. Behind them other men used shovels to pick up the rock and load it into barrows that were then trundled across to a noisy machine that was pounding away in the centre of the gallery.

Jim looked round in amazement; this was the kind of crude mining that had died out many years ago. How could these people be persuaded to work like this? At the end of the gallery on a raised platform he caught sight of Van der Merwe, sitting on a wide chair and supervising the work. The South African stood up and jumped down from his dais before walking across to them.

"Glad to see you, Mr Han, and you, too, Mr Wilson. How do you like my mine? These chinks work better than the kaffirs I had to deal with back home, but then I guess these boys are more motivated, eh, Mr Han?"

Turning around, Jim looked at the miners and then back to Han. "You must pay a small fortune to get them to work in these conditions."

Han smiled slowly. "I pay them nothing. We have an agreement: I bring them from China into the USA and they work for me for one year. Then they are free to make a new life in the promised land of America."

Jim looked at Han and the grinning Van der Merwe. "I take it they didn't know where they were going to work when they signed up for this devil's bargain?"

"True, but I think they would have come anyway. There is much poverty in the rural parts of China."

"So what about their families? How do they get them over here?"

"But they are here already, of course. I do not take children, far too much trouble. The miners' wives are here and they carry out other tasks."

Jim noticed that Van der Merwe was wearing an evil grin as Han spoke. He wondered what that signified.

As they stood there with the miners hacking at the unforgiving rock, a ragged man staggered out of a side shaft. He stopped as he reached the workings and held onto one of the scaffolding uprights. He looked slowly around him with bloodshot eyes, before doubling over and vomiting violently as he fell to his knees.

Jim instinctively moved to help the man, but was stopped by a guard's hand on his chest. The man pushed Jim back towards Han.

"Do not worry. He is not your responsibility. He will be dealt with by my staff," Han said, as he turned away and walked towards the exit.

Jim felt a shove from behind as the two guards shepherded him after the man in the business suit. "Before we go, Mr Han, just what are you mining here?"

Han stopped and turned back towards Jim. "Why, Major, you disappoint me. I thought an engineer such as you would recognise the rock."

"I'm a civil engineer, not a geologist."

"Then today you learn something. Those glistening crystals are quartz; we are mining a gold reef. Which is why I pay our South African friend, for his expertise from the gold mines of his country. This could be as big as the Klondike strike to the north of here, but we will keep it secret so we are not swamped by itinerant prospectors and government busybodies."

Han leaned into a bin and pulled out a piece of rock which he handed to Jim. "A souvenir for you. Once processed and the gold extracted from the quartz, it might make a nice ring for your lovely lady, after you leave here."

Chapter 15

Megan came out of the health centre carrying the baby. The check-up had gone well and the nurse was happy that the child was developing properly. She walked across to Kelly's ageing pickup and secured Daniela in the baby seat in the rear of the cab. As she climbed into the truck next to her friend, she did not see the dark eyes watching her from across the street.

They drove slowly back up the rutted track to the cabin and parked in the lean-to at the side of the building. They carried their burdens into the house, negotiating their way through three overexcited collies that danced around them with their tails wagging furiously.

Megan called to Kelly as she came back into the main room after putting Daniela down in her crib. "Coffee?"

"I'll make it. I don't think I could stand another cup of that paint stripper you make, at least not today."

With the coffee made, they settled down at either side of the cast-iron wood-burning stove. The dogs nestled around their feet enjoying the warmth as the evening crept on. Bracken was having a dog dream with his back legs kicking in his sleep when Sam's ears pricked up and he raised his head to stare at the door. Paddy also raised his head, letting out a low growl as he stood and walked stiff-legged towards the entrance. Sam raised himself up and walked to the other side of the door before lying down.

"What's the matter with those two?" Megan asked.

"Probably nothing. There's an old bear that sometimes walks across in front of the cabin. It doesn't bother us, but the dogs feel obliged to tell it off sometimes."

"Doesn't seem to be bothering Bracken. Then nothing much bothers him anytime."

They heard a sound from outside and both dogs stood up with their hackles raised. Kelly stood quickly and walked across to pick up her 12 gauge Remington pump action shotgun.

Megan looked at her with a startled expression. "What's up?"

"That was no bear, sweetie. There's somebody out there trying to keep quiet. Never a good sign."

Megan stood and walked quickly to her room. She returned, cradling the Winchester 94 that had saved Jim's life, in the hands of his nephew, all those months ago. Both women nodded and each moved silently to one of the windows that flanked the door. Each of them peeped around the edge of the window, but in the dark night they saw nothing.

With a loud crash the door smashed open and swung back on its hinges. The first man through the door met two flying dogs and screamed as two sets of angry teeth sank into his arms. He dropped the submachine gun he was holding as he struggled to fight them off. The second man ran past the rolling mass of fur and screams on the floor and swung his weapon around as he searched for a target.

Kelly did not hesitate and fired the powerful shotgun from the hip. At that range the full force of the shot lifted the attacker off his feet and slammed him back against the open door. He slid down to the floor with blood pouring through his ruined jacket from a mass of tightly packed holes. His weapon fell beside him.

Megan jacked a round into the chamber of the Winchester and moved to cover the door. She looked outside again, but could still see nothing. At that moment she heard the crashing of glass and the tearing of wood as a window was smashed open. She spun round and ran towards Daniela's room. She was passed by a flying blur of black and white fur as Bracken dashed to protect the baby.

By the time Megan reached the door the attacker was trying to climb back out of the window with a furious dog savaging his leg. He saw her and raised a large automatic pistol towards her. The dog attacking him threw his aim off and the bullet flew past Megan's head to bury itself in the wooden wall. She raised the rifle and fired one round followed rapidly by a second. The attacker was thrown out of the window and landed in an unmoving heap against the wall of the cabin.

Megan smiled down at the dog now sitting next to Daniela's crib wagging his tail. She patted his head and ruffled his ears before checking the baby, to find that she had slept through everything. She walked back into the main room and went to close the door.

As she did so the full moon came from behind a cloud and spread a silver light across the track outside. There was the fourth attacker with an automatic rifle in his hands. He raised it to the aim, but Megan was quicker. She snapped off a shot that struck the man in the throat. He went down in a spray of bright blood and stopped moving in seconds.

"Nice shooting, lady," Kelly said as she walked up alongside her. "I guess Daniela is OK or you wouldn't be here?"

"She's fine. How are these other two?"

Kelly looked down. "The one who took the shotgun round didn't make it. I think I stopped his heart for him. And by the look of things the dogs have put paid to the other one as well."

Megan looked around at the pools of blood on the wooden floor and the crimson stains all around the dog's muzzles.

"That's going to take some cleaning," Kelly said.

"Are you all right?" Megan asked.

"I'm fine. At least I didn't lose my dogs this time. How about you, how do you feel?"

"It's just starting to hit me." She slumped into a chair and looked up at her friend with tear-filled eyes. "These bastards were going to kill my baby. They got what was coming to them, but what if more of them come back?"- She saw that her hands were trembling and couldn't control the waver in her voice. The reaction to almost losing Daniela had really started to kick in.

"Does that mean we have to get out of here now?"

With a visible effort Megan pulled herself up in the chair. "Not this time, Kelly. These were the four that were guarding us to keep Jim in line, wherever they have taken him. None of them is going to trouble us, but we might want to go through their pockets to see if there is anything that will help Geordie and Ivan to find him."

Kelly dragged the two bodies out through the door and dumped them on the veranda before coming back inside. She patted the two dogs that waited for her and then turned back around to look out of the open door at the dark forest around them. "I think we need to be careful in case these aren't the last."

Megan sat back in her chair, starting to relax a little. and looked up at her friend. "You're right, of course. They could have called their boss when they found us gone. Still, with the dogs watching, too, this is still the safest place to be until we get Jim back."

Kelly nodded as she closed the door and shot the bolts across. "And now you need to get some sleep. You've had one hell of a scare. Maybe you should sleep in Daniela's room tonight."

Megan smiled and forced herself to stand. Her knees were trembling, but she bent and picked up the Winchester before walking slowly into Daniela's room.

Chapter 16

As Megan spoke, many miles to the north, Ivan and Geordie were pulling into a cabin in the forest edge just outside Prince Rupert. They climbed stiffly out of the pickup truck; it had been a long hard drive. They stood and looked out over the broad waterway at the bottom of the hill and then at the carvings on the building.

"This looks like the place, mate," Geordie said.

"It certainly does. Got to give it to these people, they really are damn fine wood carvers."

"And damn fine shots," the voice behind them said. "Who are you and what are you doing on my land?"

Ivan, with Geordie, turned around slowly to face the dark-complexioned old man who stood behind them. The rifle in his hands was held very steadily and both men were careful to keep their hands in plain sight.

"I'm Ivan Thomas. We're friends of David Red Cloud from way down the coast."

The man grunted. "And the black one?"

"I'm Geordie Peters and I'm a friend as well."

The rifle swung upwards and away from them as the man turned and walked towards his cabin. "You're the ones I was told to expect. Come on in and tell me what you need."

Ivan hesitated. "Should we bring the weapons in?"

"No need. Nobody round here is going to touch them, not if they have any sense and most do."

Geordie shrugged at Ivan and together they followed the old man into his cabin. As they walked in the stunning carvings carried on. Every beam above them had ornate painted carvings of fish and animals. On the walls hung weapons from the past and present. They were waved to a couple of comfortable-looking rocking chairs by the open fire.

The old man sat opposite them and looked at each of them in turn. "Why are you really here?"

Ivan looked at Geordie, who nodded. "I'm elected, it seems. We are both ex-soldiers from the British Army. For years we have been working with an officer that we have huge respect for. He was taken away and is being forced to do something we don't know about because he fears for the life of his child and his partner. We have got them to safety and now we need to find him."

"Why here?"

"He got a partial message out that said 'North of Fifty Four'. His Beaver floatplane was taken with him and there are any number of lakes around here where it might have landed."

"So you are guessing?"

"Truthfully, yes, we are, but there have been a few, just a few, odd things happening around here, so we are hoping they are linked."

"Not much to go on."

"No, but it's all we have and we have to try somewhere."

The old man nodded very slowly, his creased face locked into an expression of concentration. He stood and walked over to take a map down from the wall and brought it back close to the fire.

"The three sons of my brother have not returned from a hunting trip. Their canoe was found here," he said, pointing at the map. "Their favourite area to hunt was around here." He pointed again. "We have searched and found nothing."

"Could they just be lost or maybe they are staying out because the hunting has been poor?"

"No. These men know the area. They would not be lost and they all have jobs in the fish canning plant and families to come back to. They would not stay away and lose those jobs for a hunt."

"So what do you think has happened?" Ivan asked.

"We do not know, but we fear for their safety. Something is not right in the forests, although we do not yet understand what it is."

Geordie sat forward and studied the map. "We were also told about a boat travelling up and down the waterways without lights. Is that around here?"

"It is. It has been seen sailing up and down this inlet late at night."

Ivan and Geordie looked to where the old man was pointing. It was close to where the three men liked to hunt. They looked at each other and nodded.

"If we can borrow a boat we'll start exploring that area and see what we can find," Ivan said.

"We have searched there already, but maybe you will see something we missed. Go to the docks at the end of this road. There is a small boatyard there with a carved canoe on the gatepost. Tell them Binesi sent you. I am of the Gitanyow people, but my mother was of the Ojibwe and gave me that name. It means 'thunderbird' in that tongue. They will lend you a boat. Do you need weapons?"

Geordie smiled. "No, but thank you for the offer. David Red Cloud of the Heiltsuk people is a good friend and he gave us weapons, which he acquired when helping us out of a difficulty some while ago."

The old man nodded thoughtfully "He is a good man and his are good people. Tell me that story when you come back from your search."

Chapter 17

The black iron bars across the windows were solidly mounted. There was no way out through there and, with the guard sitting at the end of the corridor, the door was not much of an option either. He lay on the bed and contemplated the roof beams above him. The heavy-duty timbers that had been used to build the house did not seem at all promising to someone with no tools to work on them.

Jim swore quietly under his breath; this was going to take more thought. Even if he could break loose and try to make a run for it through these northern forests, the risk to Megan and the baby was just too great. For now he would have to bide his time and try to be ready when an opportunity presented itself.

The timid knock on his door brought Jim out of his reverie and he rolled off the bed and went to open it. Standing in the passageway carrying a tray covered in a snow-white napkin was an attractive young Chinese woman. She bobbed her head and walked into the room to set the tray down on the small table. She deftly removed the cloth to reveal a steak dinner with all the trimmings. She paused for a moment looking down at the food and then looked up and bobbed her head once more.

"Mr Han say you eat in your room tonight. He want to be alone."

Jim walked across and pulled out the upright dining chair. "Thank you, this looks good."

As he sat down he noticed that the young woman had seated herself on the chair opposite him. She looked back at him and gave a hesitant smile.

"You don't need to wait. I can leave the tray downstairs in the morning if you like."

"No, is OK. When you finish Mr Han say I am for you."

Jim put his knife down beside his plate. "I'm sorry, what does that mean?"

She gave him the same hesitant smile again. "I am to stay with you. I am for you tonight."

Realising what she meant, he pushed his plate to one side. He put his elbows on the table and rested his chin in his hands as he looked at her. She really was beautiful, but seemed very nervous, so he assumed she was no whore. He noticed that her eyes strayed to his plate again as he looked at her.

"Are you hungry?"

She gave a small nod. "Little bit."

"Well then, you'd better share my dinner. There's way too much for one anyway."

He sliced the steak in half and divided the rest up equally, before sliding his half into the plate that had been used to cover and keep the food warm. He sliced his half of the steak into bite-sized pieces and handed the cutlery across to the young woman.

She shook her head. "Is not right. Mr Han he will be angry. Food is for you."

"Mr Han will never know and anyway I'm not that hungry. It would only go to waste. So eat yours and don't worry about it."

She pulled her chair closer to the table and began to eat. He noticed she took small bites of everything and ate delicately. This was clearly no peasant girl from the rice paddies of China and her English was pretty fair, with only minor errors.

"So isn't it about time you told me your name and what you are doing out here in the wilds?"

The woman dabbed her mouth with the napkin and set it down. "I am Chen Pam. I am usually called Chen. I came here with my brother. He works in mine and I have been chosen to be your companion while you are here."

"Don't you mind that?"

"It is better than being chosen for the other white man. He likes to hurt women. I think he also whips men if they not work hard enough."

"So what have you been told being my companion means?"

"I am to do whatever you tell me. I bring your food, I clean your clothes and I share your bed and do what you say. Mr Han says you are to be kept happy."

Jim sat back from the table and looked at the shy young woman. He could only imagine what she was fleeing in China to make this sort of slavery acceptable. He shook his head sadly.

"Well, Chen, it isn't going to work quite like that. To start with, I don't want you to share my bed."

"You do not like me?"

"Chen, you are a lovely woman, but I have a woman of my own and she is the mother of my child. It may be old-fashioned, but I cannot betray her."

Chen swallowed and looked even more nervous. "Then he will give me to the other white man. I am afraid of him. He will beat me."

Jim thought for a moment while he looked at the frightened young woman. "No, that won't happen. You will sleep here each night, but not in my bed. What I need you to do is to tell me everything you know about this place and what is going on here. Is that a deal?"

She nodded quickly, like a sparrow pecking. "Is a deal. You are good man. I think I will not mind too much if you want me in your bed later. Your woman would never know."

Jim gave her a small smile and shook his head slightly. "That may be true, but I'd know."

Chapter 18

The last of the four bodies was dumped unceremoniously into the back of the pickup truck and a tarpaulin was dragged over them. The two women and three dogs watched as David Red Cloud tossed the weapons into the truck bed and then walked towards them. He mounted the steps at the front of the cabin and they all sat on the rough wooden chairs.

"You have heard from Ivan and Geordie?" he asked.

"Not a word," Megan said as she idly stroked Bracken behind the ears.

"My friend, outside Prince Rupert, tells me that they arrived and have left their truck with him. One of his friends has loaned them a boat. It may not be any use. It seems they still have no leads on where Jim has been taken. I was hoping they had told you something."

"Is it difficult country that far north?" Kelly asked.

"It is much as it is here. Maybe the wind bites a little deeper and the mountains are a little higher. There are few people and it is a big country. North of Fifty Four does not help much, even if we have guessed the meaning right."

Megan nodded towards the truck. "What will you do with them?"

David looked at her for a moment. "I think it is better they are not found. Maybe the Chinese boss man thinks they have run away to make a life somewhere else."

"So what will you do?"

"The Russian fishing fleet is working off the coast near the village. They understand these things if they are approached properly. When they head back for their home port in Petropavlovsk, the bodies will be dropped over the side halfway across the ocean. A length of chain around the waist and they will trouble nobody. Even the creatures of the deep need to eat."

Megan looked across at Kelly. "Does that worry you?"

"Not even a little. These creatures came here to kill us, or worse. If it wasn't for the dogs they might have done it as well. To hell with them."

David stood and looked down at them. "If I hear anything from my friends I will call you. Even with these four gone you should be careful. Look after the dogs and keep your weapons loaded."

As he spoke another of the Heiltsuk villagers came around the corner carrying a canvas tool bag. "OK, Megan, that window is fixed. Maybe not as good as new, but it will keep the wind out until you can replace it properly."

"Do you two want a coffee before you go?"

The two men looked at each other and grinned. "No thanks. We've tasted your coffee and you know firewater is bad for the natives, eh!"

Megan smiled as David and his friend walked to their truck and climbed in. The engine started with a rattling roar and a cloud of black smoke. Then they jerked into gear and headed down the rough track towards the highway.

Kelly looked at the slowly dissipating cloud of exhaust smoke. "If that truck doesn't make it they are going to have to do some fancy talking to explain four bodies in the back."

Megan grinned. "They'll make it. David's old truck has been like that for years, but it just keeps on going. It's held together with bits of wire and duct tape."

"He seems a useful friend to have around here. What about his family?"

"Oh interested, are we? He has one daughter, Mary, a lovely intelligent girl, but deaf. She manages pretty well, though. His wife died about four years back. Nasty accident. He doesn't like to talk about it."

"So he has emotions then? You'd never know from his face."

"Like a lot of our people he doesn't show emotion deeply, but it's all there. You get him talking about what is being done to the forest and the coastal waters and then you'll see the feelings all right."

"An environmentalist? Better and better."

Chapter 19

Through the binoculars it could be seen that the thick forest that came down to the water's edge gave no clues as to what might be going on within that mass of trees. Ivan lowered the glasses and wiped his eyes. From the steering position Geordie pointed to a small cove with a rocky beach.

"How do you fancy pulling in there for a break and a regroup?"

Ivan nodded tiredly. With no information to go on, cruising these meandering waterways had seemed the only option. They had not truly appreciated the sheer size of the quest they had given themselves. Ivan walked to the bow and opened the locker that held the anchor and its line. As Geordie brought the borrowed boat to a stop, he tossed the anchor into the clear cold water and secured the line to the bow cleat.

Geordie opened the box that was stowed behind him and brought out the thermos flask. He poured two cups of coffee and handed one to Ivan. Then the two of them sat in silence looking at the wall of trees while they sipped at the brew.

Ivan put the plastic cup down. "You reckon you can get us right into that beach without damaging the boat?"

"Probably. Why would we want to?"

"Because the lack of a bathroom on this boat is causing me a problem and I need to unload."

Geordie chuckled as he stood up and restarted the engine. Ivan hauled in the anchor and the boat moved forward slowly with both men checking the bottom through the cold clear water as they neared the shore. Geordie brought the boat in alongside a massive fallen tree trunk and secured it with lines from bow and stern. Ivan climbed out and walked into the forest edge.

As he sat waiting for his friend to return Geordie scanned the map of the area. Three days of driving the boat slowly up and down the waterways had barely scratched the surface, but what else was there to do? They could wait for a miracle, but neither of them had the patience to wait for information to drop into their laps. He looked up as he heard Ivan walking towards him across the rocky foreshore. Something was wrong; he had seen that look before.

Geordie stood up and shielded his eyes from the dropping sun. "What is it?"

"Come and look," Ivan said as he stopped.

Geordie picked up the rifle from beside the steering position, then climbed onto the tree trunk and walked across to the big Welshman. Ivan turned without a word and led the way into the trees. The temperature dropped as they walked out of the sunlight into the shade and their footsteps became silent on the carpet of pine needles.

Ivan led the way to a dip in the ground and stood on the edge of it. Still without a word, he pointed into the small valley. Geordie came alongside him and looked down the slope. For a moment or two he could see nothing out of the ordinary and then he realised there was something there. He walked forward towards it until he could see that he was looking at the back of a drab green fatigue jacket. He stopped and looked left and right.

He felt his stomach drop as he realised what he was seeing. Half covered by the leaves and branches that had fallen from the trees and pulled this way and that by animals were three bodies. He knelt beside the first one as Ivan walked up beside him. The line of three bullet holes stitched across the man's jacket was all too clear. Looking at the other two, he could see that they too had been ripped by fast-flying metal. Each had multiple holes across their bodies.

Geordie looked up at the stony-faced Ivan. "What do you reckon? A sub-machine gun?"

Ivan nodded. "Maybe or maybe something like an AK47? In any case, it was no hunting rifle to do this."

Geordie stood up slowly. "I guess these are the missing brothers. They don't have their rifles with them, so this was no accident. Somebody took their weapons after they killed them."

"That's the way I read it. I don't think we leave the boat unarmed again."

"No way. Now what do we do with these lads?"

"If we report it to the authorities they are going to be all over this place like fleas on a dog and we daren't have that until we find Jim. On the other hand we can't just leave them; their families have to know."

Geordie paused. "How about we have a quiet word with Binesi? I get the feeling he has quite a bit of pull with the First Nation peoples around here. They can deal with this in the way they see fit and, if we are not involved, then there's no added risk to Jim."

Ivan looked down at the three tangled and torn bodies. "That's the best way I think. Let's get the hell back to that dock and speak to him. Maybe this will get his people looking more seriously, if they know their own are being attacked."

"Well, we know something, at least," Geordie said, looking around him.

"What's that?"

"It's a fairly safe bet we're in the right area."

Chapter 20

"They bring us from a small dock to the south of the main Shanghai harbour. We are packed together in the cargo hold, little food and water, nowhere to wash and stinking buckets in the corner. Is not a good voyage. When we get close to shore we must climb down the nets into a smaller ship and it brings us through the river to a place in a bay. From bay we must walk through the forest. We must carry heavy packs on our backs. When we get here, men go to work in the mine. They must live in there and work every day for one year. Women must work also. They must carry the packs to the boat and bring food from the boat through the forest to here every time the boat comes. When boat not comes they must work in the big sheds to get the gold out of the rock."

Jim listened as Chen she told her story. "And you?" he asked when she paused for breath.

"Mr Han, he line up all the women. If he think you pretty enough he brings you into house to do other things."

"So how long have you been here?"

Chen looked out of the window as the sun came from behind a cloud. "Only one week. You are first man I have been told to serve. I think I am lucky."

"Have you seen your brother since you got here?"

She shook her head. "Nobody is allowed in mine and miners not allowed to come out. Is difficult for wives when husbands in the mine."

"So where are these sheds you spoke about?"

There are two. Both are in ravines where the water run through. Sheds are built over small rivers. One is for gold and other is for something else."

"Something else? Do you know what that is?"

"No. I know women who work in there get sick. Hair falls out and they have much headache. If women are lazy or not obey Mr Han he moves them to work in the sickness shed."

Jim sat back. He recalled the man who had stumbled out of the side tunnel and vomited. His hair had been in clumps and his skin had looked pale and clammy. What the devil was Han doing here? What could have that effect?

"Does anybody run away?"

"There is a story about two women who tried to go. The guards chase them. They bring them back and tie them to tree by the lake. They stay there until they die. First the guards bring husbands out of mine and shoot them in front of women."

Jim stood up and walked the window. "Bloody hell," he muttered under his breath. Now he had no doubt about the danger to Megan and Daniela. This was a damned mess. He turned back and looked across the room at Chen who sat with her head bowed and her hands between her knees.

"Maybe you should go and pick up breakfast for us. I think I'd like to eat here rather than with Han."

He watched as Chen bobbed her head and scurried out of the room. He heard her talking to the guard as she left, but he could understand none of their words. He picked up the cushions from the floor and put them back on the chairs, then threw the extra blanket back onto the bed. Not the most comfortable sleep he had ever had, but better than some he had experienced during his army days.

He had finished his shave by the time Chen reappeared in the doorway. "Mr Han he say you eat with him. He has job for you."

Jim sighed and put on his old leather flight jacket and as he walked out of the room he patted Chen on the shoulder. "I'll see you later."

As he walked down the stairs he could see that Han was sitting at the head of the big table, with Van der Merwe at the other end, already shovelling food into his mouth. Jim walked across the room and took a chair midway between the two of them. The waiter appeared at his elbow and put down a full English breakfast.

Han smiled at him. "I took the liberty of ordering for you. I thought you should have a big breakfast this morning, Major. You will be flying in about an hour."

"And where will I be flying to? I'll need to plan the trip, fuel levels and such."

"That will all be taken care of by my people. All I need you to do is to fly the aircraft."

Jim put down his knife and fork slowly before turning in his seat. "Mr Han, that may have been acceptable for your previous pilot, but you may recall he is now fish food somewhere at the bottom of this lake. You forced me to come here to fly for you and I'll do that, but on my terms. I check the plane. I check the route and the weather and I check the loads."

Ham looked at him calmly. "You seem very insistent for somebody who has little choice."

"I intend to get out of this alive and back to my family. To do that I'm going to fly that aircraft professionally and that involves checking everything properly."

Han bowed slightly. "Very well, you may check what my people have done. You will find they are very thorough. Failure is not a comfortable option for them."

Chapter 21

Geordie and Ivan stood quietly at the back of the group of people who had paused at the lip of the depression and were looking down at the remains of the three brothers. Ivan winced as one of the two women in the group began a high wailing cry of mourning. The men started forward and gently lifted the three bodies out of the leaf mould and onto the stretchers they had brought.

Binesi turned away from the group and looked at the two of them. "The one who cries is their mother. Their sister is all she has left now. Her husband died last winter."

Geordie took a deep breath. "She has every right to mourn then. What will they do now?" He nodded towards the group of silent men.

"First we will put our people to rest. They are a traditional family, so it will be done in the old ways. Then we will come here and try to track the killers."

Ivan looked around at the thick forest. "It's been some days. Will there be any sign left?"

Binesi shrugged. "It will be difficult, but we may be lucky. Though it will be three more days before we can start."

"In which case, do you mind if we try now?"

Binesi looked surprised. "You are trackers?"

"Not as good as your people, but we have been shown some of the skills."

Binesi shook his head doubtfully. "If you are not skilled you may cover up more sign than you find. It is better you leave it for us."

"In three more days, more sign will be lost and you may find nothing."

"I will track for them," a voice from behind them said.

The three men turned to see a lovely dark-haired young woman standing there with her hair tumbling to her shoulders. Her dark eyes were reddened by weeping, but held a determined look.

"Leah, you should see your brothers to their rest."

She looked steadily at the older man. "And will I sing at the side of the next ones to die as well? These two are hunting their friend and, if they find the killers of my blood on the way, I think they will help me take revenge." She addressed Ivan and Geordie. "Is that true?"

Geordie glanced at Ivan, then spoke for both of them. "Aye, bonny lass, we'll do that."

She paused then nodded once as she turned back to the old man. "I have my knife. I need a rifle."

Binesi stood very still, thinking. He came to his decision and nodded just once.

"It is good. I will bring you my rifle from the boat. Leave sign as you go so we can follow your path when the ceremony is done. Tell your mother where you are going. She will understand."

The four of them walked back down to the rocky beach where the brothers were about to be taken into one of the three boats that waited there. Ivan and Geordie hung back, not wanting to intrude on family grief. The men's mother spoke to her daughter at the waterside and then walked awkwardly across the stony foreshore towards them.

"You have found my sons and I thank you," she said as she reached them. "Now you go to bring them peace while I lay them to rest, so I thank you again. Promise me you will keep my only child safe."

Ivan put out a hand and rested it gently on the woman's shoulder. "I will guard her as if she was my own and if I come back, she will come with me."

The older woman looked at him with watery eyes. "Those are good words. Be safe in the forest and trust my daughter, Leah knows the ways of this country."

The older woman walked slowly back to the boats and climbed into the one that bore all her sorrows. Leah walked across the beach with a rifle in her hand and a small pack on her back. The three of them stood together and watched as the three boats pulled slowly away from the shore and set off across the waterway.

Leah sighed and looked at the sky. "It will be dark in two hours. We need to move now to find the start of the trail. Are you ready?"

Geordie gave her his widest grin. "Ready, willing and able, bonny lass. Best we follow you then, eh?"

She looked at him steadily for a second or two and then smiled back. "Watch where you are stepping and don't spend the whole time looking at my ass."

Chapter 22

The camouflage covers were off the Beaver and Jim had checked that nothing on the aircraft had been damaged by the lightweight fabric being pulled off. Once satisfied with that, he checked that all the control surfaces were moving freely and then checked the fuel load was as it should be. Earlier he had watched as the Chinese ground crew weighed the bags of cargo and then lashed them down to the floor of the plane.

Finally satisfied, he walked to where Han was standing with an amused smile on his face. "Well, Major, did I lie? My people know that mistakes are punished severely. Losing your aircraft would be an inconvenience for me and they do not want that."

"Everything is fine, but I will still check everything before I fly in the future."

"As you wish. Now these are the coordinates you will fly to. Your GPS instrument has already been programmed. It is approximately one hundred miles from the coast. You will find a cargo ship waiting there. I have spoken with them and they assure me that sea conditions are near perfect. You will land next to the ship and they will take the cargo from you. At no time are you to fly into or near US airspace. Do you understand that clearly?"

"I do, but how will you know where I fly?"

Han sighed. "Do not take me for a fool. That aircraft has been equipped with a GPS transmitter; your position will be monitored at all times. I also have my people listening to the US air traffic control frequencies."

"Fair enough. Anything else I should know?"

Han gave Jim a thin smile. "I have also had a remote-controlled explosive device installed in the belly of that aircraft, next to the fuel tanks. Should you attempt to fly away from a reasonable course it will be detonated from here. Have a good flight, Major."

Han turned on his heel and walked away up the beach towards the house. Jim watched him go. All the plans he had been formulating as he delayed this flight had now fallen in a heap. Han had second-guessed him and now he needed to come up with a better escape plan that did not involve the aircraft.

Jim stepped into the waiting support boat and was ferried out to the aircraft that was sitting on the still waters of the lake with its picture perfect reflection below it. He stepped out of the boat and on to the port float before climbing up into the pilot's seat. He set the three control levers in the centre of the panel and started the engine. Once the nine cylinder Pratt and Whitney rotary engine had settled down to its steady beat, he signalled the boat's crew, who detached the mooring lines. He waited until the boat had pulled clear and gently advanced the throttle. The aircraft moved to the area where he had decided to begin his take-off run. He made one last check of the instruments and that the lake was still clear, then he pushed the throttle wide open.

The powerful propeller dragged the aircraft to flight speed rapidly, the floats carving white wakes into the dark water. As soon as his air speed indicator reached the correct point he eased back on the control column and the Beaver soared eagerly into the air. He stared ahead to where he must start his climbing turn to escape from the valley that the lake filled. As he worked the control column and the rudder pedals the engine never missed a beat and then he was around the difficult turn safely.

The aircraft continued to climb smoothly and he settled it onto the course that the GPS screen gave him. Once above the level of the mountain peaks he could relax and enjoy his own company. He regretted that the ground crew had removed his radios. It gave him no chance to warn any air traffic monitors of his situation.

He flew on a steady course until the ocean came into view. It seemed Han had been right: the water was remarkably smooth and the day was gin clear with good visibility. He checked his watch. He should be seeing the freighter in around forty minutes if it was in position and waiting for him.

The Beaver droned on with no other aircraft in sight, just a few scattered fishing boats on the flat calm ocean below him. A dark smudge on the horizon slowly morphed into a freighter as he approached it. He flew once round the rust-streaked and stationary ship before lining up for a landing alongside it.

The aircraft sank towards the surface of the sea as he throttled back. The floats kissed the water and threw plumes of snow-white spray behind him. As he completed his landing and turned towards the cargo ship a boat was already on the way towards him. He sat in his seat and waited with the engine ticking over. The cargo door opened as one of the boat's crew climbed onto the starboard float and pulled on the handle. The swarthy-faced man climbed inside and without a word to Jim started to unfasten the cargo tie-downs. As he freed each canvas sack he handed them out of the door to a second man, who was now on the float. He in turn passed them on to a third man in the boat.

The slick and practiced operation was completed in moments and Jim prepared to open up the throttle for the return journey. As he did so the man in the cargo area tapped him on the shoulder and shook his head, holding up one finger to indicate Jim should wait. A white cardboard box was passed up from the boat to the man behind Jim, who then passed it to Jim.

He opened the box to see it was filled with confectionery. He turned to the man behind him and shrugged his shoulders.

The man leaned forward and shouted over the noise of the engine. "For Mr Han. He has a taste for Iranian sweetmeats." With that he turned and climbed back out of the cargo door onto the float and back into the boat.

Jim watched as the boat pulled clear and then, putting the box of cakes and cookies safely down on the floor in front of the co-pilot's seat, he turned back to the controls. He adjusted the propeller pitch and advanced the throttle. The aircraft picked up speed more rapidly without the heavy cargo and, as he pulled back on the control column, lifted effortlessly into the clear air. He swung the Beaver around the freighter, then set course for the return to the lake and settled in for the boring part of the flight.

    Again, there was no air traffic near him, just the scattering of inshore fishing boats as he approached the land. Then he lined up on the jagged mountain and made his approach to the elbow lake.

Chapter 23

Leah was awake before dawn and was surprised to find Geordie already out of his sleeping bag and cooking breakfast over a small fire. The two hours before nightfall had been productive and her remarkable tracking skills had impressed the two ex-soldiers as she picked up the tiniest of signs.

"Aren't you worried about the smoke giving us away?" she asked as he handed her a metal plate.

"Not really, bonny lass. The wood is dry, so doesn't smoke much and we're under a nice big tree, so any smoke gets dispersed by the branches. Did I pass the test?"

Despite herself, she returned his wide grin. "I just needed to know how far I can trust you not to screw this up."

Geordie smiled again. "Fair one. Maybe we should have told you we are both ex-army so, although our tracking skills are not up to your standard, we're not complete dummies."

"Where's Ivan?"

"Down by the stream over there. He's filling the canteens in case we need them later."

"There's no shortage of water in these hills. It's just extra weight to carry."

Geordie turned over the slice of tinned meat he was frying. "Maybe so, but Ivan is a careful man. He doesn't leave much to chance if he can help it."

She shrugged. "As long as you don't want me to carry things we don't need, it's up to you."

Geordie nodded. "Well, OK then, so how about you tell me about you, while we wait for Ivan?"

"Not much to tell. I was born around here and I've lived here all my life. One of my uncles runs the fish cannery and I work for him. My brothers used to work there, as well as helping out on the boats when the big shoals come through."

"So how did you learn to track like that'?"

"I used to go hunting with my brothers. Our father taught us all the same way. He wanted to make sure we knew our heritage and didn't adopt just the ways of the Europeans."

Geordie nodded again. "Yeah, good for him. Half of my folks came from the Caribbean. My Mum made us learn Caribbean cooking and music for the same reason."

"What about Ivan?"

"Ivan comes from good solid Welsh hill farm stock. Best damned soldier you could wish to meet and you can't imagine a better friend."

Leah was quiet for a while, eating her breakfast and looking around at the trees. "So who is it you are trying to find?"

"The boss? Oh well he was our officer when we were in the army. We three got involved in some fairly hair-raising tasks over the last couple of years and now he's in trouble, so here we are to get him back out of it."

"You are risking your lives for him. Is he worth it?"

Geordie put down his plate and wiped his hands down his trouser leg before looking at Leah.

"Oh yes. When you've been through some of the stuff we have then you owe each other. He's not just the boss, he's a friend."

"Would he do the same for you two, though?"

"Without a doubt, C*ariad*." Ivan's deep Welsh voice came from behind her.

Leah spun round to find the big man standing behind her. "You move quietly for such a large man. Are you sure you aren't related to my people?"

"No, lass, Welsh to the core. Now are we going to sit round gassing all day or shall we move on?"

Chapter 24

The scream from outside the window woke him. He rolled out of the cushion bed on the floor and went to look outside. In the early light of dawn, before the sun crested the mountains, he could see a crowd of people standing in lines. He saw one of the guards recoiling his whip as a woman was helped to her feet by two others. There was blood across her shoulders and the fabric of her dirty jacket was torn.

Jim dressed quickly and left the room. He brushed past the corridor guard, who rose to stop him, and went down the staircase to the main room of the cabin. As he stepped through the front door he found that Han was there before him, standing on the wide veranda, looking out over the silent crowd of women.

He moved alongside Han. "Didn't you see that?"

"See what, Major?"

"One of your damned guards whipping a woman."

Han shrugged and turned towards him. "Major, these people are peasants; they respect authority when they know there is instant punishment. It is necessary to maintain discipline."

"Discipline does not need to be brutal."

Han shrugged. "You do not understand these people. If one is whipped then hundreds will learn the lesson and not cause any trouble. Examples must be made if this venture is to be a success."

"Just what is this bloody venture of yours? I took your gold out to the ship, but what are these women carrying in those packs?"

Han shouted something in Chinese and one of the guards grabbed a pack from the ground and brought it to the foot of the steps. He stopped when Han held a hand up, then opened the bag and took out some pieces of black powdery material.

"I advise you not to touch it, but that is processed pitchblende. We came here to mine it and found the gold seam above it. An added bonus. As far as we know, it is the only place in the world where these two minerals occur together. The pitchblende is deeper in the mountain and takes more work to get it ready to be walked out to the boat that comes into the waterway beyond that ridge."

Jim looked down at the material the guard was holding in his outstretched hand. "So why have me here flying the gold out, when you could walk it out with these people to your boat?"

Han snorted lightly. "The people who run my supply boat have no way of dealing with this. They take it out to the ship you flew to yesterday and it is left in the cargo hold. They probably have no idea what it is, but gold is different; they know what that is and it would be a huge temptation for them to steal it. As you can see, there is too much of this to fly out in your little aircraft and the lake is not large enough to land a bigger one."

With a wave of the hand the guard was dismissed and took the pack back to the pile. Another wave of the hand and the lines of women started to pick up a heavy bag each and to walk towards the edge of the forest, with the guards hurrying them along. Jim watched them walk by. He could see the ones who were new to this and the ones with the bent necks and the pale skin who had obviously been doing it for longer.

The guards each had an AK47 assault rifle on their shoulder and a leather whip on a belt loop. Their boots were shiny and their fatigue uniforms gave them the look of experienced soldiers. They were clearly practiced at herding the unwilling workers to their task.

"So Mr Han, what happens to them next?"

"They walk over the ridge and down to the waterside carrying the pitchblende to where I have had a small dock built and then they load it onto my supply boat. It is an inshore trawler so it looks as though it belongs here. They unload the food and other supplies that the boat is bringing and they carry them back here. It takes them most of the daylight hours as it is a steep climb on the way back."

"Some of those women do not look capable of making it."

"They are peasants, Major, bred to a life of hard labour and, if some do not make it, the others carry their load and there are less mouths to feed."

Jim looked at Han. "That seems pretty cold."

"I have an almost endless supply of labour trying to get out of China to the promised land. They volunteer to pay for their passage by working here. They know the work is hard and still they come. A few losses are nothing. Now it is time for breakfast, I think. Do you join me this morning?"

Jim hid his disgust as best he could. "Thank you for the offer, but I will eat in my room this morning."

"Ah yes. Chen is a pretty little plaything, is she not? I hope you continue to enjoy her."

With that, the elegantly dressed Han turned and walked back through the wide front door of the cabin. Jim paused and watched the end of the column of women walk into the forest edge, then he walked through the door and took the stairs back to his room.

Chen was dressed and waiting when he got there. "Chen, can you bring some breakfast up here, please? Make sure it is enough for two."

She bobbed her head and left the room as Jim walked across to stare through the barred window. His mind was racing as he tried to remember what the hell pitchblende was used for. He knew he had heard of it, but what the devil was it?

The lake was calm as he looked along it, with the Beaver sitting quietly on its floats, again covered by camouflage sheets. He wondered if he could get into the aircraft without being seen, to disable the GPS tracker. Getting into the fuel tank bay below the floor would be hellish difficult out on the water, but if they didn't know where he was maybe he could divert somewhere and land before the explosives were ignited.

Chen came back into the room while he was still contemplating his options. She set down the tray on the table and waited for him to join her. He sighed as he sat down.

"What is wrong?" she asked. "Is the food not what you wanted?"

He picked up his fork and then smiled at her. "The food is just fine. I'm trying to remember what a particular ore is used for and I'm drawing blank."

"Which ore it is?"

He swallowed the forkful he was chewing. "It's the stuff those women were carrying. Han called it pitchblende. I'm sure I've heard of it, but I'll be damned if I can call it to mind."

Chen laid her fork down carefully next to her plate. "Han was wrong. Pitchblende is what they dig out of the mine. After it has been through the processing shed it is called Yellowcake, even though most of it is not yellow."

"Yellowcake? But that's the stuff that makes …"

"Uranium, yes. I think Han is selling it to someone who is not supposed to have it."

Jim put his elbows on the table and rested his chin on the back of his interlaced fingers. He looked across at Chen, who looked back at him calmly.

"I knew you weren't some Chinese peasant. No worker from the rice paddies would know about pitchblende or yellowcake. Oh, and you should be careful, your accent slipped and your English improved all of a sudden. So who are you really and what the hell are you doing here?"

She gave him a small smile. "I knew as soon as I said it that my cover was blown, but I am going to have to trust you. I am a federal agent in the FBI. I am on assignment to track the illegal trafficking of people from China into the USA. Unfortunately, as you can see, it has not gone exactly to plan."

"And your brother in the mine?"

"He is not my brother; he is another agent who was working with me."

"I take it you don't have any means of contacting your people?"

She shook her head a little sadly. "We had to ditch everything when we saw that people were being searched before they got on to the freighter that brought us from China."

"So is this a Chinese government operation?"

"No, not as far as we know. It appears their government want to stop this almost as much as we do. I don't have the proof, but we think this is being run by the Triads, a Chinese criminal gang like the Yakuza in Japan or the Mafia in the US."

"I wondered, because the guards had a military look about them."

She smiled. "Well spotted. They are all ex-People's Liberation Army. Han hires them because they are useful in this situation, where his street thugs would not be."

"I thought the FBI only operated internally. Shouldn't the CIA be doing this?"

Chen smiled a little. "The CIA has bigger problems than people trafficking. Their main focus is on terrorism and espionage. The FBI does operate in foreign countries, just usually with the local government's agreement."

"So you were deep under cover?"

"Until now, yes. The Chinese government did not want us involved at their end, but we were concerned that their people were not taking it as seriously as we hoped."

"I guess we'd better make sure your cover is not blown. Han seems to be quite ruthless, so you'd better be careful of that accent."

She nodded. "I will and maybe together we can work out a way to get away from here to alert our people."

Chapter 25

Leah sighed and turned back towards the two men who had been waiting patiently while she crossed and recrossed the broken rock of the scree slope at the side of the mountain. She stopped and looked up at the wide expanse of tumbled rocks that rose up the mountainside. Her shoulders sagged as she turned back.

"I've lost the trail. There's nothing here at all, as far as I can see."

Geordie looked across at the rock slide. "Could we walk around the edge and see where they came off it?"

"We could, but it would be a long shot. The sign is getting difficult anyway and we could miss it completely."

"So what do you want to do, Ivan?"

The big Welshman looked at them both and then stood up slowly from the fallen tree trunk he had been sitting on. "We know the rough direction they were travelling, even though they have wandered about quite a bit. So I say we take a compass direction and head that way to see what we find."

Geordie stood and shouldered his pack before picking up his rifle. "You don't seem impressed, Leah?"

"They could have gone anywhere from here and you could end up lost in the forest. It is better to go back and try another way."

Ivan shook his head and he picked up his own weapon. "Can't do that, *Cariad*. The boss is in trouble and we need to find him. Even if going this way proves fruitless, it means we have covered an area we don't need to search again."

Geordie smiled at her. "Surely you can't want to leave two handsome guys like us lost in the deep dark woods?"

Leah shook her head resignedly. "If I don't go with you you'll only end up in trouble, probably lost in the forest and making a meal for the bears. Which way are you going to go, Ivan?"

"Due north. Then, if we find nothing, we can go east or west for a couple of miles before we take you home. That should cover a good piece of real estate."

Leah sighed as she picked up her own pack and rifle. "This is a waste of time, but if you insist on going on, then I'll come, too."

Geordie gave her one of his brightest smiles. "That's good; we wouldn't want the band to break up over artistic differences, would we?"

Ivan checked his compass and started to walk out of the clearing. The slope they followed was gentle as it wound between two mountains. Geordie took up the rear and kept a wary eye behind them as they walked on. They crested a rise at the two hour point and could see the forest stretching ahead of them up and over the mountains. To their left they could just see the sunlight glinting from one of the many waterways that carved into the landscape.

Ivan signalled a break and they dropped their packs and sat around on the ground as Geordie opened his pack and drew out the thermos flask.

"It might be a bit stewed by now, but it's warm and wet." As he passed the two small cups to his companions.

Ivan sat sipping the lukewarm coffee and staring out over the landscape. He was beginning to think that Leah was right and that this was a fool's errand. Trying to search an area this big on foot and with no trail to follow was not productive, but he couldn't just sit back and wait for news. He knew Geordie felt the same. Neither man was good at waiting.

"Sounds like you were right then, Ivan," Leah said quietly, her head cocked to one side.

"Right about what?"

"Can't you hear it?"

Ivan paused and listened. "No, nothing. What did you hear?"

"Huh, city boys. I don't know what it is, but over that way there's a noise that doesn't belong in these forests. It's faint, but constant."

Ivan stood and hefted his pack back into position. "How far away, would you guess?"

Leah listened and shook her head. "Hard to tell, but probably somewhere around a mile, I guess, maybe a bit less."

"Pack up, Geordie, we're back on the trail, with just a little bit of luck."

Chapter 26

"So then, Chen, what kind of escape plan have you come up with?"

She sighed. "We can't just escape; the cost would be too high. Even if we could alert the authorities, Han would kill the miners before they could be rescued."

"Surely he doesn't have enough men to do that and make sure he gets everyone?"

She smiled sadly. "I thought you had been in the mine? Didn't you see the pipe running along at the side of the entrance shaft?"

"The ventilation pipe? Yes, I saw it. So what?"

Chen shook her head. "That's not for ventilation, that's a water pipe connected to a small lake further up the mountainside. If the workers rebel or the operation is discovered they lock the iron gates and open the valve. They flood the mine and drown all the witnesses."

"Hell's teeth! So if we report what's going on we could be responsible for hundreds of men being killed."

"Not just the men. The plan is for the women to be driven in there by the guards, as well, before the gate is shut and the water starts to flow. Then Han and his men leave to enjoy the spoils of their work here. That's why they take the uranium ore out of here in batches so they have their nest egg ready for when it all ends."

Jim sat back in his chair. That made his plan to escape useless. There was no way he could make a run for it knowing it would cost all these people their lives.

"How do you know all this? Are you sure about it?"

Chen nodded. "I'm sure. The women in the kitchen talk. They tell the newcomers like me so that we don't put their men, or them, in danger."

Jim thought for a moment. "There's a flaw in this. What happens when one of the workers or a batch of them has done their year of labour? How does Han control them when they are gone from here?"

Chen stood and walked to the window, pausing as she looked out across the still lake waters. "Nobody leaves here. The arrangement of people working for a year to pay for their passage is a lie. The woman who prepares Han's food has been here since it began over two years ago. Her husband was put to work in the lower workings; she has not seen him for many months. She believes he is dead and she has nothing to live for."

Jim walked across the room and stood next to Chen. He took her hand and together they continued to stare through the window. His situation was worse than he had imagined and with this level of coldness from Han and his thugs he had to worry about what was happening to Megan and the baby.

"Whatever plan we come up with, Chen, it has to include all the workers."

"What are you thinking of?"

"Right at this moment, I'm fresh out of ideas, as you Americans say. Han seems to have covered his bases rather well, but there must be a weakness somewhere. We just have to find it".

Chapter 27

Ivan eased himself forward on his belly to peer between two of the small bushes that grew in the cracks of the rock outcropping he was lying on. To his right was Leah, and beyond her, Geordie. All of them strained to make out what was causing the noise in the shallow valley below them.

Their walk through the forest to this point had been careful and quiet until they found this observation point. Now they waited as the noise approached them from up the hill to their right.

Geordie hissed to attract Ivan's attention and when the big man looked across he could see him pointing down to the valley. He eased forward again and saw the movement through the trees. Whatever it was seemed to be big. Then he realised what he was looking at as they came closer. People, lots of people, all walking together, but not speaking. The sound they had heard was the mass of footsteps tramping across the debris of the forest floor.

As they came closer Ivan realised they were all women carrying heavy packs on their backs. Then he saw the men walking to either side with AK47 assault rifles over their shoulders and leather whips on their belts. He watched and noticed that they moved like soldiers. Relaxed but watchful. They could only be guards. Then he noticed that they weren't watching the trees around them, they were watching the women. So not guards, but jailers.

He heard Geordie whisper from the other side of Leah. "Have you noticed?"

"Noticed what?"

"They all look like they are Chinese, just like that guy you dropped back at Megan's cabin."

Leah turned to look at Geordie. "Dropped?"

"Yeah, only put him out for the count. He didn't hurt him."

"A shame. Do you think some of those with guns could be my brothers' killers?"

Ivan nodded as he watched the trudge of people passing by. "Could be. Those weapons are automatic rifles so they could have made those wounds on your brothers."

Leah moved and brought her rifle forward to take aim. Ivan stretched out his hand and gently pressed the weapon down.

"Not yet, love. By the look of these people you'll get your chance, but just not yet. Now more importantly, we need to know where they are going and then where they came from."

Leah relaxed a little. "When we find the right ones you let me take them out, is that a deal?"

"If we can, yes, but for now, do you know this area?"

She nodded. "Where they are walking will take them down to the waterside. There is a deep inlet that eventually leads out to the ocean. Where they have come from I do not know. There are no villages out that way, just forest and mountains with a deep lake or two."

Ivan tapped Geordie on the shoulder. "What do you make of those?" he said, pointing.

Geordie eased forward to see more clearly. "Two double-ended handcarts by the look of them and they have forty-gallon drums on them. Four on each, I think."

Ivan slithered back off the rock and waved the other two to come with him. When they were down into deep cover behind the outcropping they sat cross-legged and spoke quietly.

"Right now, we need some answers. First, where are they going and why? Next, where have they come from and what are they doing there? We could also do with knowing what's in those packs and the forty-gallon drums."

"OK, so how do you want to play this?" Geordie asked.

"We let this column of people go past and you, Geordie, follow them down the hill. Keep well out of sight and watch what they do and where. Leah, while they are heading down the hill you and I will follow their trail, back to where they've come from. With all those people I reckon even an engineer can follow the trail."

Leah looked at both men. "So how do we meet up again afterwards?"

"Good point. I'm guessing that after they've finished what they are doing down the hill, they will come back up again, at least I hope so. Geordie, you keep following them and at some point Leah and I will be off to one side of the trail, waiting for you. Does that work for both of you?"

Geordie smiled. "Works for me, but don't jump out on me and shout boo! You know how nervous I get."

"Maybe I should go with Geordie if he is nervous?"

Ivan patted Geordie on the arm. "Leah, that's a pathetic attempt at a joke. Martin Peters doesn't have a nerve in his body."

Leah looked puzzled. "I thought your name was Geordie?"

Geordie grinned. "Well, bonny lass, you see I come from Newcastle, up in the North-East of England and in the army anybody from up there gets called Geordie. Just like people from Wales get called Taff. Except Ivan, of course. Nobody would dare."

Leah shook her head. "I don't understand. Why Geordie?"

"Well, lass, it's like this: George Stephenson, the Victorian engineer, was a Geordie boy like me and it's down to him that people from the North-East are called Geordies in the first place."

Leah smiled. "Go on then, tell us the story."

"It came from the coal mines. George Stephenson developed a safety lamp for miners and then Davey developed what he said was a better one. All the coal mines changed over to the Davey Lamp, except up in the North-East where they stayed with the lamp they called the Geordie Lamp and so the Geordies got their name."

"Is that true or just one of your tall tales?"

"As true as I'm off down the hill following these people. See you later."

Chapter 28

Chuck Colton stood looking down through his window at 9th Street of Washington DC. For some reason he didn't understand, watching the traffic and the people going about their daily business calmed him. Maybe it was because they had no idea of the troubles being dealt with here in the Hoover Building. He turned round from his window as the door opened behind him.

"Agent Mason is here for your four o'clock meeting, sir."

"Thank you, Kate. Please send him in and hold any calls while he is here, if you could."

Deputy Director Colton resumed his seat behind the impressive desk, which his position entitled him to, and waited. He heard the gentle tap on the door and then it opened for his personal assistant to show the young man in.

He stood and waved to a chair on the other side of his desk. "Come in, Peter, and tell me what you've got."

"Thank you, sir," Mason said as he sat and opened the blue folder he carried. "We don't have much, I'm sorry to say."

"Don't apologize; just tell me where we are."

The younger man nodded and cleared his throat. "We had our last report from the two agents just over four weeks ago. That was when Agent Chen called in with an update. They had made contact with the smuggling gang and were about to be taken to Shanghai docks to board a freighter. Since then we have heard nothing from them."

"Do we know why not?"

"Yes sir, we do. We tracked the signal from the GPS chips in their phones. We sent another agent and she found that the phones had been pushed under a shipping container, along with various other items that might have been able to identify them as being FBI."

Colton sat back into the leather of his chair. "Do we know why they would do that?"

"Again, yes sir. The agent asked around and managed to find a dock worker who had seen a group being loaded onto an older freighter. He saw that they were all being searched before being allowed aboard."

"Shit! So we have no way of tracking them. OK, what about the freighter itself? What do we have on that? Do we know how many of these illegals they were carrying?"

The younger man eased his finger around his collar, nervous of the Deputy Director's famous temper. "We have virtually nothing. We don't have a name or a flag for the freighter and we don't know when it sailed. We have a window of probability of around four days, but with the amount of traffic in and out of Shanghai we can't narrow it down. The witness thought there were forty or fifty people being taken aboard, but he wasn't sure."

"Do we have access to the port records? Could they tell us what ship was in that particular berth?"

"The only way to do that would be to ask the Chinese authorities. As you know, they are co-operating, to some extent, but they did forbid us to put agents into China. They were due to handle that end of the operation."

Colton stood and went back to the window. He looked at the scurrying people crossing the street outside and then turned around and leaned back against the cool glass.

"So did they?"

"Did they what, sir?"

Colton sighed. "Did they handle their end of the operation? Do they have any assets on the freighter? Are they tracking likely targets? Have they worked out where people are being landed and how? Anything?"

"Erm, I don't know, sir. They haven't sent us anything on this group."

Colton walked back to the desk with his fists balled. He put those fists down on the desk top and leaned over them to the young man opposite. He paused to control his anger.

"Our people are in danger and may already be dead and you are sitting waiting for a report from the Chinese? Get back downstairs to your office and find out now. Contact the Chinese liaison officer and ask him directly what they know and what they've done. I want a full report from them today. I don't care how little or how much they have to tell us, I want it all. We don't leave our people hanging out to dry. Now get the hell out of here and get me my answers!"

The younger man was heading for the door when Colton yelled after him. "And get me satellite surveillance of Shanghai docks for the target four days!"

Chapter 29

"Megan, I've got to go and check on my bear cubs. Should I leave the dogs with you?"

"Bear cubs? Near here?"

"That's right. There's a den a way up the hill in a small ravine. The Mama Bear is raising two cubs. I've been taking photos of them since they first emerged from the cave they were born in."

Megan came through from the kitchen wiping her hands on a dishcloth. "Isn't that a bit risky? You know how protective the bears get when they have cubs."

Kelly smiled. "It's not so bad; I climb up, so I am looking down from a cliff. I use a long lens so I don't worry them, and if the bear starts to climb up the cliff towards me I can get out of the way before she gets near. Anyway she's seen me before and never bothered, so I think she knows I don't mean her babies any harm."

"Any chance I can come with you? I'm in the first stages of cabin fever, stuck round here all day."

Kelly paused. "What about Daniela?"

"If I have her in her sling across my back she goes straight to sleep and she'll stay that way until we get back. Anyway, she needs to get used to bears. We have an old male that comes by the cabin when Jim's fishing. He sits and waits until he gets thrown a fish and then he wanders off. I think he's a bit old for hunting and we owe him a debt anyway."

Kelly smiled. "In which case get your boots on, sister. We're going on a bear hunt with Daniela. You'll have to tell me about this debt to a bear when we get back."

Fifteen minutes later they were ready with the three dogs getting more excited as they realised there was a walk in the offing. Kelly picked up her shotgun from the rack by the door and walked outside into the thin sunshine.

"Kelly, do I need the Winchester?" Megan asked.

"Always best to bring it. The noise will chase the bears away if they are having a bad day and come towards us."

Megan picked up the rifle and hung it over her shoulder on the leather sling. She walked outside to find that Kelly had the dogs sitting in an expectant row, all wagging their tails and panting.

Kelly smiled at Megan, then turned back to the dogs and swung her arm. "Off you go!"

Three black and white blurs exited the clearing in the direction she had waved. Then the two women started to trek after them at a far steadier pace.

"Won't the dogs upset the bears?" Megan asked.

"No. They'll keep running back to see where I am and, once we get close, I'll get them to lie down and stay a good distance away."

"What about Bracken? He's not as well trained as your two."

"He's getting there. I've been giving him some extra training around the cabin to pass the time. He's a quick learner, like most collies."

The trail climbed up through the trees on the hill behind the cabin. As predicted Daniela fell fast asleep almost as soon as the walk started and, also as predicted, the three dogs kept reappearing out of the undergrowth to check on the two women before dashing off again. Twenty-five minutes into the walk the trail steepened and Kelly called the dogs to her. She made all three lie down and then sternly gave them the instruction to stay. Bracken whimpered a little as Megan walked away, but stayed where he had been told.

The two women climbed higher until they came out of the trees at the top of a cliff overlooking a small ravine. Kelly pointed out where there was a small hidden cave entrance and almost on cue a small black nose appeared from the dark. The nose was followed by a Black Bear cub as it ventured out into the sunlight and sat down to enjoy the warmth. A second cub joined it moments later and then the bushes were shouldered aside as the adult bear appeared.

Kelly spent around half an hour photographing the bear family while Megan just watched them in wonder.

"Lord, how I love this country," Megan whispered to Kelly.

Kelly tapped Megan on the arm and indicated they should leave. They silently withdrew into the trees and walked back down the rough path. The dogs were laying exactly where they had been left and jumped up as soon as Kelly gave them the command.

As they neared the cabin Kelly's dogs, Paddy and Sam, stopped and lay down with their ears pricked up. Bracken sat between them, happily wagging his tail. Kelly dropped to one knee and motioned Megan to get down as well.

"What is it?" Megan whispered.

"Might be trouble. The dogs have seen something they don't like. Stay here and let me cut round to one side to see what it is."

She disappeared into the undergrowth and Megan stayed still on the path, waiting. After three or four minutes Megan stood up to see if she could see anything. Blissfully unaware of any problem, Bracken barked to get her to hurry up.

There was a rustling in the bushes ahead of her and a dark-haired man stood up and turned towards her. His eyes opened wide in surprise as he started to raise the ugly AK47 in his hands towards Megan. She slipped the Winchester off her shoulder and rapidly jacked a round into the chamber, knowing as she did so that she was too late. The automatic rifle in the man's hands swung towards her and three rapid shots roared out.

Megan was stunned not to have been hit when she realised the man had vanished. As she stood there with the rifle in her hands, Kelly stepped back onto the path. The slight trace of smoke from the barrel of her shotgun told its own story. They walked forward and looked down at the body in the bush. The first shotgun blast had taken him by surprise, so he'd paused in firing, the second had ripped his arm and the third had virtually destroyed his chest.

"I wonder how he found us." Kelly asked as she slid three replacement shells into the tube magazine of the shotgun.

Before Megan could answer, four rounds, from across the clearing, cracked close overhead. She snapped the Winchester up to her shoulder and scanned through the telescopic sight. The attacker reappeared from behind the tree and took aim again. Before he could fire, Megan took the shot and he fell backwards with a scream as his weapon flew out of his hands.

The sound of the rifle, so close to her, wakened Daniela and she was crying loudly as Megan walked across the clearing in front of the cabin to check on the second attacker. Her shot had taken him directly in the heart and he had probably been dead before he hit the forest floor. Megan picked up the AK47 and walked back towards the cabin as she comforted the crying child.

"I've had a look round and I can't see any more of them. So what now?" Kelly asked.

"I need to get Daniela inside to safety just in case there are more of these bastards. Then coffee, I think. It's been quite a tiring walk," Megan answered.

Kelly stopped and looked closely at her. "Did you feel anything when you shot that man?"

Megan nodded. "Recoil."

"Nothing else? I thought you were more affected last time we were attacked."

"I was, but I seem to be past worrying about that now. These people took the man I love to God knows where, to make him do God knows what. They tried to kill me and you and, more importantly, they tried to kill my baby. In my book that means they got everything that was coming to them. So the emotions are gone for now."

Kelly shrugged. "I envy you. I feel a bit sick after that. I guess there may be some nightmares tonight." She hefted the shotgun onto her shoulder and turned towards the cabin. "But coffee now, then. Does that mean we have to get that handsome friend of yours back up here for the bodies, eh?"

Megan laughed. "I'll get you another chance to talk to David Red Cloud all right. Maybe we should get him to stay for dinner this time? That way you get a bit more time to work on him. Poor man doesn't know what he's getting into."

As they sat drinking coffee in the cabin with Daniela settled down and sleeping peacefully, Kelly looked across at her friend and smiled.

"What?" Megan asked.

"I was just thinking. Now I know why Jim calls you Mama Bear."

****

Megan lay in her bed in the early hours of the morning listening to Daniela snuffling in her sleep and Bracken lying by the door breathing softly. The dog had refused to sleep anywhere except the baby's room since the first attack on the cabin. He seemed to understand the danger had not gone away.

Despite her brave words to Kelly, the reaction had set in and she was trembling all over. Her forehead was wet with sweat and the tears forced their way out of the corners of her eye then ran down to drip onto the pillow. The picture of that man's face through the telescopic sight on her Winchester was burned into her consciousness. He had looked so surprised and vulnerable as the high-powered round had ploughed into his chest.

She felt Bracken's cold nose lift her hand from the bed cover as he tried to sneak onto the bed. She let the dog climb up and then snuggle alongside her for comfort. He licked the tear from her cheek and then settled down, a warm protector in the night.

She hated herself for the weakness, but she really needed Jim here to cling onto in the darkness. She prayed a little before she eventually fell into a fitful sleep.

Chapter 30

Geordie lay on a small cliff overlooking the waterway below him. Even without binoculars, he could see fairly clearly what was going on. The fishing boat tied up alongside the crude wooden jetty had its hatches open and the lines of women were operating in chains, unloading large backpacks from the hold. The armed men had spread out and were keeping watch on the women and out across the waterway. It seemed not to have occurred to them to guard inland.

The backpacks from the boat were being stacked at the edge of the forest, while the packs they had brought down the rough trail with them were piled up down at the waterside. Geordie kept watching until it became clear that the fish hold was now empty. There was shouting from the deck of the fishing boat and the women walked wearily across to the other pile of packs. They formed their chains again and started to load the heavy bags into the boat.

Two rubber tubes were run out from the deck of the trawler and connected to the metal drums on the first handcart. Two drums were filled from one hose and two from the other. For the second cart, all four drums were filed from just the one hose. Just as the filling ended some of the fluid splashed across the arm of the woman standing on the second cart and holding the filler nozzle. She screamed and leapt from the cart then ran into the waterway and plunged her arm into the frigid water. The nearest guards yelled at her and pulled her from the water before pushing her back towards the cart.

Geordie took his chance and moved quickly towards the unguarded pile of packs that had just been unloaded. As he got close he placed his own pack and rifle behind a tree and slithered forward on his belly, with only the Colt M1911 strapped to his leg for protection. If the guards with their AK47s spotted him that would not be a lot of use, but it might just get him enough time to make a run for it.

He moved forward cautiously until he reached the edge of the pile. Reaching a hand through one of the low bushes he pulled a pack towards him and looked inside. The bag was full of brown rice. He pulled another one from the pile and checked in that. This, too, was full of rice. Now what the devil did that mean, he wondered.

He slid back across the rough ground and only lifted off his belly when he reached the tree where his pack and rifle waited. He slipped the pack onto his back and made his way to a hidden vantage point where he could see the trail the women had used on the way down the hill. He settled down and made himself comfortable to wait for the return trip to start.

At the same time, Leah and Ivan were following the trail that had been made by hundreds of weary feet passing up and over this ridge countless times. Keeping close to the treeline and watching warily for any of the armed guards, they walked carefully up the hill. As the trail crested the ridge they saw that it angled away across the next valley and disappeared into the densely packed trees. They withdrew into the forest and spent a long ten minutes scanning for any sign of movement in the valley before they continued.

Satisfied that they were alone for the moment, they walked briskly across the clearing and followed the trail into the forest. Even though it was darker under the thick canopy of fir trees, the trail could not have been clearer. They walked on in silence listening for any untoward sound that might warn them of an enemy.

They moved forward as the trail started to climb another ridge and slipped deeper into the trees as they neared the crest. At the apex of the ridge they stopped and looked from the cover of the forest. Below them they could see the trail led down to the end of a narrow, steep-sided valley with a lake filling it. To the left they could see a decent-sized wooden cabin raised on cut down tree trunks to lift it from the cold ground. The thin trail of smoke from the chimney at the back of the building told them they had found their destination and the armed guard patrolling at the front of the cabin confirmed it.

"OK, Leah, this is where we wait for Geordic. I don't want to wander down there blind. There's no way that cabin is big enough for all those women. There must have been two hundred or more of them."

"So we wait for them to make the return trip and see where they go. I counted two hundred and fifty-seven, with fourteen guards."

"How the hell did you manage to count them all?"

She smiled. "It's a quirk I have with numbers. Pretty useless up to now, but I'm sure of my count."

"Well OK, then. Somewhere there is a place where two hundred and fifty-seven exhausted women can lay their tired heads. Damned if I can see it from here, though."

Leah's smile lit up her face again. "We can certainly see where that many people go. Maybe we should pull back into the trees a bit further. We can move forward again when they are past so we can catch Geordie following behind."

Ivan nodded and shouldered his way through some low branches and into the forest where they found a small depression filled with pine needles. "Perfect place to catch up on some sleep. I'll take first watch if you like."

"Why would we need to sleep now? It is two hours to dark and we need to be alert for danger."

"Fourth rule of soldiering, never stand when you can sit, never sit when you can lie, never stay awake unless you have to and take every opportunity to brew up. Bottom line, we might have a long night ahead of us, depending what we find, so get some rest now."

"What are the first three rules?"

Ivan gave her one of his rare smiles. "Never get separated from your weapon, always keep something to eat later and never march on Moscow."

She nodded. "Those sound like sensible rules. What about the brew-up?"

Ivan smiled. "Can't risk the fire being seen or the smoke being smelled. We'll have to wait for Geordie and his flask if there's any left."

Chapter 31

"Ah, Major, I am glad to see you are up and about this morning. I hope Chen has not been tiring you too much."

Jim turned to see Han walking across the beach towards him. He had been standing silently, contemplating the lake and trying to work out how to get to the Beaver, without being seen by the ground crew, to disable the explosives. With the fuel tanks mounted below the cabin floor it would be difficult without removing the floor panels and without being caught doing it.

"What can I do for you, Mr Han?"

"There is another batch of my special cargo to be delivered to the cargo ship."

Jim turned and looked at the waves being whipped up on the surface of the lake. If the wind was creating them down here in this steep-sided valley the ocean was going to be difficult, if not impossible to land on.

He shook his head at Han. "Not the weather for it. The wind is too strong and it looks like we could be in for heavy rain. Best to leave it for another day."

Han gave a small smile. "If it was going to be easy flying my cargo I could have used any pilot. I chose you to be able to handle the difficult days. You will not be landing this time. My ground crew have fitted a stores release system under your wings. It was used on the military variants of the Beaver and we obtained two from the Internet some time ago."

Jim turned. "So you want me to fly over the ship and drop the cargo onto the deck?"

Han chuckled. "Not quite. I doubt if the Captain would be amused at having his ship dive-bombed by you. No, the cargo is attached to a flotation tank and you should drop both of them as close to the side of the ship as possible. The ship's boat will be ready and will pick them up."

"Two of them?"

"That is correct. You will have one under each wing. It should have little effect on the performance of the aircraft."

"And when do you want this delivery to take place?"

"In about three hours. The ship should be back at the right coordinates by then and you, of course, will want to check your aircraft before you go."

"Tell your men to have the aircraft ready for me. I'll go and get a jacket and be with them shortly."

With that he turned and walked back towards the main cabin. Han watched him go and then strolled along the beach to where the ground crew waited for their instructions.

As Jim mounted the stairs to get to his room he heard a muffled cry from in front of him. As he reached the top of the staircase he could see the corridor guard was smiling at something and clearly enjoying himself. He turned into the corridor to see Van der Merwe had Chen pinned against the wall with one hand over her mouth and the other firmly clamped over her left breast.

He said nothing as he strode towards the pair and the solid punch to his right ear took the Boer miner by surprise and knocked him to the floor. Jim took Chen's arm and pushed her gently towards the door of his room. As she moved past him, the mine boss recovered from his surprise and stood up.

"So then, sweet on the little chink whore, are you? I'll have to cure you of that."

Jim waited calmly as the bigger man approached. He noted the balled fists and the flaring nostrils. He would have preferred room to move, but this corridor would have to do.

The South African's attack was fierce and fast, with a large scarred fist aimed at Jim's face. The Englishman rocked back out of the way and let the momentum carry the miner half past him. Then his own strike to the throat followed by the knee to his belly put the angry man on the floor gasping for air.

He waited until the miner had got his breathing under control to see what would happen next. As he expected, the thug climbed halfway up before launching himself at Jim, with his head low and aiming at his stomach. Again Jim waited until the last instant before changing position and smashing the side of his stiffened hand down on the back of the man's neck. Van der Merwe went down face first and skidded along the wooden floor, leaving a trail of blood from his crushed nose.

"Are we done yet?" Jim asked.

His answer came in another roaring charge from the South African. The one, two combination punch that Ivan had taught him stopped the fight. The left jab brought the bigger man to a halt and the right cross put him down again, crumpled against the corridor wall.

Jim stood over the beaten man and waited until he looked up. "Now I think you might find it a good idea to listen for a change. If you touch Chen again or if I hear you have hurt any more of the women around here, in any way, then Han is going to need a new mine boss. Is that absolutely clear to you?"

Van der Merwe nodded and spat a gob of blood onto the floor.

"And let's be clear here," Jim said. "Next time you and I tangle, I won't stop when you go down."

He turned and walked into his room without a backward glance. Chen was sitting by the window with a worried look on her face that cleared as he came in. He walked to the sink in the small bathroom and rinsed his damaged knuckles under a stream of cold water.

Chen came and stood beside him, looking at his face in the mirror above the basin. "Thank you. I have been worried about him trying something for days now. I just didn't expect it with the guard watching."

"I hope that puts him straight, but you need to be careful around that bastard when I'm not here. He'll be wanting revenge."

Chen nodded. "I know that. I'm pretty sure I could have taken him, but with the guard watching that would have blown my cover. A Chinese peasant using FBI unarmed combat moves would have raised suspicions."

Jim looked into her calm dark eyes reflected in the mirror. "You'd have let that attack continue just to maintain your cover? You really are quite special. You know that? I think my Megan is going to like you when we get out of here."

Chapter 32

They lay absolutely still in the debris of the forest floor as the exhausted women trudged past with the large packs on their backs. In front of them one woman stumbled and fell to her knees. As she put her hands down to push herself back up a whip whistled and cracked across the back of her calves. She screamed and fell forward. Two of her companions helped her up and she stumbled on, with one of them each side to support her.

Ivan felt Leah stiffen and she hissed at him. "That one, whip boy, he has my brother's knife on his belt."

Ivan looked through the undergrowth. "How can you tell?"

"I made that leather sheath when I was thirteen. I made one for each of them, for Christmas. I still have the scar on my thumb where I cut myself doing it."

"So now we have our answer. These people are the ones that killed your brothers."

"But why would they do that?"

Ivan sighed. "Whatever these people are doing has got to be hugely illegal to act like this. My guess is that your brothers ran into a patrol intended to keep people away."

Leah started to move forward until Ivan put a hand on her shoulder and pulled her back. "Put the knife away. It's not his time yet. If we take him down now it will be like kicking over a wasp's nest. Our turn comes later."

Leah relaxed and then turned her head towards the big Welshman. "Sorry, I wasn't thinking, but when the time comes I want him and whoever was with him."

Ivan nodded. "I can see where you would want that, but look, the end of the column is arriving. Keep an eye out for Geordie and I'll move to the edge of the treeline and watch where they go."

He slid forward on his belly until he could see down into the valley where the column of weary women walked slowly towards the end of the lake. The guards were spread out to each side of the column and moved as though they knew their business. Ivan watched as the column wound around to the back of the large cabin and then he saw them continue on, but this time without their burdens.

Now he moved to the right to be able to see further in the direction the column was shuffling towards. From here he could now see what looked like low wooden barrack huts set back in the trees. The column split up, with the women walking into the three huts he had counted. Unless they went back much further than they appeared to it was going to be damned crowded in there, he thought.

He heard a low whistle to his left and a couple of moments later Geordie and Leah dropped down to either side of him. Ivan rolled to one side and looked at Geordie who grinned back at him.

"So what did you find out?"

Geordie pointed down into the valley as the last of the column disappeared around the corner of the cabin. "Those packs they are carrying are full of food. A lot of it seemed to be brown rice and then there were quite a few bags of dried fish."

"Any idea what they were carrying on the way out?"

Geordie reached into his jacket pocket and brought out a piece of crumbly brown material. "One of the bags split a bit and this fell out. It looks like nothing I've seen before. Any ideas?"

Ivan touched it and crumbled a little between his fingers before shaking his head and passing the lump to Leah. She sniffed it and rubbed the sandy surface before passing it back.

"Not seen anything like that around here before, but with that flat surface on the top and bottom I wonder if it's something they make down there. It doesn't look natural, at least not for anything I've seen in these mountains."

"What about the drums, Geordie?" Ivan asked. "Did you find out what they are carrying in them?"

"Not for sure. I got the smell of gasoline when they were first pumping, so I'm guessing it might be fuel for the Beaver. That was just in two drums, I think. The others are more of a puzzle. Some poor soul got some splashed on her and it looked like it hurt quite a bit."

Ivan frowned. "What the hell fluid hurts just from being splashed on you?"

Geordie shrugged, but Leah spoke quietly. "Could it be an acid?"

Ivan looked at her for a long moment. "Maybe, but why would you need drums of acid out here in the middle of nowhere?"

"Well, damn me." Geordie said, pointing into the valley while he looked through the telescopic sight on his rifle. "Would you look who that is?"

Leah followed the direction of his finger. "Who what is?"

"The tall guy who just walked out of the front of the cabin wearing a brown leather jacket. Leah, may I introduce you to Major James Wilson, late of the Royal Engineers and the one we came to find!"

"He doesn't seem to be under guard. Does that mean he is working with these people?"

"No, bonny lass, it means he is trying to keep Megan and the baby alive. As far as he knows, they are still being guarded by a couple of thugs and if he steps out of line they get the chop."

"So what do we do now?"

"Now we keep watch on this place to see what they are doing and, after dark, we take a little walk and see if we can spring the boss out of there. Geordie, you take first watch and wake me in two hours."

Geordie continued to watch through his telescopic sight. "Looks like the boss is going flying."

Ivan looked up at the sky. "Pretty bloody awful weather for an aircraft that size. Still, he usually knows what he's doing."

Chapter 33

The ground crew took the camouflage covers off the aircraft with Jim watching to make sure they did not snag on anything that might cause him a problem. He checked again that the underwing cargo clamps were holding securely before he climbed through the narrow doorway into the pilot's seat. He ran his eyes over the instrument panel and set the three central levers into the right configuration for take-off.

Satisfied, he started the engine and allowed it to settle into a steady beat before signalling to the boat crew that they could unfasten the mooring lines. Once they were out of the way and heading for shore, he moved the aircraft across the choppy water to the best position for his take-off run. One last check to see that the lake ahead was clear and he pushed the throttle to the stop to give him maximum power.

The short sharp waves running down the lake towards him made the acceleration run uncomfortable, but the churned water allowed the floats to unstick that little bit earlier and he pulled the control column back to gain altitude before his turn around the cliff. As the cliff lashed past, just to his right, he spun the control yoke over and pressed the rudder pedal to take the willing aircraft around in a tight climbing turn.

Once clear, he settled the old plane down on to its preplanned course and sat back to let the earth pass by below him. The deteriorating weather seemed to have driven the fishermen home and he saw no sign of their boats this time. The loaded and threatening clouds drove him lower and the squalls of pounding rain obscured his vision. He relied heavily on his navigation instruments to get him to his target and was relieved when the dark bulk of the freighter loomed out of the shrouded horizon.

He took a low pass along the ship to make sure he had the right one before lining the aircraft up ready to drop the cargo from under his wings. He approached as slowly as possible. He saw the ship's boat already pulling clear of the lowered companionway ladder and punching into the waves. As he came abreast of the stern of the ship he pulled the release lever and felt the jerk through the airframe as the two packages fell clear of their mountings. He turned slowly around to the left and circled back to check that the packages were actually floating as they were supposed to. The two small flashing beacons on top of the yellow floats stood out clearly against the dark and forbidding ocean, and then he turned back towards the shore.

Just over an hour later he was back over the elbow lake. Weather conditions had deteriorated still further and the rain was lashing the mountains in vicious bands. On his first approach he ran into one of these squalls and was forced to abort his landing. He circled back to try again and again his timing was off, as yet another squall forced him to apply more power to take the aircraft into a juddering climb and to go around again.

On the third approach he was luckier and there was a gap between the blasts of wind and rain. He slowed his air speed and lined up with the top end of the lake. As he came abreast of the cliff where the lake turned he spun the control column to the left and pressed on the rudder pedals. The old Beaver turned as sweetly as she had ever done and he managed to line her up for a landing as another squall struck and the lake below him disappeared in a grey turbulent haze.

With ragged cliffs all around him and no useful visibility he dare not attempt to fly out of the valley, but held the aircraft on course for a blind landing. With water streaming across his windshield, the floats touched down before he saw the churned surface of the lake. He cut the throttle and allowed the floats to sink onto the water as quickly as possible. The squall passed as rapidly as it had arrived and the misted shore came into view. He taxied the Beaver to the mooring buoy and cut the engine as the boat crew secured the mooring lines.

For a moment he sat in his seat and allowed his racing heart to steady before he unfastened the safety harness and eased open the door. As he climbed down onto the float and into the waiting boat he could feel his legs trembling. That had been a closer call than he wished to try again. He sat in the boat and gripped his hands together so the crewmen would not see them shaking.

Up on the ridgeline Geordie and Ivan had watched the landing on the lake below them. They looked at each other and Geordie shook his head.

"Bloody hell, that was a hairier landing than the one he did in Gibraltar. Are we sure he isn't, just the slightest bit, out of his mind?"

Ivan grinned. "Madder than a box of frogs, but then I think he always has been. You'd have to be to take that job looking for lost submarines."

Leah sat beside them and looked over the valley before she spoke. "Submarines and hairy landings in Gibraltar? Sounds like you two owe me a couple of stories tonight. In any case, I've found us a small cave to shelter in. With a few branches across the entrance it should be warm and dry enough for us and I think we can risk a fire."

Geordie sat up. "That'll be welcome after all this damned rain. I'll cook, but we are running low on meat."

"Not a problem," Leah said, holding up a pair of squirrels by the tails. "I took these while I was scouting around. Throw them in a stew and they'll be fine."

Ivan smiled. "They'll be my first squirrels. Geordie can cook them while we tell you the tales of our tasks for Jim Wilson. And after that, Geordie, I think we need to tell the boss we've arrived. You up for a bracing walk in the moonlight?"

Chapter 34

The weather had moderated by the following morning and Jim walked down the beach to where the ground crew for his aircraft kept their support boat. As he neared the boat the two mechanics trotted across to him. Although unable to speak each other's language, Jim managed to make them understand he needed to check the Beaver after the rough landing of the day before.

The two men climbed into the boat and started the small engine. Once Jim had followed them they released the mooring lines and steered out to where the plane waited under its camouflage sheets. They nodded and smiled when Jim held up ten fingers and waved to tell them they should come back after this many minutes. Thankfully he was dealing with intelligent people and they understood almost immediately.

As the boat pulled away from him he climbed into the aircraft and started checking that the instruments had survived the hard landing. As his eyes scanned across the dials he noticed faint writing on the panel that he hadn't seen before. He leaned in to see it more clearly and smiled. The word was "*Ubique*", the motto that had been on the collar badges of his dress uniform for sixteen years. One of the mottos of the Royal Engineers. He spat on the heel of his hand and rubbed the word out. Now he knew that, somewhere nearby, the two best soldiers he had ever served with were waiting for their chance. They may have retired from the army, but those unique skills don't stop when the uniform comes off.

He finished checking the aircraft and was pleased to see that he had not damaged it during his daring landing. He leaned against the wing strut whistling quietly to himself. It was a moment or two before he realised that he was whistling "Wings", the quick march of the Royal Engineers. He smiled at that and looked around, wondering where they were right now.

On the ridge above the valley Geordie was laying beneath a scrubby bush, watching his old commander through the telescopic sight of his rifle. He watched as Jim climbed out of the support boat and walked to the main cabin. He noticed that he was looking around and Geordie smiled. Message received, it seemed.

The night before, in the lashing rain, Geordie had crept down to the lake's edge and untied the boat. He had paddled it out to the aircraft by leaning over the bow of the boat and using his hands. It had been cold and uncomfortable, but it had been silent and he was almost certain that no patrols would be wandering about in that weather. Having left the message that only Jim would understand, he had put the boat back where he found it and carried on with his reconnaissance.

His silent walk to the accommodation sheds had confirmed they were full of far too many women sleeping on the bare floor with just a blanket. There had been no guards, so whoever these people were, they must be confident that nobody was going to make a run for it over the hills and through this dense, cold forest.

He had scouted further up the valley, away from the lake, and found the two workshops, set under the trees, which straddled a couple of streams that ran down the mountainside. He had walked through the silent sheds and puzzled over what they were intended for, but came up with no answer.

His last port of call had been the large cabin that overlooked the lake. Here he had found a guard, fast asleep in a chair on the porch, his hat pulled low, with a blanket wrapped around him and his AK47 rifle leaning against the wall. He had peered through the ground floor windows into the large main room and the kitchen. Then he walked silently around the outside, checking the windows on the upper floor. Here he struck lucky and found that just two windows on one corner had bars across them, while the rest were without.

Satisfied that he now had the lie of the land, Geordie slipped back up to the ridgeline where Ivan lay with the scoped rifle, covering him in case anything went wrong. They withdrew to the shallow cave shelter that Leah had found and she handed them a welcome warm drink as they settled down. The three of them sat in the shelter appreciating the warmth of the small fire while Geordie briefed the others on what he had found.

Ivan lay back on one elbow and sipped at his coffee. "So you reckon this room with barred windows is where Jim is? I wonder why they let him walk about freely during the day, but have him in a barred room at night."

"My guess would be that they don't want him wandering at night, causing any kind of mischief. The guards seem to stand down after nightfall; at least they do in the early hours of the morning. Maybe they get lazy after their boss goes to bed."

"Could be, a lot of soldiers do when the guard sergeant isn't on top of things. So that's when we try and make contact with Jim. Can we get into the house?" Ivan asked.

"We could get in fairly readily from what I've seen. Trouble is, a wooden building like that could have hellish creaky floors and I don't know if there are any internal guards."

"OK then, the window it is," Ivan agreed. "Leah, I think I've got a job for you."

Chapter 35

Chen woke in the early hours of the morning. There was no sound, except the quiet breathing from Jim Wilson, asleep on the improvised bed on the floor. She rose silently and went to listen at the door. She heard nothing. She stood and looked around the room; there was nothing that could have disturbed her.

There was a sound at the window and she saw movement. Carefully skirting around Jim, she walked to the window and looked more carefully. In the fleeting, cloud-shrouded moonlight she saw a face, framed by dark hair, below her. She hesitated, then opened the window a crack.

"Is Wilson in there?"

"Who are you?" Chen asked.

"No time to explain. Is Wilson there? Get him quickly."

Chen moved swiftly to Jim's side and placed a hand across his mouth. He came awake instantly and gripped her wrist.

"There is someone at the window who wants to speak to you."

"What?"

Chen just pointed and Jim came up out of his bed and walked across to the window in stockinged feet. He opened the window wide and looked down.

"I am Leah. I am here to help you."

Jim looked into the dark eyes. "Who's with you?"

"Ivan is on the front stoop by the door and I am standing on Geordie's shoulders. We need to talk to you. Are you able to take a walk up the ridge towards the sea inlet?"

Jim nodded. "I can probably do that."

"Tomorrow morning take a walk. The trail has been worn by many feet. We will see you and we can talk. I have to go."

Without waiting for an answer the girl dropped down from the window and Jim saw two dark shapes move away from the building. A third large shape came from the front veranda of the cabin and silently joined them. Even in the dark Jim recognised the bulk of his old Welsh Sergeant Major. He closed the window gently then turned and went back to his bed with a happy smile on his face.

Outside, the three would-be rescuers walked carefully and silently back up to their shelter on the ridge. Coming down had been more difficult since the guard in his chair might have been awake. They had moved separately with Ivan heading for the guard by the door to the cabin. Once there, he had slipped silently alongside the man and gripped his neck at the pressure point he had been shown on one of their previous classified tasks.

The guard had jerked under his blanket as the grip came on, but in seconds he had passed out completely. Ivan moved his position so he would not choke on his own tongue, then adjusted the blanket and left him. He would awake about an hour later with a splitting headache, but probably with no memory of the big man who had laid him out so neatly.

Leah and Geordie had slipped around the back of the big cabin to approach the barred window from the other side. Once there the native girl had climbed onto his shoulders and reached up to tap cautiously on the window. The conversation had been quick and simple by necessity. Hopefully they could have a longer talk the next day, with much less risk.

Once back at their shelter in the forest, Geordie had added a little wood to the fire that kept them just warm enough to sleep, without showing a light to the outside world.

"My turn to watch, I think," Leah said and settled herself by the entrance with a blanket around her shoulders.

Knowing how capable she was, neither man argued and both settled down to catch up on their sleep.

Chapter 36

The morning dawned bright and clear with only a gentle breeze from the west. "A shame we didn't wait a couple of days, Major. Your flight would have been much calmer."

Jim turned to Han, who had come out onto the veranda of the cabin behind him. "It would have been a damn sight safer. Maybe we can talk about scheduling your deliveries later on. You wouldn't want to lose your aircraft, now, would you?"

Han paused, then nodded. "A wise precaution and having seen your skill at landing during that storm, I think I do not want to lose my pilot either."

Both men stood and looked along the tranquil waters of the lake for a moment or two.

"My guard tells me that you and my mine chief had a disagreement over the plaything I gave you. You should know that I need him to run my mine and I can always get you another companion."

Jim turned. "And you, Mr Han, should know that I object to the way you treat people. If you expect me to keep flying for you, then you should ensure your tame South African keeps his paws off Chen."

Han smiled and shook his head. "Ah, your sense of honour, no doubt. I have spoken to Van der Merwe and explained that I will be annoyed if he damages my pilot. You should also be careful. That sounded almost like a threat and you know I have two very important bargaining chips in this game. You would not want me to have to tell my men to hurt your woman or your child."

Jim managed to stop his hands balling into fists as he looked the smug criminal in the eye. He turned away and said nothing, but he could feel the hate bubbling up inside him.

"No flying for you today, Major, so how will you pass your time?"

"I was going to try my hand at a little lake fishing, but all these stinking fish carcases on the foreshore don't make that seem too inviting."

"An unfortunate by product of the processes we undertake here, I'm afraid. Still there are many lakes in this area so one without fish is a small price to pay."

Jim looked at Han and didn't comment on the fish. "You seem to be killing the trees around the lake as well, so unless you object I'm going to take a walk up that trail to the west. I'm not good at sitting still, doing nothing."

"Should I send one of my men with you in case of bears?"

"I would prefer not. I like to be able to think while I walk. You have no need to concern yourself, I won't run away. As you say, you have two very good reasons for me to stay here."

"Indeed I do," Han said, as he turned away. "Enjoy your walk."

Jim waited until the door closed and then zipped up his scuffed leather jacket and walked down the short flight of steps in front of the cabin. He carried on walking up the trail, which had been beaten by so many feet, towards the ridge. As he went he scanned around him to make sure none of the guards were following him. Once he was convinced he was alone he upped his pace and strode up the slope.

He reached the treeline and paused, looking back into the valley below. Even though he knew where it was, it was difficult to make out the Beaver aircraft sitting on the lake. He checked again for any followers before he carried on over the ridge and along the trail. As he walked a few paces down the trail, under the shade of the overhanging trees, the valley dropped out of sight.

He was fifty paces from the ridgeline when he heard the low whistle from his left. As he looked in that direction the face of Geordie rose out of the undergrowth, his dark complexion wreathed in smiles.

"Hey boss, fancy meeting you here."

Jim strode across and gripped the strong hand held out to him. "Is Ivan with you?"

"He's up on the ridge, watching in case anybody decided to follow you. Follow me and you can meet Leah a bit more formally while I go and get him."

Geordie led the way through the dark trees to the camouflaged shelter. Inside Leah was rolling up the blankets and fastening them to the packs that stood against the wall. She stopped as Jim came in.

"Let me finish this. Ivan wants everything packed when not in use, in case we have to move out quickly."

She fastened the last blanket to a pack and turned around. She sat down and then studied Jim's face before she smiled shyly.

"I guess you must be Leah? It's a little difficult to recognise you from last night."

"And you are Jim. I saw you through the telescopic sight on Geordie's rifle yesterday."

"Nice to meet you. How did these two reprobates manage to convince you to come with them?"

"I come for vengeance for my family. These people owe me a blood debt. I will tell you about it later maybe. Now we need to get you away from here."

Ivan pushed the covering away from the entrance and he and Geordie came into the shelter. Their bulk seemed to fill the space. They sat down on either side of Leah and looked at Jim.

"Hi, boss. I heard what Leah said. Are you ready to hike out of here? It's about a three-day walk back to where we left our boat," Ivan said.

Jim shook his head. "I can't leave yet or people will die."

"No, that's OK, we've got Megan and Daniela clear. They are staying with her photographer friend, Kelly, in her cabin out in the backwoods. You remember where that was? Leah was supposed to mention that last night, but in all the excitement she forgot."

Jim felt a rush of relief flow through him. "I guess I owe you another one. Thanks, that's a huge load off my mind. I'm afraid it's worse than that, though. If I get away the boss man down there will assume I am going straight to the authorities and he will close the operation down and vanish into the woodwork."

"Why do we care about that? The RCMP can pick him and his thugs up later."

"It's not that simple. They've got a mine down there with iron gates across the shaft. If they decide to close down and make a run for it, the workers get locked in there and then they flood the mine. We can't just leave and let something like six hundred people drown."

Geordie was the first to speak. "The boss is right. I got stuck down a mine once before I joined the army. There was a cave-in and the gallery started to flood. It's a bloody awful way to go. How do they manage the flooding, though?"

Jim sighed as he sat back. "It seems they have a small lake above the mine with some kind of floodgate or valve. They just whack that on, then the water shoots down a pipe into the mine and does the rest."

Ivan spread his hands in front of him. "Sounds pretty grim for the miners. So what's the alternative?"

"We have to get them out and away before we make our graceful exit."

"Sorry, boss," Ivan said, "but what the hell are we supposed to do with six hundred or more people?"

"Nothing. We get them out and they make a run for it if we tell them which way to go. We can't take them with us. It's not good, but it gives them a chance and it's a damned sight better than the alternative."

"That's a big ask, boss. Getting that many people away is going to be a trick worth watching, but then having them wander the forests with those armed guards after them ... Sounds like a recipe for a disaster," Ivan said.

"Maybe I can help?" Leah said quietly.

"How would you do that?" Jim asked.

"You find a way to get these people out and set them off heading in the right direction. I will go home and get my people to come the other way. We meet them and get them to safety. They will have to be handed over to the authorities, but at least they will be alive and in Canada they will be treated decently."

"OK," Jim said. "You say it takes three days to get out of here on foot and then it will take you, say, a day to get your people on the move. So we need to spring these prisoners on day five and in the interim we need a plan. Does that work for everyone?"

Geordie spoke into the brief silence. "And if we can't come up with a decent plan, what the hell do we do then?"

Jim looked at him for a moment. "To be truthful, right now, I don't know, but then you two have never let me down yet."

Ivan rubbed his chin. "We'll work on it. There must be a way; at least, I bloody hope so."

Chapter 37

Deputy Director Colton sat at the head of the table in the briefing room. The massive screen at the other end of the room was showing satellite images of the ships that had left Shanghai in the four days they had targeted. There were just so many and they were heading in all directions.

"Narrow this down for me, Mason. We can't chase every damned ship on the ocean."

Mason shifted in his chair. "The Chinese intelligence people are going through the dock records now. They say they will be back to us by the end of today, their time, so we should have more in the morning. However, the weather bureau has a satellite watching the mid-Pacific area and we are getting their images at the moment. If these ships are doing what we think they are doing then we should be able to spot the ones coming to the US and put search teams aboard."

"And the problem is?"

"I don't understand, sir."

Colton sighed. "The Chinese manufacture vast quantities of consumer goods that they send to the US by sea. The number of ships moving back and forth is large. Just how many ships do you think we can stop and search? These things have dozens, if not hundreds, of massive containers stacked on the decks. It would take days to search each one. We don't have the manpower."

"I see your point, sir. So we have to hope the Chinese can tell us which ship was in the right dock at the right time."

"Brilliant! And in the interim my two agents are still hanging in the wind. Your team is not leaving tonight. I want the Chinese information in here the minute they send it and you go back and reinforce the urgency to them right now."

Mason and his two staff members left the room hurriedly and Colton sat back in his chair, looking at the plain white ceiling. Two of his people were out there and he had sent them. They had put their necks on the line to infiltrate this people-smuggling gang. If they died it would be his fault alone and he had no excuses for himself.

Chapter 38

The three men stood and watched Leah vanish into the forest on her way south to get help from her people. "Are you sure she'll be safe, Ivan?"

"As safe as anyone. That's a capable young woman and I'm damned glad she's on our side in this."

"That's high praise coming from you. Is she really that good?"

Ivan met Jim's gaze. "She stood over her three brothers' bodies and, instead of getting weepy or falling apart, she picked up a rifle and helped us track the bastards that did it. Capable enough for you?"

"Sounds pretty hard-core."

Geordie sighed. "She is, and speaking of hard-core, when do you need to get back? I guess they'll come looking if you are too long?"

Jim nodded and checked his watch. "I really ought to be reappearing over that ridge shortly."

Geordie grinned. "Then we need a quick plan of next steps. Oh and by the way, don't call me shorty."

Jim and Ivan shook their heads. "Dear Lord, do you still think that's funny, after all these years?" Jim said.

Geordie chuckled. "So come on, boss, what's our next step?"

Jim stood still and thought for a moment. "Right, first job is for you two to recon the whole site. How many guards are there and where? What patrol patterns are they using? Find a time when there are minimum numbers of them on duty and that's when we make the break. Don't forget, there is at least one of them manning the gate across the mine shaft. So we need a way to take him out without the rest knowing. And don't forget either that they are all ex-PLA soldiers and they are all armed."

"On the plus side, "Ivan said, "if they have any plans against attack they'll be expecting an RCMP SWAT team or maybe an infantry type assault. They won't be expecting a couple of sappers sneaking about. So asymmetric warfare is our ace in the hole."

"Sounds like you have a plan already, Ivan?" Jim said.

"Maybe the germ of an idea. We'll work on it in the early hours once the place has settled down for the night."

"I nearly forgot, there are two FBI agents here as well. One in my room most of the time and one stuck in the mine. They have to come out with us."

Geordie grinned again. "I hope the pretty one is in your room."

"She is, and don't start adding two and two to make five."

"Boss, you cut me to the quick. Would I do a thing like that?"

"Yes, you damn well would. Right, I'm off back to the madhouse before anyone down there starts to get worried and comes looking for me. You two be careful, these guys are serious and they clearly have no problem killing people."

"You be careful, too, boss. These guys can always get another pilot. Keep your head down and we'll work this out."

Chapter 39

"Can you get a message to your colleague in the mine, Chen?"

She looked up. "What message?"

"I need him to have all the miners ready to leave sometime in the next four days. There probably won't be much notice, so they need to move as fast as they can."

"Jim, they have virtually no clothing. In the heat of the mine they don't need it. They have no food. Where are they supposed to go? They'll just die in the forest, even if they get past the guards."

Jim nodded a little sadly. "I'm afraid some of them may die, but if we don't do this the chances are they will all die when the mine gets flooded. Maybe not today or tomorrow, but Han will never let them leave here. He's playing for higher stakes than just money."

Chen put down the shirt she was sewing. "What do you know that I don't?"

"I'm not certain of this, but it's my best guess. I think the ship off the coast is Iranian and the fishing boat is ferrying yellowcake out to it. The USA has a treaty with the Iranians not to develop nuclear weapons, so why would they need all this yellowcake? I believe this material is going to Iran, once the ship is fully loaded, to go through their centrifuge program and to then build weapons. My guess is that they will smuggle it in so no American or UN inspectors are aware of it. Once they have those weapons they control the

Middle East and with the oil under their control they can dictate terms to the rest of the world."

Chen's mouth hung open as she realized the enormity of what Jim had said. "I had been concentrating on the people-smuggling issue. I hadn't thought about the wider implications. If you're right, we have to stop it. How will running away from here do that?"

"We need to get the information to people who can do something about it. If you or I make a run for it there is a strong chance that Han will flood the mine, with all the workers in there. I can't live with that, so we have to give them a chance."

"But how will they survive? Surely you are just condemning them to a slower death?"

He smiled. "We've thought of that. If you can get the women to collect any clothes they can and blankets, they can give them to the men when we get them out. We'll try and hit the food stores on the way as part of the distraction. There's no shortage of water in these hills. Better than that, I will have people coming up from the south to help."

"What people? Not the police?"

"Better still. These will be people from the First Nations. They've lived on this coast and in these forests for ten thousand years. If anyone can get these prisoners out, it's them."

"Sorry, what are First Nations?"

"The native people who were here long, long before the Europeans arrived. Resourceful people for the most part and they already have a grudge against Han and his thugs."

Chen sat very still for a minute or two. "I agree. I fear we will still lose some people. I think they will accept the chance at life, though. How will you get them out of the mine?"

"We haven't worked that out yet."

"You have said 'we' before. Who else is there?"

Jim smiled down at her. "I should have told you from the start. The girl who came to the window was not alone. She was with two friends of mine. Two of the finest soldiers I have ever served with. They were both Royal Engineers, as I was. Both are intelligent and tough men. They are going to work out how to get the miners out and then give us the word to start them running."

"So we have a real chance?"

"I think we do and we have to take it. One more thing, though: I need your promise."

"What promise is that?"

"I need you to promise that the information about the Iranians goes no further."

"But why? We need to stop them. I have to report what I know up my chain of command within the FBI."

"You're right, we do need to stop them, but if we can get away from here I think I can arrange that quietly. If we allow the US government to get involved it could cause a huge problem, maybe even another bloody war in the Middle East. Will you trust me?"

"I already trust you, but, as I said, I work for the FBI. I will have to pass this intelligence on to my superiors."

"Chen, if the US are backed in to a corner and forced into a war an awful lot of young Americans could end up dead or savagely injured. My way means we can avoid that, but still get the job done. Is it worth trusting me to save those lives?"

Chen sat silently, looking at him. "And if your way fails?"

"If my way goes wrong then I will tell you and you can then report what we suspect. I promise I won't leave it too long. There will still be time for the US to act to stop the nightmare scenario."

She nodded very slowly. "With that promise then, yes, nobody will hear it from me until you give me the word, but be sure your way will work, and don't leave it too long."

Chapter 40

Geordie skirted silently around the back of the big cabin aiming to check out the isolated accommodation shed where he thought the guards might live. His dark clothes and dark skin made him almost invisible in the thin, cloud obscured moonlight. He froze as he saw the light of a cigarette come around the corner of the building. He lowered himself slowly to the ground so that his movement did not attract any unwanted attention.

Lying as still as a rock on the ground, he could now see the faint silhouette of the guard who stood at the corner of the main cabin with the AK47 rifle across his back. Geordie smiled to himself. Any sergeant major would have ripped that man a new one for giving away his position like that. He waited until the guard had finished his smoke and moved away before he continued his reconnaissance.

He reached the accommodation shed without any further alarms and lifted his head cautiously to peer in through the barred window next to the door. In the faint light through the other windows he could see that the room was laid out like barrack blocks across the world, with single beds neatly lined up down either side. He counted twenty beds, some occupied and others empty. So, unless they were hot bunking, he now knew how many armed thugs they had to deal with.

He checked the door and found that it opened outwards. That would give him an advantage later. He circled the shed and confirmed that there was only the one door. Although he did find there was a latrine block to one side and by the smell it was a deep trench type that was not being maintained properly. He puzzled over the barred windows and then thought they might be there in case the prisoners ever rioted. Armed men could wreak havoc on unarmed people through those bars.

Moving on, he approached the three sheds that the women were forced to live in. He circled wide through a stand of trees to come in from behind them. He paused and observed, time and again, to try and spot any guards around these sheds, but saw nothing. Han and his security detail must have assumed that the women would stay put out of fear.

Geordie carried on down to the beach where the support boat was tied to a small wooden jetty. He crawled under the jetty to wait for Ivan to complete his part of the night reconnaissance.

Up above the mine the big man was moving to the small lake that instilled such fear in the workers. He reached the end and found the crude spillway below a large old-fashioned valve, with a cast-iron wheel on top of it. A set of rough steps had been cut into the rock to allow access from the valley below to the heavy valve. Judging by the size of the mechanism, the flow would be powerful once the valve wheel had been spun to the fully open position and the mine would flood rapidly.

Shielding his small flashlight in his hand, Ivan examined the mechanism before drawing a lock knife from his pocket. He worked on the valve system for around ten minutes then straightened up and looked down into the valley beneath him. Somebody was in for a surprise if they tried to drown the miners.

Using the crude steps, he made his way down to the valley floor and along to the mine entrance. This was the most difficult part of the night's mission, which was why he had allocated this task to himself. He eased himself alongside the entrance and took a peek inside. Most of the shaft was dark with a dim light coming from somewhere inside the mountain.

Ivan pushed himself away from the cliff wall and walked into the tunnel entrance. Using his uncanny ability to move silently, he walked along the shaft towards the light in front of him. As he came closer he could see the iron barred gate that closed off the tunnel. Then, as he came around the slight curve in the tunnel, he saw the guard on duty. The man was sitting in a chair with his AK47 across his lap and his feet resting on a crosspiece of the gate. The light came from two lamps set up on the far side of the iron bars to illuminate any worker coming that way and to leave the guard in sheltering darkness.

Unlike the guard who manned the veranda of the main cabin, this one was awake. Ivan turned slowly and slipped back out of the mine shaft into the still night. He waited for his eyes to fully adjust to the darkness and then made his way down to the lakeside and around to the jetty, where Geordie waited.

Geordie rolled to one side as the big Welshman dropped down next to him. "Find what you needed?"

"I did. The flooding valve is out of action, or at least it won't flood the mine without a repair job, and I know where the mine guard is. How about you?"

"Not bad. Got the guard hut spotted and I have an idea of how to slow them down. There are no guards by the womens' sheds, so that makes them a little bit easier to get out. I did find out there is a roving patrol we haven't seen before, though they seem overconfident as far as I can see."

"And the food store?"

"Nope. Couldn't get there because of the wandering sentry. Pretty sure I know where it is. I just need to find out how to get in there."

Ivan grinned. "Maybe you can use those lock-picking skills our burglar friend taught you when we rescued the Prime Minister."

"That's what I'm counting on. I can't imagine they have anything clever holding the door shut, can you?"

Ivan tapped Geordie on the arm. "Time to get the hell out of Dodge. We've had our fun for tonight. Tomorrow we work out a plan and find a way to run it by the boss before we execute."

Chapter 41

They sat in the shelter in the woods sipping at the coffee that Geordie handed around. "We need to execute this plan a bit quick, boss. We're running out of coffee and you know how crabby Ivan gets without a regular caffeine fix."

Jim smiled. As long as Geordie was making jokes he knew they were both firing on all cylinders. He paused while he ran through their proposed plan again in his head. It was risky, he knew. He also knew that if anyone could make it work it was these two.

"Are you sure about them having explosives mounted in the aircraft?" Ivan asked. "It would make it a damned sight faster getting back to civilization if we could fly out of here."

"Not certain, but Han and his people seem to be pretty bloody ruthless, so it's a good bet they would do something like that. I've been wondering if that's what happened to the previous pilot."

"I thought you said that was an accident during landing?" Geordie said.

Jim nodded. "That's what Han told me, but maybe it's something more. His supervisor or whatever you call it in a criminal gang was coming in for a look at the operation. Now, if Han is off the reservation and feathering his own nest, maybe he didn't need the scrutiny. An explosion just as the aircraft went by that damned cliff would be difficult to differentiate from a crash and with the plane at the bottom of the lake who would ever know?"

"Interesting idea. What do you reckon he's skimming?"

"From what I've seen, the pitchblende they are mining and turning into yellowcake is what they are taking out to the freighter. The gold could be Han's little bonus on the side."

Geordie looked up. "That's the first time you've mentioned yellowcake. Is that what those women are humping down to the fishing boat?"

"That's right."

"I thought yellowcake was the start point for uranium? So what the hell are they going to do with it?"

Jim paused and looked down into his coffee mug before he spoke. "I'm not sure about this, but my guess is that the ship hanging around out there is Iranian and will be taking this stuff back home once they have a full load. My fear is that it will be used to make nuclear bombs."

"I thought the Americans had a treaty with Iran to stop them doing this kind of thing?" Ivan said.

Jim put his mug down. "They do and the US monitors quantities and facilities as part of that treaty. However, if some of the centrifuges they need for processing are mounted somewhere in secret and this material can be smuggled in without the monitors noticing, it could be a hell of a mess."

"If they get nukes it would change the whole balance of power in the Middle East," Ivan said.

"And the Yanks would be forced to take action to safeguard the flow of oil," Geordie said.

"If they don't, Iran could end up dictating to most of the bloody world."

Ivan grunted. "If the Americans go in then we would be dragged along with them. The Iranian troops are a bit more useful than the Iraqis. It would be way worse than Iraq or Afghanistan."

"And hundreds or maybe thousands of Allied troops would end up dead or maimed, not to mention the Iranian casualties," Jim said. "Plus, if it goes wrong and they drop a couple of buckets of 'instant sunshine', the oil fields would be unusable for years."

"So then," Ivan said. "Once we get these slave labourers out of here and heading south, how do we stop Han and, more importantly, that bloody freighter full of yellowcake? Maybe we just call up the Mounties? I have a satellite phone in my pack."

"I have an idea about that and calling in the authorities would scupper it, so we'll keep your phone back as the option of last resort, I think. As soon as we are clear of here, and the workers are being moved to safety, we need to get to Seattle or Vancouver. I need to find the nearest British Consul and I know they have one in both those cities."

"Probably a stupid question, but why?" Geordie asked.

"Because I would be very surprised if he or she did not have a secure phone connection to the UK and we need to report this back at the highest level if we are going to stop another Middle Eastern war."

Chapter 42

Ivan checked his watch again. He always hated this part of any operation; the waiting wound him up, though he knew as soon as things started he would calm down. Geordie lay in the bushes beside him completely relaxed. He envied his friend's ability to maintain his calm no matter what was going on.

At five minutes before the agreed start time Ivan tapped Geordie on the arm and watched him flick to instant alertness. He rolled into a sitting position without speaking and checked his weapons one more time before turning to Ivan.

"Right then, mate. Time to go and cause a bit of trouble, eh?"

Ivan nodded. "And keep your head down. I'm not carrying you out of here through this bloody forest."

Geordie grinned and the moonlight reflected off his brilliant smile. "If you check the record, the guy who keeps getting holes in him isn't me."

Ivan reached out and tapped the trunk of a fir tree superstitiously. "I've been lucky since that job in Dubai. Don't want to jinx it this far from a hospital."

"Just be careful, you old bugger. I just hope we don't lose too many of these Chinese guys in the forest. They've had a pretty rough time of it."

Ivan stood up slowly and moved his equipment into the most comfortable place. "That's going to be up to us to discourage these ex-PLA bastards. If we give the labourers enough time to get clear that's about the best we can do for them."

The two men looked down into the valley from their position on the ridge. The clear moonlight was unwelcome, but it did let them see there was nobody walking about and it might help the prisoners to get away. Without another word, they shook hands and stepped out of the trees to start moving to their planned tasks.

Ivan cut to the right to take the path along the edge of the lake, towards the mine entrance. Geordie went left, to head for the guards' building and then on to the main cabin. Both moved silently and took advantage of any cover they could.

Geordie was the first to reach his objective at the guards' shed and he carefully peered in through the barred window. All was quiet inside, with the guards sleeping peacefully in their narrow bunks. He dropped down from the window and moved across to the door. Taking the stout branch he had prepared earlier, he slipped it through the handle of the door and then through the second handle on the wall at the top of the flight of three steps. A large plank of wood left over from the construction of the shed, which he had spotted during his earlier reconnaissance, was lying beneath the steps. He heaved it out and rested one end under the door handle, with the lower end pushed firmly into the ground. If nothing else, this should slow down the guards when the excitement started.

Satisfied with his action, Geordie moved back from the accommodation shed and started towards the main cabin. Ivan was making his way along the lake edge in front of the cabin, shielded by the low ridge that ran across most of the valley at this point. He reached the small jetty where the support boat was moored and paused to check around him. The night was still, with no sign that any of the guards were alert. Their overconfidence was what was making this risky plan possible. Content that he had not been seen, he moved on towards the mine entrance.

Inside his dark room, Jim and Chen stood at the window watching for any signs of movement outside. The door had been locked as usual and would not be opened again until the corridor guard decided the time was right, in the morning. Chen touched his elbow lightly and pointed across to the jetty where he saw a dark shape move swiftly into the shadow of the mountainside near to the mine. He smiled, admiring the stealth that such a big man could achieve.

Jim turned to Chen. "Well, we've started. You're sure the people know what to do when it all kicks off?"

Chen smiled up at him. "The women have been told to be ready and to have extra clothing for the men. One of the women who takes food into the mine has passed the message on to my partner. He will have the miners ready. Now we just have to rely on your two friends. I just hope they are as capable as you think they are."

"No worries on that score. They only retired a short while ago from the army and they are two damned fine soldiers."

Chen looked back out of the window. "But are soldiers what we need tonight?"

"These two are. As well as being soldiers, they are highly intelligent engineers. Whatever goes wrong, they will find a way around it. Never fear."

"I hope you are right. A lot of lives depend on them. If the mine is flooded it would be a tragedy."

Jim looked out of the window and said nothing. The risks were high, but higher still if they did nothing. At some point Han would close this operation down and the labourers would be doomed to a terrible death in the mine. Even if some didn't make it tonight, it would be a price worth paying. Or at least he hoped it would be.

At the end of the veranda, in front of the main cabin, Geordie stood in the shaded darkness and waited until he spotted the guard sleeping peacefully in the chair against the front wall. Knowing that his target was properly asleep, he stepped onto the wooden deck and made his way slowly forward, testing each plank for sound as he did so. He reached the man's AK47 rifle standing against the wall and carefully laid it down so it would not fall. He had never mastered the nerve pinch that Jim had been taught during one of their earlier tasks for the Prime Minister, so he had to use his own method.

He lined himself up to deliver the rabbit punch to the man's exposed neck. Having picked his spot he swung his arm with the hand forced into a rigid blade. The side of his hand powered into the man's neck at just the right point. There was a grunt and then the guard's body went limp. Geordie grabbed him before he could fall and gently lowered him to the floor. He turned the man over so he would not choke on his own tongue and then put his blanket back over him.

Leaving his own rifle beside the front door, Geordie slowly pressed down on the handle and swung the door open. The warmth from the still-burning log fire in the main room greeted him as he moved inside and silently shut the door behind him. He paused in the dark and listened. The downstairs area was silent and then he heard the sniff and cough from upstairs. He smiled in the darkness and started to carefully mount the wooden stairs to the upper floor.

He reached the landing at the top of the stairs and could see the feet of the corridor guard. He sidled along the wall until he was just at the entrance the corridor, then scratched on the wood panelling. There was no response so he scratched again, louder this time. He heard the guard's chair rock forward and heard it creak as the man stood up to investigate the odd noise. As he appeared through the doorway a powerful black fist emerged out of the night and connected with his jaw. The strength Geordie had built up during his days as a coal miner and the years of army training had not deserted him. The guard was lifted off his feet and slammed back against the wall of the corridor before collapsing unconscious in a heap.

Geordie rubbed his knuckles as he walked forward into the corridor and went through the man's pockets to find the key to Jim's room. The key was on a cord on the guard's belt and Geordie snapped the cord and stood up. As he turned to walk down the corridor he heard a door open and tensed. He was expecting Han to appear, but instead a bleary-eyed blond man walked into the corridor rubbing his cheek.

Van der Merwe stopped and looked at Geordie open-mouthed. "Hey, Kaffir, you're a long way from home. Come to steal from us, I guess, eh?"

Geordie knew this man had to be silenced before he could raise the alarm and walked forward with his hand held out.

"Hey baas, Mr Han told me you'd be glad to see someone from home when he hired me. Seems he wants another miner to keep these Chinks motivated."

Van der Merwe didn't fall for it and stepped forward ready to attack the approaching black man. "You're a liar, Kaffir. I'm going to enjoy this."

The South African's big scarred hand swung forward, aimed at Geordie's face. The ex-soldier stopped and swayed to the right. He felt the air move by his cheek as the blow missed him. His next step forward brought him in range of the off-balance white man and his left knee powered up into his testicles.

The South African collapsed to the floor in agony and rolled to one side. Geordie dropped to one knee beside him and lifted the man's head.

"Sorry it couldn't be longer, baas," he said, as he delivered a powerful right cross and knocked the mine boss into the middle of next week.

Geordie stood and turned to the door behind him. He unlocked it quickly and pushed it open.

"Are you two going to stand there all night or would you like a romantic stroll in the moonlight?"

"Nice to see you, Geordie. Any problems?" Jim said, guiding Chen towards the door.

"Not really, boss. Just make sure you don't trip over my new friend out here."

Chapter 43

By the entrance to the mine shaft, Ivan stood in the deep shadows listening. Once satisfied that there was no movement inside, he started to walk very slowly and silently into the shaft. The dim light from in front of him gave him enough to avoid tripping over any of the loose stones strewn across the floor. He paused as he came in sight of the iron gate that was closed and secured across the mine shaft. He leaned forward slightly to peer around the gentle bend in the mine tunnel. The guard was there in his chair, his back towards the tunnel entrance, with his AK47 across his lap and his feet up on one of the gate's crossbars.

Ivan had hoped this guard would be as confident as the others and would be asleep. Unfortunately, this one seemed to understand what his job was and, although comfortable, he was alert. Ivan had no choice; he had to act now or the whole plan would fail. He stepped forward and for once his ability to move silently failed him. A small stone he hadn't noticed rolled away from his boot and caused just enough noise to alert the guard.

The man's chair rocked forward and he came rapidly to his feet with the AK47 swinging round towards Ivan. He was fast, but the big Welshman was that little bit faster and had surprise on his side. He moved rapidly towards the guard, closing the distance so that he could grab the barrel of the automatic rifle before it could be pointed at him. His massive fist pounded into the smaller man's face and slammed him back against the bars. The guard collapsed to the floor after two such powerful impacts, but not before his finger had clamped onto the trigger of his weapon and sent a long burst of 7.62mm bullets flying along the mine shaft towards the entrance.

The bullets ricocheting off the stone walls of the tunnel did no damage. The problem was the noise echoing in the rock shaft that was going to be heard all over the mine site. The surprise they had planned on was gone. Ivan dropped to his knees next to the fallen guard and searched him for the gate key. Nothing. He looked up as the first of the miners arrived at the other side of the gate.

"It's over there on a hook in the wall," the worker told Ivan.

Ivan leapt to his feet and grabbed the heavy key from the wall hook. He forced it into the massive padlock and turned it. The key spun without difficulty and Ivan pulled the hasp out of the door loops to allow the gate to open.

"You speak good English for a peasant farmer from the rice paddies."

"No rice paddies in Los Angeles, my friend. I'm Junjie, the other FBI agent you were told about."

"Nice to meet you. We need to get your people moving fast. The rest of the guards will have heard those rounds going off, so we are going to have trouble in minutes unless we are damned lucky."

"They're right behind me, but some of them are in poor state. The ones digging the pitchblende have been badly affected by radiation, so they're pretty weak," Junjie said.

Ivan swore under his breath. "Get the strong to help the sick, but for God's sake get them to hurry. We are rapidly running out of time."

He turned and ran towards the mine entrance, leaving the FBI agent to hurry the miners along. As he ran Ivan picked up the M4 rifle he had left leaning against the wall as he entered. He slid to a stop at the entrance and scanned for movement. He saw nothing, but then heard the pounding of boots to his left as someone climbed the steps to the flooding valve above the mine.

He heard the squeak as the valve wheel was spun and then the scream as the massive jet of icy water blasted the man off the platform, instead of rushing down the pipe to flood the mine. He saw the screaming man fly past him, with the moonlight reflecting off the silver torrent of water that carried him far out from the cliff. The scream stopped abruptly as the guard's body was slammed down onto the rocky beach at the edge of the lake. Even with the flow of water jetting across him, Ivan could see that the man had crumpled backwards over a boulder at an impossible angle. There was no way he could have survived that mutilation.

Ivan turned as the first of the miners panted up the shaft behind him with Junjie in the lead, carrying the fallen guard's AK47 assault rifle. "Good man. Now take a look across the valley. You need to take your people across the end of the lake in front of that big cabin, then up to that ridge beyond. Get them over the ridge and into the cover of the trees to the left of the track. We'll be there as soon as we can to get your people moving in the right direction from there."

"And what will you be doing?"

Ivan hefted his rifle. "Trying to slow the guards down so your people don't get cut to ribbons. Now, as fast as you can, get them moving."

"What about their women?"

"If the rest of the plan has worked, your partner Chen is on the case and they should be on their way to join up with you over the ridge."

With that Ivan turned away and left the mine entrance, angling to the right towards the various buildings tucked into the forest edge. He looked back over his shoulder as he moved and saw that the miners were now streaming and stumbling out of the mine entrance and heading in the right direction, with Junjie urging them on.

Chapter 44

Jim and Geordie stepped through the front door of the main cabin, with Chen just behind them, as the burst of weapons fire from the mine echoed across the valley. The two men paused and looked at each other.

"Damn! So much for a stealthy escape. Never mind, we are committed anyway. Chen, can you get the women moving and Geordie, you get into position to do your thing."

"OK, boss, and I've got a bonus gift for you."

Geordie leaned down and scooped up the AK47 that the sleeping veranda guard had left lying there. A quick check of the still comatose man produced three spare magazines for the weapon which Jim pocketed gratefully.

"A long time since I've fired one of these, but it might come in handy. I'll cover the front right of this cabin, so I should be out of your way, but just keep an eye out for me when the shooting starts."

Geordie grinned and took Chen by the arm to hurry her towards the sheds where the female prisoners were kept. The two of them disappeared around the left corner of the building and Jim turned to move to the opposite end. From here he hoped to be able to disrupt any attack on the fleeing column of miners that were approaching along the beach. He watched them struggle along across the uneven rocks. They were moving more slowly than he had hoped for. As they came closer he could see why. There were sick and emaciated men being supported by others, who were not in much better shape. The treatment in the mines had been worse than he had realised. He took up his position where the moonlight cast a deep shadow and waited.

Chen went to the door of the first shed and called the women to come out. They were waiting, with whatever warm clothes they had been able to get hold of for the men from the mine. She set them off to take a wide sweep around the back of the guards' cabin and then to reach the ridge from out of the trees. This way they should be mostly out of sight and away from where they expected the guards' attention to be focussed. Once she was sure they were moving and going in the right direction she moved quickly on to the next shed and then the third.

Geordie had left Chen to do her part and had climbed up onto the roof of the first big shed. His dark clothes and dark skin helped to make him all but invisible as he took up his position to cover the escape. He jacked a round into the chamber of the rifle he carried and settled down to wait for his moment. Away to his right he could hear the angry shouting from the guards' hut as they pounded on the door to get out. His blocking of the door had held for longer than he had dared to hope and had allowed the miners to get further across the valley.

He heard the splintering of wood as the upper half of the door finally gave way and the shouting got louder as they threw the beam off the door and boiled out, carrying their weapons. There was a moment's confusion before one of them spotted the crowd of miners down by the lake side, silhouetted by the moonlight. The first man to raise his rifle did not know what hit him as Geordie controlled his breathing and dropped the man with a single shot to the head.

The others automatically dropped to the ground and started to crawl into cover. There was a pause before one of them raised his head to assess the situation. Through the powerful telescopic sight Geordie took aim and put his second round through the man's shoulder. The scream through the night sent the rest of them scurrying further back into cover to regroup.

No matter that they were criminals and thugs, these former Chinese soldiers did not lack courage or skill. The burst of automatic fire from beneath the accommodation shed came uncomfortably close to Geordie's head. Even if they were firing blind, they had identified roughly where he was hiding. Another shot from here would give away his position and bring down a hail of 7.62mm rounds.

Geordie saw a group of four men break from cover and make a dash for the shelter of the main cabin. They chose the right-hand side, where they could see the majority of the miners making their painful way across the valley. Once they were confident they were hidden from Geordie's position they stood up and took aim at the fleeing men. A burst of fire from Jim's borrowed AK47 swung across the group and all four were hit. Two died instantly and one fell to the ground with no further interest in firing his weapon. The fourth took only a minor wound and went down only to scramble to his knees to open fire on where he had seen the muzzle flashes. He was too slow and a single round from Jim took him down permanently.

Seeing that Geordie had controlled the guards to some extent, Ivan left his position at the base of the cliff and went after the fleeing miners. He caught up with the stumbling column quickly and walked alongside them, forming a barrier of sorts between them and their attackers. As they walked on he came up to where the FBI agent, Junjie, was standing.

"Have we lost many?" Ivan asked.

Junjie smiled. "So far none. Your friends have run good interference for us; if they can keep that up we might get them all clear of here."

Ivan looked around him. "Try and keep them moving. We are still vulnerable until we get into the forest edge."

There was an explosion from out on the lake where the Beaver sat on its floats. Then a roar as the three fuel tanks in its belly erupted into a massive fireball. The old aircraft was blown to pieces with the fuselage almost completely destroyed and the wings flung out to either side. There would be no quick escape in that direction. The burning fuel on the surface of the lake and on the floating wreckage illuminated the fleeing men even more than the moon and brought rifle fire from beside the guards' hut.

The covering fire from Geordie and then Jim had kept the gunmen at a distance, but the miners were still in range and the rounds cracked past just above their heads. A second burst of fire, this time from the upper floor of the main cabin, knocked four men to the ground. Ivan dropped beside them to try and help. Three of them were beyond any earthly help, but the fourth had been lucky and two other miners picked him up and helped him on the way.

Ivan turned back to find Junjie had taken up a position behind the low bank at the top of the rocky beach and was scanning the upper windows of the cabin. He saw a movement and put a short controlled burst of fire through the window. There was no cry from there, so he had to assume he had missed. Ivan took a position beside the FBI man and readied his automatic rifle.

The Welshman waited with his teeth clamped. He was anticipating the pain if the unseen gunman managed to hit him. His memory of previous bullet wounds was not comfortable.

"Are you any good with that rifle?" Junjie asked quietly.

"Not as good as Geordie, but at this range I can do some damage. Why do you ask?"

"I'm going to stand up and fire to make myself a target. You drop the bastard when he comes to the window to fire."

Ivan shook his head. "You've been watching too many cowboy movies. Stay down and watch."

Junjie smiled at him. "Can't do that. These guys are moving too slowly. If we don't stop this guy he can take a lot of them down from up there, even now they are crouching behind the bank."

Without waiting to argue further, the FBI agent jumped to his feet and fired a burst of five rounds towards the cabin. Cursing under his breath, Ivan brought the rifle to the ready and watched for any movement. The flickering light from the burning fuel was enough to show him a pale patch of skin and a weapon coming up to the aim. He fired twice in quick succession and was rewarded by a piercing scream from the upstairs window.

"And you say your friend Geordie is a better shot? He must be something quite special. Now help me get these last few out of danger before it gets any worse round here."

Ivan turned around in time to see one of the exhausted men sink to his feet. The radiation and the overwork had done for him. The big man slung the rifle across his back and took the three paces to the fallen miner. He scooped him up in his powerful arms and carried him after the retreating column. In a few minutes they had reached the top of the low ridge without further interference and they walked into the dark cover of the trees.

Chapter 45

Jim and Geordie arrived at the rendezvous point, just beyond the ridge, together. They found Ivan giving first aid to an injured miner, so they waited for him to finish.

"There you go, mate. You'll be good until your next thousand-mile service."

The uncomprehending Chinese man nodded his thanks and then, leaning on his wife's arm, he limped away. Ivan sat back on his heels and looked around him. All through this part of the forest were the women who were now helping their menfolk with injuries or giving them warmer clothes or blankets to wear for the trek through the trees. The big man stood up, collected his rifle and walked across to Jim.

"What's the score, Ivan?"

"We lost three on the beach. They were shot. Two were wounded, but can walk. One died of heart failure, I think, on the way up the ridge and quite a few are in bloody poor condition."

Jim nodded. "Must be the radiation in the lower part of the mine. This weather isn't going to help them either. Looks like the bits of clothing the women managed to scrounge together won't be enough. Not for these hills anyway."

Geordie, who had been looking down into the valley, turned around. "So what do we do with them? We can't just let them die of exposure out here and they've got at least a three-day walk, even for the reasonably fit ones."

"I've been thinking about that. Now that this mining operation is blown, Han and his thugs are going to want to get the hell out of here before the RCMP or the Canadian Army arrive. I guess it was Han who set off the explosives in the Beaver to make sure we couldn't use it for a getaway. So all that leaves them is a hike over this trail and down to the waterway to meet up with their supply boat."

"How does that help us?" Geordie asked.

"Once they are clear we can take the ones in the worst condition back down into the valley and use the buildings as shelter from the weather."

"Good idea, boss," Ivan said. "But if they come up here, while we are still here, we are going to have a bloodbath."

"Sadly true. So we are going to have to delay them until all these people are out of the way. We need to move them into the forest and try and keep them as warm as possible until Han and his gang have left. Then we bring them back."

Geordie lifted up his rifle and scanned the valley through the sight. "We've got company. They are starting to assemble in front of the big cabin and some guy is giving them a pep talk by the look of it."

"Shit! I was hoping they'd be slower. OK, you two get into a good position and slow them down. I'll get our two FBI friends to get this crowd moving. I'll be back as soon as I can."

Without a word the two ex-soldiers moved to the edge of the treeline and took up positions where they could see into the valley without being seem themselves. Jim hurried through the milling crowd of tired and disorientated people, searching for the two FBI agents. He found them by the side of a small stream tending one of the men who had been wounded.

"Chen, I need you and your friend to get these people deeper into the forest as quickly and as quietly as you can."

The taller-than-average Chinese man turned and looked at Jim. "And you are?"

"This is Major Jim Wilson, the one I was telling you about," Chen said and turned to Jim. "Why do we need to move them? They are in poor condition and need to rest."

"Han and his scum are getting ready to come up the trail any time now. I'm guessing that the supply boat will be waiting for them by the time they get there. If they find all these people here we are going to lose more than a few."

Junjie stood and picked up the AK47 from beside him. "I can hold them back for a while."

"Thanks, but I've already got that covered. I need you two to get these folk on the move as soon as you can. We don't have a lot of time and they really do need to go now."

"How far do we have to take them?" Chen asked as she finished tying off the improvised bandage.

Jim looked around. "With the forest being this thick, I reckon a kilometre, or maybe a bit less should do it, but for heaven's sake keep them quiet, whatever happens. Once the thugs are gone we'll take the weakest back down to shelter in the buildings until help gets here."

He watched as the two FBI agents rounded up the exhausted and injured people and started them moving further into the forest. The stronger ones helped the weaker, but progress was slow. Way too slow.

As he walked back to where he had left Ivan and Geordie he saw Ivan coming towards him. "Any way we can hurry these people? The thugs are on the move and it looks like they mean business."

"How so?"

"They're not just hiking out of the valley. They've formed a skirmish line and they are on the way with weapons at the ready."

"How long before they reach the treeline?" Jim asked.

"Less than five minutes, even if they move carefully. When they get to the top of the ridge there's no way they can miss the tracks all these people left as they came off the main track and went into the forest."

As they reached Geordie, Jim looked out across the valley towards the big cabin. He dropped down next to the bush that Geordie was using for concealment and tapped him on the shoulder.

"Mind if I take a look through your scope?"

Geordie rolled over and handed the scoped rifle to Jim, who steadied it and studied the valley floor. He sighed as he looked back over to where the released prisoners were struggling away from him.

"Geordie, I think we need some of your skill. As the snipers say, 'I need you to reach out and touch someone'. Just slow them down and make them think again."

Geordie grinned and took back the weapon. He snuggled down into his improvised sniper nest and scanned the ex-PLA soldiers who were coming towards him. He could see now that the guards had split into two groups and his practiced eye identified the two section leaders. One of them had his arm in a sling from one of Geordie's previous shots, but the other one seemed hale and hearty, judging by the shouting and arm-waving he appeared to be doing.

Geordie waited until the section leader stopped and turned to yell at a man who was falling behind the skirmish line. Then he stopped his breathing and took careful aim before firing a single shot. The high speed round flew exactly where Geordie had aimed and tore into the back of the section leader's thigh. They could hear the scream up on the ridge as the man fell to the ground with blood soaking his trouser leg.

The rest of the guards dived to the ground and brought their weapons up to the aim. With the moon just dropping behind the trees in front of them, Geordie's shaded position was invisible and they had nothing to fire at. The other section leader was the first to recover and started the men back up the slope again, while two men were detailed to assist his fallen colleague. Through the powerful scope, Geordie could see the reluctance of the men in advancing toward an unseen enemy. He didn't blame them and now he would add to their troubles.

He picked his man and took aim. This time the bullet was little off and smashed into the butt of the AK47 type rifle his target carried. The butt was blown into a dozen pieces with fast-flying wooden splinters slashing the man's face and arm. The weapon spun away into the air and the man screamed and grabbed his face. He was lucky; the splinters had missed his eyes, but the blood and pain sent him reeling backwards, followed by the rest of his section, who had realised there was nothing but death and pain waiting for them if they continued up the open slope.

The three men on the ridgeline watched as the confused men moved back into the cover of the main cabin. Two rounds would not stop them, but they would make them careful and slow them down considerably.

Chapter 46

The guards mustered behind the main cabin, away from Geordie's all too accurate rifle. The three men on the ridgeline watched to see what they would do next. As they waited Jim checked on the progress with moving the captives out of harm's way. They were still moving, but painfully slowly. The hike up to the ridge had virtually finished men who had suffered the radiation in the mine for the longest time. He went back to his two companions.

"Any movement?"

Ivan looked across at Jim. "Some. They have sent a couple of men out to the left, presumably to see if there is a way round that way."

"And they are just coming back now," Geordie said, pointing down into the valley.

The three of them settled down again to watch for developments. "If they go left and into the forest on that side, they could be up to the trail and across before we could do anything about it," Ivan said.

Jim nodded. "That's true and with only three rifles, at short range we would be swamped."

Geordie grunted. "That seems to be what they are doing. There they go now. Keeping low, but heading out to the left. I can drop a couple if you want, boss?"

"No, let them go," Jim said. "We want them out of those cabins and away, so we can get the sick and injured into cover before nightfall. Have you seen any sign of Han?"

Geordie shook his head. "We don't know what he looks like, but all I've seen are the guards or at least people who look like guards. Would Han stand out in some way?"

"Not if he's wearing a guard's uniform. Any sign of our South African friend? He might be staying close to Han on the way out."

"Not seen him yet. Hang on; they're entering the edge of the forest over there. If they turn left towards us they could be here in five minutes or so."

Ivan heaved himself up. "Time for a fighting retreat, I think."

"You're right. OK, spread out and move back into the trees. Find good cover and snipe at these guys if they come after us. Whatever you do, stay between the injured and the enemy."

"Right then." Ivan picked up his rifle. "Fifty meter spacing and keep your heads down. Fire and move, don't let them pin you down."

Geordie grinned. "We know all that, mate. We'll be fine."

Ivan gave him one of his rare smiles. "I know you know it. For a minute there I was back in Sergeant Major mode. Just be careful, eh?"

The three men moved back quickly and quietly into the trees and found concealed positions. They waited. Behind them they could hear the sick and injured moving away, then in front of them they heard the guards burst out of the trees and onto the trail. There were some shouted commands in Chinese. They didn't understand the language, but they had been soldiers long enough to guess what they were about.

The Chinese guards were angry. They had forgotten some of their caution and advanced across the trail and into the forest way too quickly. Jim was the first to see the approaching line and put a burst from his borrowed AK47 into the middle of them. He didn't wait to see the results, but pulled back before the answering fire shredded the tree trunk he had been concealed behind.

The line moved forward, but stumbled and stopped when fire came from both sides as Ivan and Geordie caught them in a crossfire. As they turned outwards to deal with these new threats, Jim's AK47 chattered again and sent the line of men into cover. The guards were returning fire in three directions now, but their targets had slipped away and headed deeper into the shaded darkness of the forest.

Finding new positions, the three men waited again. The Chinese guards were wary now and moving cautiously. Jim was spotted by one of the attackers and fire ripped into his position while he hugged the ground. Geordie had a clear shot and placed a single round into the side of the man's head. The powerful bullet smashed through skin and bone, then blood, mixed with brain matter, exploded from the other side of the victim's head. The man fell to the ground without the chance to scream, his blood forming a pool on the forest floor before it slowly sank into the broken ground.

At the same time, Ivan fired from the other side and a second guard took a round through his shoulder. His weapon fell from his nerveless hands and he screamed loud and long. The section leader realised this was a fight he could not win in these conditions and started yelling at his men. They fell back towards the trail, taking turns to fire randomly into the forest at imagined targets.

As soon as he had them back on the trail, the section leader set them off down the slope, at the double, towards where the support boat was due to pick them up. The three friends advanced slowly to make sure there was no chance of the attackers sneaking around behind them. Geordie reached the man he had killed and, picking up the fallen man's AK47, he slung it across his back with the strap across his chest. A quick check through the man's jacket revealed the usual three spare magazines, which he pocketed.

Jim and Ivan came upon the wounded man, who had been left behind in the rush to get out of the killing ground. Ivan picked up his weapon as Jim helped the man to sit up as gently as he could. He took the small pack from his back and dropped it to the ground before applying a crude dressing to the wound. The man had been lucky. The bullet had passed through without smashing any bones. It would hurt like hell, but it shouldn't kill him.

While Jim was dressing the wound Ivan opened the pack and checked inside. There was nothing personal in there, just a couple of small sacks, which he opened to find semi-processed gold. He took one nugget for a souvenir and closed the bag up again. Together they walked the injured man to the trail and helped him put the pack over his uninjured shoulder. They pointed him down the slope and waved him on his way.

As he stumbled down the trail Jim turned to Ivan. "A bit surprised you gave him his pack back."

Ivan nodded towards the retreating man. "He may be useful to us at some point. I slipped my satellite phone under the gold bags. Maybe we can get the authorities to track its signal and pick the lot of them up."

"Nice thinking," Jim said, as Geordie walked out of the trees towards them. "And nice shooting from you. I take it the owner of that AK won't be walking out?"

"No. Had to give him a headshot. I didn't think I had time for anything clever."

Jim nodded. "You're right and I'm losing track of the number of times you've saved my life."

Geordie grinned. "All part of the service. Anyway I'm going to call that marker in one of these days."

"That sounds like you have a plan."

"I do and I'll tell you when things get a bit calmer round here."

Chapter 47

Colton looked up from his computer screen, irritated at the interruption. "What do you want, Mason?"

The younger agent came into the room and cleared his throat. "Ah, I may owe you an apology, sir."

"For what?"

"I think I have exceeded my authority and the cost could be significant."

Colton turned away from the screen and sat back in his chair. "Well, spit it out and we'll see if you still have a job."

Mason looked alarmed at the threat. "Well, sir, you said you wanted answers and the report from the Chinese intelligence people was pretty thin, so I asked for help from elsewhere. I used your name to get an NSA surveillance satellite repositioned."

"So where did you get it moved to?"

"It's going to be in geostationary orbit above the west coast of Canada in about three hours' time. The reports should be coming in a few moments after that."

"And why have you put it where you have?"

Mason cleared his throat again and mopped the sweat from his palms. "Well, sir. The major ports in the US are on alert. We have our agents monitoring all ships coming in from China. Plus, we have alerted the ICE people to a potential major shipment of illegals and they are on high alert, too. The problem area is the Canadian coast and Alaska. There are hundreds of islands, inlets and waterways that we have no way of covering fully. The Coast Guard is working with the Canadians, but they just can't cover it all."

Colton looked at the younger man for a long moment. "And what will this satellite be able to scan for?"

"It can provide detailed photo reconnaissance and it has infrared capability. So any heat source, like a bunch of people moving across the cold ground, will show up."

Deputy Director Colton steepled his fingers in front of his mouth as he thought. "OK, that's good. Keep me informed of everything you get. How long can we keep the satellite there?"

"The NSA has given us five days unless there is an increase of tension somewhere else."

"Five days. Not much, but we may get lucky. OK, Peter, you keep your job for now. That's good work."

Chapter 48

The three of them waited until they were sure that the Chinese guards were not trying to circle around them and then set off after the escaping prisoners. Chen and her colleague had managed to get the sick and injured away, but now they had been forced to stop. The more healthy ones had pushed on as they had been told to. They could only hope that Leah and her people were coming the other way to help them.

Jim handed Chen one of the AK47 rifles they had captured and Geordie gave another to Junjie, who passed it on to one of the fitter miners. They gave them each three spare magazines. The five of them now sat down with their backs against trees to decide on their next move. Clearly this group of people, who had been so weakened by the radiation in the pitchblende mine, could not go much further and the cold of night might well finish some of them.

"We need to get this group back to the main cabin down in the valley," Jim said. "With shelter, warmth and a decent meal inside them, they are going to have a better chance of survival."

Chen looked up. "But what if Han and his thugs come back? Or has Han even left there? He could be waiting with more of his guards to slaughter us."

Jim looked at her for a moment. "That's all true, but either way these people are going to die if we don't do something. These northern forests are unforgiving. We three will go down to the mine site and check it's safe. You two get the weaker ones moving back. Even if we can't use the cabins for some reason, we can get them down to the waterway at the end of that track, and they can be picked up from there in a day or so."

Junjie shook his head. "That way some will die for sure. We need the shelter down in the valley. I will go with you to check around. Chen can shepherd the people back there. It will be slow, but once they get to the downward slope it should be easier for them."

Jim thought for a second or two. "OK, that sounds like we have a plan. Us four will search the cabin and the sheds to make sure there is nobody waiting for us and then Geordie can get a meal on the go for when Chen gets the people down to us."

"What about the rest of them? The stronger ones. Should we call them back?"

"I don't think so," Jim said. "We have enough to do to look after the sick and injured. The rest should be fine once they run into Leah and her people. They know these forests well and they'll take care of them."

Ivan stood up to forestall any further discussion. "No time like the present and we're going to run out of moonlight soon if we don't get a move on."

Chen clamped her mouth shut and swallowed her objections as the three other men pushed themselves to their feet. She sat and watched as they walked away and vanished into the gloom of the forest. She sighed and stood up. Slinging the rifle over her shoulder she set off to try and rouse the exhausted people to one more effort.

Jim and his companions reached the edge of the treeline and stood still, while Geordie scanned the valley below them through his telescopic sight. He could see nothing moving, just the wisp of smoke coming from the smouldering remains of the support boat and jetty that had both been doused in burning aviation fuel when the Beaver floatplane exploded. Beside the small jetty, the remains of one of the aircraft's wings had drifted ashore and the tip of the tail fin lifted just above the smooth surface of the lake.

Geordie turned and nodded to Jim. They moved out of the cover of the trees and spread out, to make a more difficult target should there be anyone lying in wait for them. They walked slowly down the slope towards the mining camp with their weapons at the ready and their eyes scanning all around them. They saw no sign of any danger and there was not a sound from the scattered buildings.

Ivan was the first to reach the main cabin and he stepped up onto the wide veranda and peered in through the window nearest to him. The house was still and silent. He gave the thumbs-up sign and Junjie followed him on to the veranda as Jim and Geordie swept around to the side of the house to check the food store.

The FBI agent walked past Ivan and gripped the door handle. As Ivan saw what he was doing he shouted to him.

"No, don't! It could be ..."

He was too late. As Junjie pulled the door open he saw a thin line from the inner handle to a box on the floor. The box erupted with a roar and searing yellow flame hit the door, ripping it off its hinges. The splintering wood smashed into the FBI agent and carried him out onto the stony beach in front of the building. He groaned once as he landed and then lay still. Ivan was at his side in a heartbeat, but could see there was nothing he could do. A large jagged fragment of the heavy wooden door had slashed open Junjie's throat. Other pieces had pierced him deeply all over his body and the flash had burned him where the shattering door had not sheltered him. Ivan checked for a pulse. There was nothing. The FBI man was gone beyond help.

Ivan turned back towards the cabin as Jim and Geordie ran towards him. The explosion had started a fire which was taking hold and burning fiercely in the wooden structure. They had no chance of putting that out without any fire-fighting equipment. The three men stared down at the twisted body before them and then back at the cabin.

Geordie was the first to react. "The food! We need to get into the food store and save some before the fire reaches it."

Jim swore under his breath as he started to move. "Ivan, give us cover while we two get the food we need."

With that the two men ran back around the side of the building to where the food store was located. They arrived in front of the stout wooden door with its massive lock. They tried the handle more in hope than expectation.

"No dice, boss, and despite what Hollywood tells us, I doubt if shooting at that bloody big lock is going to help."

Jim nodded grimly. "Time for your party trick then, Geordie. Can you pick it?"

"To be honest, boss, I'm not sure. It's a damn sight bigger than those locks Dusty taught me to pick when we were on that job for the Prime Minister."

"The principles must be the same though, surely?"

"I'll give it a go, but, boss ..."

"What?"

"Don't call me Shirley."

Geordie chuckled at his own favourite joke and dropped to his knees in front of the lock. He fished in his pocket and withdrew the set of lock picks he had been carrying ever since Dusty, the professional burglar, had taught him how to use them while they were waiting to break into a large country house in the north of England. He inserted the odd tools and felt for the levers inside, just as he had been shown.

"It's a shame about Junjie," he said as he worked. "He seemed a decent guy and he sure as hell didn't deserve that."

Jim looked around to make sure they were alone. "No, he didn't. I'm guessing that was Han's idea and maybe his handiwork."

Geordie grunted as he moved the first lever. "Heavy going this. I wonder where Han is? We haven't spotted him yet. Could he still be around here, do you think?"

"We'll settle with him later if he turns up. I was wondering where our South African friend has got to. Han might have sneaked out with the guards, but Van der Merwe would stick out like a sore thumb."

Geordie grunted. "Got it."

He stood up and pulled open the door to the food store slowly as he checked for any other booby traps. Satisfied, he swung the door wide and moved inside. Bags of rice were stacked along one wall with bags of dried fish and canned goods along the other side on a row of wooden shelves.

"How much do you think we are going to need?" Geordie asked.

"No idea. I'm not sure how many people Chen is going to bring down here or how long we are going to have to keep them supplied. Let's just shift as much as we can before the fire gets here."

"Should I get Ivan to help?"

"No, Geordie, I would rather have him watching our backs in case of any other nasty surprises."

Geordie picked up the first big sack of rice and, heaving it up on his shoulder he walked briskly away to a spot well clear of where the fire might reach and dropped the bag. As he walked back towards the store Jim passed him going the other way with another rice bag. Working together, the pile grew steadily. Jim concentrated on the rice while Geordie switched over to the other foods and added them to the pile.

Chapter 49

Chen kept the people moving as best they could. It was easier once they cleared the forest and started down the slope towards the cabin. From the ridge they could see that the fire was taking a firm grip on the wooden cabin walls and flame was licking all around the lower floor. The billowing smoke made a white roiling column up into the clear sky.

Ahead of them Ivan stood with his rifle scanning all around in case any of Han's thugs had been left behind. He saw the column of people stumbling and limping down the slope towards him and was considering whether he could risk going to help them when he heard the scream.

At first he could not place where it had come from and then a breeze cleared the smoke a little, to let him see the upper windows of the cabin. There, behind the barred window, he saw a face. The window glass smashed and two hands gripped the bars in useless panic. Those bars were far too strong to be ripped out by any human hand.

The man saw Ivan and screamed at him. "Get me out! I'm locked in! Don't let me burn!"

The South African accent was clear. Han was cleaning house in the worst way. Ivan stood rooted to the spot for maybe three seconds as he considered his limited options. He dropped the rifle to the ground and ran for the front door of the cabin. With an arm over his face he ran into the burning building and turned towards the stairs. He slid to a stop as he saw that the wooden staircase was burning fiercely from top to bottom. There was no way he could reach the upper corridor to open the door.

He ran back outside with his jacket already smouldering as the staircase crashed down behind him. His mind raced as he cast around for any other way to reach the trapped man. The screams from the top floor never stopped, but he had to ignore them while he thought. In front of him, down by the water's edge, he spotted an untidy coil of rope and dashed to it. He grabbed the rope bundle and ran back to the cabin, untangling it as he went. Once there, he threw an end up to the window. The desperate hand that reached through the bars missed and the rope fell to the ground.

Ivan coiled the rope and threw again and again, until Van der Merwe managed to grab it and haul it through the bars. "Don't tie it off. Pass it through and drop the end down to me."

Van der Merwe did as he was told and Ivan pulled the two ends of rope out and away from the wall of the burning building. Dropping the two ends, he ran around to the food store with the South African's wails ringing in his ears. He was back in only a few seconds with Jim and Geordie close behind. The two newcomers took one of the ropes while the big Welshman took the other. Together they heaved backwards, hoping to tear at least part of the window bar out of the wall.

A steady pull didn't work, so they tried to jerk it out by heaving on it rhythmically. The bars did not budge and Ivan was beginning to give up hope when he felt the rope being lifted behind him. He spun round to find that the Chinese labourers had arrived and without a word had picked up the rope to try and save their tormenter. They were sick, they were injured, but they were still human and they had to try.

The added weight on the rope and the extra pull began to have an effect and the bars started to give way. Then the bars bent outwards and ripped from the wall. The whole set of bars fell to the ground with a crash and the exhausted labourers fell to the ground a second later. Van der Merwe slung his leg over the bottom of the window and then dropped to the ground. It wasn't an elegant landing, but he was alive.

Jim looked around at the Chinese people scattered around him and turned to Ivan. "Nice save there. Now how about some help with shifting the food for these people? Bring that scumbag with you." He pointed at Van der Merwe. "He owes them a bit of labour."

Chapter 50

Special Agent Mason ran into Deputy Director Colton's outer office. Mrs Spelling was not there, so he summoned up his courage and knocked on the inner door. Without waiting for a response, he walked in to the lion's den.

Colton looked up from the file he was reading. "It's normal to wait for Kate to announce you before you walk in here."

"Sorry, sir. She's not there and this might be important." Mason walked over to the large desk and laid out a pair of large photographs.

"What am I seeing here?"

Mason pointed at the first print. "This one, as you can see, is infrared and we have a massive heat signature that just appeared. This is a normal visual view and you can see that there is a building on fire at the head of this L-shaped lake."

"OK, so tell me why I care."

Mason lifted a rolled-up map onto the desk and spread it out. "We care because according to this map, made only a little over three years ago, there are no buildings here. Yet if you look more closely there are seven buildings, including the one that is on fire. There are spoil heaps outside two of them and there is a spoil heap falling down the hillside at the side of the lake where we have seen a cave or an opening."

"Interesting, but where is this and again, why do I care?"

"You care, sir, because here in front of the burning building you can see a cluster of smaller heat signatures. We thought at first they might be debris from the fire, but they're not. Those are people. People who shouldn't be there."

"Where is this and how do you know the people shouldn't be there?"

"OK, so this is in Canada, inland from the bottom end of Alaska. And those people shouldn't be there because there is nothing there. This L-shaped lake is in a deep gorge in the forest. There is no logging going on there and the Canadians have no record of any settlement in that area."

"Are the Canadians involved?"

"Not yet, sir. I was waiting for your go-ahead before I tell them what's going on in their backyard."

Colton sat back in his oversized chair and held the two photographs up. He studied them carefully, then turned to the map and examined it in detail. He put his finger on the normal photograph and looked up at Mason, who stood nervously in front of the desk.

"There's a distinct trail here that seems to lead into the forest. That's not on the map either. It seems to lead down to one of those waterways that run in from the ocean."

He paused while Mason looked at the trail over the ridgeline. "All right, young man, you may have something here. Not protocol, I know, but I am sick of sitting in here while two of my agents are missing. Contact the Canadians and tell them we are coming. Ask for their assistance, and ask nicely. Then round up your sidekick, Turner, isn't it? The three of us are going to see what's going on up there. Get Kate to make any bookings you need and get it done fast. I want to be up there tomorrow morning, so if there are no commercial carriers going that way get her to book an FBI corporate aircraft."

Chapter 51

Geordie and Ivan had checked the other buildings for booby traps before allowing the labourers to take shelter in them. Inside the door of the guards' cabin they had found a small charge of plastic explosive attached to a drum of aviation fuel and rigged to explode if the door was pulled open. They defused this device and decided that this building would be the best place to house the injured, as it had beds and a wood-burning stove installed.

The exhausted Chinese labourers had been helped into the chosen cabin and had collapsed onto the beds. Within minutes all of the thirty-seven worst cases were fast asleep and Chen decided they should be left to recover. They could feed them later once they had rested a little.

Geordie worked to set up a crude field kitchen outside the accommodation ready for when he needed to cook for his guests. Ivan went to help Jim question Van der Merwe about what had happened after the prisoners escaped.

"So what happened with Han?"

Van der Merwe looked up from where he was sitting on a fallen log. "As soon as he realised the water solution into the mine had failed and the miners were loose, he went crazy. Screaming at everyone and firing out of the window. He thought you would use the floatplane to get away, so he triggered the explosives on it."

"And then what?" Jim asked.

"And then he ordered the guards to get up the hill and round all of them up. They were to be brought back down. Any who resisted were to be shot on the spot, to encourage the others."

"So why did you get locked up in my old room?"

"I made two mistakes. The first one was to advise him that we should make a run for it and take what we had before the RCMP or the Canadian Army got here."

"What was the second?"

"The second was to have the same skin colour as you two. Han decided I had been in on it from the start and had been plotting with you. I got cracked on the back of the head and woke up in the room with the barred windows. I tried the door, but couldn't bust it down, then I smelled the fire."

He looked at Ivan. "I owe you for that, man."

"I think you owe the Chinese labourers more," Ivan said. "It was them that made the difference and they knew damn fine it was you in there as well."

Van der Merwe nodded and looked down at the earth between his feet.

"So where is Han now?" Jim asked.

"I don't know, but when I saw him last he had a guard's uniform on and an AK47 across his back. I guess he was going to join the hunt for the prisoners."

"So what do you know about who Han was working with?"

"He's part of a Chinese criminal gang. Something like the Mafia, but without the compassion. The original mine was just to get the pitchblende out of here. Then we found the gold reef above it and I think he decided to go into business for himself."

"Yes, I know all that, but who are the end customers for the yellowcake?"

Van der Merwe looked up. "I had nothing to do with that. They just hired me to run the mine."

Ivan took a step forward and Van der Merwe's eyes switched to the big man. "The boss asked you 'who', not what you did or didn't do."

Van der Merwe sat up straighter and sighed. "I think it's the Iranians, I'm pretty certain. Han never told me, but there were the odd clues and a document I found on the big table one morning. They've got a ship off the coast that steams around and comes back when there is a delivery to pick up. The fishing boat hides in a creek somewhere and then comes in to get the stuff and ship it out. The plane was just for the gold and in case Han needed to make a quick getaway."

"What happened to the original aircraft Han had here?"

"Ah, now there's a story. The gang has a hierarchy and Han is not a top boss. So they sent someone in to check on what he was doing. Han guessed someone on the cargo ship had mentioned the aircraft deliveries and raised suspicions. He put a bomb on the plane before it left and triggered it remotely during the return trip when it was on final approach. That way it fell in the lake and went to the bottom."

Ivan shook his head slowly. "Charming."

"And what are the Iranians planning to do with the yellowcake?" Jim asked. "Did Han tell you that?"

The South African nodded. "He didn't say, but as I said, I found a document when he was away. They've got a hidden plant out in the mountains near Isfahan, which the Yanks don't know about. A full processing plant with centrifuges and everything. They had it hidden before the treaty was signed and the monitors know nothing about it. The treaty with the Americans is going to be bypassed and they won't know that until it's too bloody late to do anything about it. They won't dare invade a nuclear-armed Iran."

Jim looked at Ivan. "And then the whole balance of power in the region shifts."

Ivan looked thoughtful for a second. "They could blackmail just about the whole damned world, or at least everyone who needs oil from the Middle East."

Chapter 52

The dawn found Geordie working in his improvised kitchen, putting together a meal for the labourers who had collapsed into their beds last night, too tired to even think about food. Chen walked slowly across and stood watching him work.

"How are you holding up, bonny lass?"

She raised her eyes and looked at the hills around them. "Not well. I had dreams about Junjie all last night."

"It's tough when you lose one of your own. We've lost people in Iraq and Afghanistan, so we do understand."

"He has nobody to cry for him. That is sad. And to die so far from home with nobody to know about it is sadder still."

Geordie stood up with the long stirring spoon still in his hand. "We know about it and we know he died doing something important. Hundreds of people owe him their lives and they won't forget too easily. That's not a bad way to go."

Chen stood very still and her eyes dropped down to Geordie's honest face. "I think you are a good man and your friends, too. You have risked your lives for people you didn't know. You could easily have taken your friend and left here with no risk."

Geordie smiled. "That's true, we could have, but every morning when you shave you've got to be able to look yourself in the eye, in the mirror. If we had left these people we could never do that and I look terrible with a beard. Now then, how about you go and wake the folk in the shed and we'll start getting them fed and watered."

Chen nodded and walked across to the cabin and up the short set of steps. She went inside and walked from bed to bed gently wakening the people. They came awake bleary-eyed and wary, but then realised they were safe and their expressions brightened.

As they came outside they were greeted by a smiling black man with mugs of hot sweet tea. "Pretty feeble tea compared to the sort I am used to, but the British Army has been surviving on something like this for centuries."

Chen translated for them and soon there were smiles as they warmed their hands around the steaming mugs of tea. Ivan and Jim walked up as Geordie was about to start ladling out the breakfast he had prepared. They stood by and watched as the line of people shuffled by and then squatted down to eat the concoction Geordie had made for them.

Ivan put a hand on Jim's arm. "Can you hear that?"

Jim listened. At first there was nothing, then he felt rather than heard the low pounding in the air. "Helicopters?"

Ivan nodded. "I reckon so. Three, maybe four of them and coming straight at us unless I miss my guess."

Jim paused and slowly slipped the AK 47 from his shoulder. "It can't be the Chinese or they would have been using them here before now, instead of kidnapping me."

"So that leaves the Canadians. Probably military or Coast Guard, I would guess," Ivan said.

Jim thought for a moment then slung the rifle back over his shoulder. He set off down towards the stony beach, the obvious place for helicopters to land, with Geordie and Ivan close behind him. As they walked the three aircraft appeared at the end of the lake and started their landing approach. One by one they flared into a landing on the beach and Canadian soldiers boiled out and formed a skirmish line, with weapons at the ready.

Jim and Ivan slipped the weapons from their shoulders and laid them down on the ground. The three men stood calmly facing the troops with their hands well clear of their bodies and the holstered pistols that Geordie and Ivan wore. The soldiers moved quickly forward and collected the rifles from the ground before removing the two pistols from their holsters.

A young officer walked forward and stood before them. "Good morning, gentlemen. I am Captain Buchan and I would really like to know what the hell has been going on here. For a start, who are all those people behind you? And who is this rather attractive lady walking towards us?"

A voice from behind the captain answered one of his questions. "That, Captain, is FBI Special Agent Chen Pam. She works for me and somewhere here is another one of my agents, though I don't see him yet."

Chen walked up alongside Jim and looped her arm through his. "Good morning, Mr Colton. Nice to see you again. Maybe I can answer all your questions."

The Canadian Captain looked to Colton for confirmation. Colton nodded and the captain told his men to lower their arms.

Jim turned to Geordie. "Have you got enough tea on the go for all these people? Then maybe we should go and sit by the fire, for a warm, while Chen brings her boss up to date."

Jim turned and led the newcomers to the fire where the labourers were just finishing eating. Buchan took in the situation at a glance and ordered most of his men to start rendering what first aid they could for the injuries he could see. The remainder sat down on logs and boxes near the fire to listen to Chen.

"As Deputy Director Colton knows, we were sent undercover to China to try and track a people-trafficking gang operating out of Shanghai. We did that, but lost our communication equipment in the process. We ended up here with an awful lot of other Chinese people being used as slave labour to work in the mines and to process the ore. I don't know how long we would have survived had Major Wilson and his two friends not freed us. There was certainly a plan to flood the mine at some point with the workers still inside."

Colton cleared his throat. "First question, where is your partner, Junjie?"

Chen swallowed then looked at him. "He died yesterday trying to find shelter for the sick and injured."

Colton turned and looked at the labourers being treated by the Canadian soldiers. "So these are just the sick and injured? Where are the rest?"

Jim held his hand up. "I can answer that. They are walking south through the forest to try and meet up with some people of the First Nations, who, I hope, are coming the other way to help them."

"And just who the hell are you really?" Colton asked.

Jim smiled. "As Chen said, I am Jim Wilson. I work for the University of Vancouver. Until relatively recently I was a Major in the British Army and these two," he said, indicating Ivan and Geordie, "were two of my soldiers."

"So how the hell did you get involved in all this?"

"Mr Colton, I guess if we do this your way I'm going to be answering your questions for days and I'm sure the Canadian authorities will be wanting the same. We are happy to answer all of your questions, but it is vital that I get to a British Consul urgently. After that you can keep us for as many days as you like, while you sort all this out."

"I don't think you are in a position to dictate terms here, particularly with the dead bodies I have seen lying around," Colton snapped.

"Mr Colton," Chen said quietly, "without these men I think I would be dead and so would many other people. I think you might cut Jim some slack here."

Colton looked at his agent steadily and then turned to Captain Buchan. "What do you think, Captain? Can we get this man to a consulate without the risk of losing him?"

Buchan nodded. "If I send two of my men with him we can take him to the British Consul in Vancouver. Once he's finished he can be taken back to CFB Esquimalt for longer-term questioning. That's where we will be taking his two men and the rest of these people. They're going to need the base hospital by the look of them."

"All right, Chen, if you vouch for him I'll buy it. Special Agent Mason will go with you, Major, and he has a vested interest in not letting you escape."

Jim smiled at Chen. "Thank you and thank you, too, Mr Colton. You have no idea how important this is."

Colton nodded. "Now I'd like to see my other agent. Chen, can you walk with me?"

Chapter 53

Jim sat across the desk from the British Consul and explained that he needed to phone London on the secure scrambler telephone. He declined to explain why, but eventually she agreed to let him make the call. He handed her the phone number he needed and she looked at it.

"This seems familiar, Major Wilson. What phone is it?"

Jim gave her a small smile. "Downing Street. That's the number for the duty officer in Number 10."

"How the devil did you get this number?"

Mildly amused, Jim said, "The Prime Minister gave it to me during one of the classified tasks I have undertaken for him."

The Consul's mouth dropped open just a little. "Personal tasks for the Prime Minister? What were they?"

Jim sat forward and rested his elbows on the desk. "Way more classified than I can tell you, but now it's time to make that call. I promise you the PM will want to take it."

As she dialled the number she looked over the desk at Jim. "I guess you want me out of the room while you are speaking?"

Jim nodded. "Sorry to throw you out of your own office, but yes. I'm afraid this is way above your pay grade and, in truth, you really do not want to be involved."

She listened as the connection was made and the secure phone made the odd noises it usually did as it went through its routine. Then she was speaking to the duty officer.

"British Consul in Vancouver here. I have a Major Wilson, late of the Royal Engineers, here who wants to speak to the Prime Minister urgently. I'm handing you over now."

She passed the telephone handset to Jim, then stood up and left the room, closing the door firmly behind her. Jim waited until he was sure she was gone before he spoke.

"Code word is Diamond Three. Authentication Middle Wicket," Jim said.

"Just a moment, sir, I'll have to check that."

Through the phone line Jim could hear the tapping of a computer keyboard as the duty officer made his checks. "Right, sir, I have you on screen and your authentication checks out. What do you need?"

"I need to speak to the Prime Minister right now and you can tell him this is a big one."

"It would have to be a big one to use the Diamond Three code. I'll see if I can get him for you. Hang up and I will call you back."

Jim hung up the phone and walked to the window. He stood looking down at the pleasantly tree-lined Melville Street below him and waited. He had only around three minutes to wait before the secure phone trilled and he walked quickly back to the desk.

He sat in the Consul's leather desk chair and picked up the phone. "Wilson."

He heard the familiar voice from the other side of the Atlantic. "Major Wilson, I hadn't expected to hear from you again. So what trouble have you got yourself into this time and how can I help you?"

"Hello, sir. I have a little confusion to clear up with the Canadian authorities and the FBI, but I don't need your help for that, at least not yet. However, I do need to give you some information you won't like, since it may lead us into another war in the Middle East."

"Oh Lord, no. What the hell have you done?"

Jim smiled grimly to himself. "Not me this time, sir, but I have stumbled across an operation being run by a Chinese criminal gang. They are supplying a shipload of yellowcake to the Iranians secretly and the Iranians have a hidden facility that the Americans don't know about for processing it."

"Processing it for what?"

"For nuclear weapons. If that ship arrives the balance of power in the Gulf region could change dramatically and if the Americans find out that they have been led a merry dance, they may be forced to invade."

"Oh God, we don't need this with an election coming up this year. Tony Blair followed the Americans into Iraq and led us into a war for a quarter of a century. I can't let that happen. I take it you have a suggestion, Major?"

Jim paused; this was where things got really serious. "Sir, my suggestion would be twofold. One, that ship must not be allowed to unload its cargo in Iran. Two, that processing facility must be closed down before the Americans get wind of it.

And at all costs, the Americans should be kept in the dark until it's over. The President is a good man, but he would be forced to act and that could get seriously bloody."

There was a pause on the line and Jim could almost hear the Prime Minister thinking. "And how do you suggest I accomplish these two aims in secret?"

"Sorry to drop this in your lap, Prime Minister, but I'm afraid the execution is your decision."

"Bloody hell, Wilson! Sorry, Major, it's been a long day and I don't need this. But of course you are right. Now tell me how to find this damned ship and where the facility is."

Chapter 54

Phillip Morton, Prime Minister of Great Britain and Northern Ireland, sat in the apartment above Number 10 Downing Street with a glass of his favourite Glenmorangie whisky in his hand and stared at the picture above the fireplace. The portrait of Margaret Thatcher seemed to stare back at him. She had been faced with serious problems when she was in this job, but the world had become more complex since then.

He put down the lead crystal tumbler, his whisky untouched, and picked up the phone from the small table beside him.

He waited for the answer and then said, "I want the Chief of the Naval Staff in here now." He paused. "No, tomorrow morning will not do. Get him here."

He picked up his glass again and seethed. The staff in Downing Street were taking a long time to get used to his direct style. His predecessor seemed to have been far more easy-going and the staff had got used to a slower pace of life. He would have to have another word with the Cabinet Secretary. What was it the Americans called it? Kicking ass and taking names. He smiled at the recollection.

Within the hour Admiral Thomas Oliver tapped at the door to the apartment and Morton opened the door. One of the duty Civil Servants was with him, notebook in hand.

"There will be no notes of this meeting, thank you. You can go back to your cup of tea."

Damn, he would have to apologise for that rudeness tomorrow. He would have to control himself, but his nerves were wearing thin.

"Admiral, thank you for coming so quickly. Take a seat. Would you like to join me in a rather nice single malt?"

"Just a small one, thank you, Prime Minister," Oliver said as he lowered his spare frame into one of the overstuffed leather chairs.

Morton sat down opposite him and handed him the crystal tumbler of whisky. "Before we start. This meeting never took place and what we are about to do never happened. Is that clear?"

"Frankly, no, but I suppose it will become clearer as you tell me what you need, Prime Minister."

Morton contemplated the Admiral for a moment or two. "All right then. First off, do we have any submarines in the South Atlantic?"

"Yes and no. HMS *Tenacious*, a hunter killer sub, is due to be on patrol around the Falkland Islands. Or more correctly she was. Her skipper has been taken seriously ill and the boat is now heading for Ascension Island at maximum speed. Once she is within range a helicopter will meet her and take the skipper off while delivering his replacement. She will then return to her patrol area."

"Why Ascension? Why not take her into Port Stanley to make the changeover?"

"A long established matter of policy, sir. We never let the Argentineans know where our submarines are. So they never surface in Falkland

Island waters, for any reason. Plus she was on her way to the patrol area and Ascension was marginally closer."

"Got that. So where is the replacement Captain now?"

"He will be on leave at present; he is due to fly out to Ascension the day after tomorrow. Why do you ask?"

Morton took a sip of his whisky. "Because I need to give him an order personally, face to face, so there is no mistake and no confusion in his mind."

The Admiral sat back in his chair and looked across the table. "And may I know what the order is?"

"Yes, Admiral. We are going to prevent a bloody and expensive war by sinking a civilian ship in international waters."

The Admiral's eyebrows lifted just a little at this. He sipped his whisky and then set the tumbler down. He admired the way the light shone through the glass facets and coloured the amber fluid. He looked across at the Prime Minister.

"To be clear, you do know that's illegal and would get all three of us a long term in one of Her Majesty's more unpleasant prisons, don't you?"

Morton nodded slowly. "I'm fully aware of that. I'm also painfully aware that the wars in Iraq and Afghanistan have seen far too many of our young people coming home in boxes, or with life-changing injuries from a war we don't seem to know how to get out of. Not to mention the ones who have been mentally scarred and have to deal with PTSD for the rest of their lives. Sinking this ship may stop another war like that or maybe even worse."

The Admiral leaned forward and picked up his glass again. "You know this really is a very fine whisky and that, if short, was a very fine speech. We'll just have to make sure that this remains our little secret. I'll send for Commander McGee as I leave you. I suggest we both meet you here first thing in the morning, if that suits you, Prime Minister?"

Chapter 55

Commander Michael McGee of the Royal Navy put down his coffee cup very slowly and looked across the table at the Prime Minister and the Admiral. He leaned back in his chair and stroked the side of his nose with his finger as he always did when considering a problem. The two men watched him and said nothing for a minute or two.

Then he leaned forward and looked closely at the Prime Minister. "Let me see if I have understood you correctly, sir. You want me to sink a civilian ship carrying considerable quantities of radioactive material in the southern ocean. You want no warning given and you don't want me to pick up the crew. The environmental damage is of no concern to you, I take it?"

The Prime Minister looked back at the Commander steadily. "That's about the size of it, yes. The environmental damage you speak of would be dwarfed into insignificance if Iran or the US were to deploy nuclear weapons."

The Admiral cleared his throat. "Well, Commander, what do you say? Are you prepared to stop a war?"

"Admiral, I would be delighted to stop a war, obviously, but sinking a ship in the South Atlantic is serious. There is no way the crew could be rescued down there. It would be mass murder."

"Is that your only objection?"

"You mean apart from being charged with murder in ten years' time when somebody else is sitting in Downing Street?"

The Prime Minister shifted in his seat. "I think that's unlikely to happen."

"Do you really, Prime Minister? Then maybe you could explain to me why it happened to our soldiers who served in Iraq? Or maybe you could explain why it happened to our soldiers who served in Northern Ireland during the troubles, while known terrorists walk free? There is no way to guarantee this would remain a secret since my crew have to be involved in firing a weapon. The 'I was only obeying orders' defence didn't work at Nuremburg in 1945 and it wouldn't work now."

Admiral Oliver turned to the Prime Minister. "The Commander makes a good point, sir. The British government does not have a proud record of defending its servicemen and women from crooked, avaricious lawyers, or biased politicians on the make. This sort of thing did huge damage to Army morale and, in this case, would do the same for the Navy."

The Prime Minister looked at the Commander across the table, who was regarding him coolly. "Are you refusing to obey an order, Commander?"

McGee shook his head slowly and sat back in his chair. "The correct term in the Manual of Military Law is 'Refusing to obey an unlawful command', sir, and no, I am not refusing, but I am looking for some kind of safeguard for me and for my crew."

"What do you need then?"

"Written direction to carry out the attack and that should include a guarantee of immunity for the crew and commander of HMS *Tenacious*."

"Admiral, what do you think?"

"Well, sir, I think I would have to agree with Commander McGee. He could end up in a filthy prison cell for doing the right thing. At best his career would be destroyed if this became public."

"And if this becomes public, I am going to get the same sort of hate that Blair gets now. Plus, I will be criticized for issuing such an immunity letter."

"In which case, we seem to be at something of an impasse, Prime Minster," Admiral Oliver said with a deep frown. "However, there is precedent for the immunity letters. As part of the Northern Ireland peace process known terrorists were issued with them and have been kept safe from prosecution. Sadly the government of the time did not issue such letters to our own troops."

"No, unfortunately, we are not at an impasse. I may be painted into a corner by this, but I see your point, Commander, and I also know I have to stop this war. Attacking Iran would be a whole different ball game to Iraq. I cannot let this pass and then face our young people coming home in flag-draped boxes."

There was a tap at the door and one of the Downing Street staff put her head inside the room. "The Israeli Ambassador has arrived, sir. Should I ask him to wait?"

"No, Sally, thank you. I will come down and meet him now." He turned to the two naval officers. "I'll walk you two gentlemen downstairs and ask you to wait while I deal with the ambassador. You'll have your letter before you leave, Commander, but you make damned sure you keep it safe and secure."

The two officers stood and followed the Prime Minister out of the apartment and down the picture-lined staircase. At the bottom they were taken to an anteroom while the PM greeted his next visitor.

"Ambassador Malka, welcome. Would you come with me, please?" At the foot of the stairs he turned to the staff member who was following them. "That's fine, Sally. This is a personal meeting, so no need for minutes."

The two men climbed the stairs past the row of previous Prime Ministers' portraits. "Prime Minister, I don't see your picture here."

Phillip Morton stopped and turned back to the ambassador. "Oh I'm here, right at the top of the staircase by my apartment."

They carried on until they reached the savage caricature framed and hanging on the wall at the end of the distinguished row of previous politicians. "My wife, Susanne, bought the original from the newspaper that printed it and persuaded the staff to hang it here as a joke. I think it works quite well, don't you? It catches my rather large nose to perfection. However, come on in, we need to talk."

"Are we not to be joined by your lovely wife this morning?"

237

"Sadly no. My son is graduating from Hull University today and she is up there to watch the ceremony."

"I'm surprised you are not there yourself, Prime Minister."

"I wish I was, but in this job we sometimes have to do things we don't enjoy. As you are about to find out."

Morton led the Israeli into the apartment and they sat in the two brown leather Chesterfield armchairs. He pulled the thin file towards him and took a small map out of it before handing it across to the puzzled ambassador.

"I'm sorry, Prime Minister, but what is this? It seems to be a part of Iran. Why would that be of interest to me?"

"Before we go into details, Ambassador, this conversation never took place. Her Majesty's Government will strongly deny any involvement in what we are about to discuss. Our meeting was about a possible state visit by your Prime Minister. Is that agreed?"

Malka looked steadily at Morton before he spoke. "This sounds serious. I agree we spoke about a visit only. Now what are we really here for?"

"Ambassador, I have come across some information that is of vital interest to Israel, with the promises that Iran has made about the destruction of your country. That map is the closest I can come to pinpointing the threat."

"Perhaps you should tell me more?"

Chapter 56

Commander Michael McGee stood on the baking hot tarmac of the airfield on Ascension Island and contemplated the ignominious end of his career in the Royal Navy. He had agreed to carry out the mission for the Prime Minister and his immunity letter was carefully hidden away in the floor safe back at home. He was still mightily uncomfortable at the idea of leaving sailors to drown in the wide waters of the South Atlantic, so had managed to prise another concession out of the PM before he left Downing Street. Whether the Prime Minister would live up to that undertaking, or whether it was just another politician's promise would become clear later.

He looked across the airfield to the ocean. Through the heat haze he saw the Merlin helicopter lift off the aft deck of HMS *Huntingdon* and turn towards him. The aircraft flew fast and low across the sea and then across the airfield, to flare into a landing in front of him. He turned his face away from the blizzard of small stones and dust that the large rotor blades kicked off the tarmac. As he walked toward the heavy helicopter the side door slid back and a grinning crewman took his sea bag and secured it in one of the spare seats. He was still strapping himself into a seat when the helicopter lifted off and dipped its nose to accelerate across the airfield and out to sea, heading south.

He slipped on the headset that the crewman handed him and heard the pilot's voice over the noise of the three turbine engines. "Sorry to rush you like that, sir, but we have had a call from the *Tenacious* and her skipper has taken a turn for the worse. They want him in a hospital as fast as possible."

"Do we know what's wrong with him yet?"

"No, sir, but the on board medic is pretty worried by all accounts. Anyway, we'll have you out there in about ninety minutes to make the changeover. I hope you've winched down before? We can't land this beast on your new command, I'm afraid."

"One of the joys of being a submariner, Lieutenant. I'm used to it, but make it a steady drop this time, will you?"

"I'll do my best, sir."

McGee turned to the perspex side window and watched the brilliant blue waters sweeping by below them. Far calmer than the big rollers of the roaring forties further south in the Atlantic. At least he wouldn't have to worry about them as he sailed below them towards the Falkland Islands.

Despite the noise and vibration he was surprised when the crewman woke him up. He hadn't expected to doze. He looked forward through the co-pilot's windscreen to see the black hull of his new command lying on the surface of the shimmering azure sea. As they approached he could see there was a small party standing behind the conning tower waiting for them. He unfastened his seat harness and allowed the crewman to slip the winch harness around him. His sea bag was secured in the second loop of the harness so they would go down together.

As they came to a hover above the black hull, the side door was slid open and the crewman on the winch control waved him forward to the doorway. He sat on the cabin floor with his legs dangling outside in the downdraft waiting for the word to start dropping down to the submarine casing below him. The crewman tapped him on the shoulder and he pushed himself out, with his sea bag in front of him. The pilot had done a good job and he dropped gently onto the after hull of his new command. One of his sailors helped him to unhitch the harness and carried his bag forward for him.

Commander Joseph Cunningham staggered towards him leaning heavily on the arms of the sailor either side of him. He looked terrible, with almost grey skin and a vacant look in his eye. He hardly noticed McGee as they strapped him into the winch harness as gently as they could. McGee stood on the casing and watched as the winch pulled the sick man up and into the helicopter. The two ratings that had been helping stood and watched as well.

"How long has he been like that?"

"Just a couple of days, sir. It's been getting worse for about a week, though. We've been damn worried."

"Another two hours and he should be in a decent hospital. Right, you two, enough gawking. We've got an appointment down south."

McGee followed the two men along the casing and into the side hatch of the conning tower. He dropped down the ladder into the control room, glad to see that the First Lieutenant had not bothered to set up any welcoming ceremony.

His first words as he hit the deck were, "Right, Number One, let's get this show on the road. Make your course for West Falkland maximum speed. I'll see all the officers in the wardroom as soon as you can round them up."

If the First Lieutenant was surprised by this, he was professional enough not to show it. The slight vibration of acceleration hummed through the hull and settled down as the boat moved forward onto her allotted course. McGee went through to the Captain's small cabin to change into his normal seagoing uniform. His bag was already there and he wasted no time in getting unpacked.

When he reached the small wardroom all the officers except the officer of the watch were seated waiting for him. They all stood as he entered. "Good morning, gentlemen, please sit. I'm sorry to be joining you under such unpleasant circumstances and I wish it could have been a happier meeting." He looked around the assembled group. "I see a number of faces that I know and those few of you that I don't I will meet in the next day or so. I'm not going to give you the customary speech about what I expect of you. You're Joe Cunningham's crew, so I know you are already at top standard. What I will tell you is that we have been granted a training opportunity which is also designed to demonstrate our abilities and our

242

presence to the Argentinean Navy. We don't want them getting complacent."

The smiles around the group told him all he needed to know about a professional and eager crew. He dismissed them all except the First Lieutenant and the Chief Engineer.

"Right, gents, our training mission involves us finding a remote-controlled cargo ship that was on its way to be scrapped before the navy bought it and converted it for unmanned use. The exercise is to find it and sink it, simple as that. We will be using RAF and RN assets based in the Falkland Islands to find the target and once we do we will sink her, making as much noise as we can to irritate the neighbours."

The Chief Engineer cleared his throat. "Sounds an interesting exercise, sir, but why did you keep me back?"

"Very simple, Chief. We are running late and we need to get down to the target area as fast as possible. I need maximum speed all the way. Is that going to cause you any problem?"

"Not really, sir. We are just out of refit so all I need to do is to get the stokers to keep shovelling the coal as fast as they can."

McGee smiled at the joke. It was good to have a confident engineer running his nuclear reactor. "Thank you, Chief, and my compliments to your stokers."

The engineer stood and left the small wardroom. "Right, John, I need you to run a series of attack drills. We don't yet know if we will be there in time to hit her with a torpedo. If not and we are out of range we may have to use a Tomahawk."

John Fine sucked the end of his pencil before he spoke. "Sir, the Tomahawk at extreme range would not be a good option against a moving target as small as a ship."

"I'm aware of that, so, if we are late and have to fire at long range, we will be supported by the Royal Air Force from the Falklands. They will be using a laser designator on the target and that will guide the missile in."

John smiled. "That should work rather nicely. I'm quite looking forward to this."

Chapter 57

Tired and disorientated, the labourers who had been told to head south through the forest stumbled on. The small amount of food they had managed to take with them was virtually gone now and the tattered rags were doing a poor job of protecting the ones who had escaped from the heat of the mines. Some were on the verge of collapse and had to rely on the support of others who were not in a much better condition.

As the first group reached a clearing in the forest they paused and looked up to enjoy a rare bit of warmth from the sun. As they turned to trudge wearily onwards they were alarmed to see people coming towards them out of the trees at the other side of the clearing. They were just too tired to run, so stood in an abject dejection as the newcomers approached.

Leah was the first to reach them. She dropped her pack and then opened it to hand out energy bars and water. All around her the rest of her people were doing the same. As more and more of the escapers arrived they dropped to the ground and accepted the help from these people they did not know. Some cried, others just sat in silence.

One of the Chinese labourers spoke English and he was ushered to the front to speak to their benefactors. "We thought it would be the police or maybe army who came to find us."

Leah smiled at him. "No, we are the people of the First Nations. We help people in need. It's the other immigrants you need to be wary of."

"Other immigrants?"

"My people have lived here for 10,000 years. This was all our land until the Europeans arrived and stole it from us. They are the immigrants you need to worry about."

"What happens now?"

"Now we get you down to our boats and get you across the waterway to where we have shelter and proper food being prepared for you."

Chapter 58

Han stood outside the bridge on the starboard side. The vastness of the Pacific Ocean never failed to impress him. They had been sailing now for three days since they had last seen another ship. Maybe if they had been able to use the Panama Canal there would have been more to interest him, but the radiation detectors installed by the lock gates at each end were a problem. They might be able to detect the radioactivity in the partially processed pitchblende. Had it been fully processed yellowcake the radiation would have been reduced and it might have gone unnoticed. The Americans had paid for the detectors as part of their efforts to stop terrorists damaging the canal and bringing a good proportion of the world's maritime trade to a shuddering halt.

Having to go all the way around the southern tip of South America was an inconvenience, although it did take them away from the busier shipping lanes. He was not looking forward to the storms around Cape Horn, but the captain had assured him they would be no problem. If the weather looked too challenging they would take the Beagle Channel or the Drake Passage through the area of Tierra del Fuego and avoid the worst of it.

For exercise he decided to walk around the ship while the weather was comfortable. Once they got closer to the Antarctic pack ice the cold and wind would be limiting factors. Dropping down the bridge ladder, he walked slowly along the starboard deck until he reached the bow. He had started to develop the habit of standing here right at the front of the ship watching the waves as they parted to allow their passage. He found it fascinating to watch the sea life that interacted with the ship. Sometimes the dolphins would swim along with them to play in the bow wave and then, at other times, the flashing wings of the flying fish would move these strange creatures out of the way. He found it most relaxing and he was glad that the crew and his own people left him to his solitary contemplation.

Today there was nothing to see except the tumbling white water of the bow wave. He left the bow and continued his walk along the port side of the ship. He saw a small knot of his guards leaning against the rail. Happily, they saw him and cleared out of his way. They were still wary of his anger at losing the mine before the gold seam had been fully worked out. He had calmed down, now that he had counted how much gold he had amassed and stored in his cabin, but they did not need to know that.

At the stern of the ship he stood and watched the pure white wake that trailed them across the crystal blue water. Maybe he would buy a large yacht of his own after this and live his life in far more comfort. It was an amusing thought and it would have the advantage of keeping him away from his compatriots back in China.

As the sun dipped towards the horizon he walked slowly back to his cabin. It was nearly time to force down the filth that the ship's cook had the gall to call food. He found it faintly disgusting and, if there had been any alternative, he would have dumped his over the side for the seabirds.

This voyage was beginning to be tedious, though his welcome in Iran would be a triumph. He would make considerable profit from the investments he had made in the knowledge of what the Iranians were planning. They would become a major power on the world stage and he would rise with them. The thought comforted him as he entered the cramped dining room and saw that the pig slop was already being ladled out.

Chapter 59

Aasim Kraskov sat with his Special Forces section in the darkened briefing room in a military complex just outside Tel Aviv. He and his people were staring hard at the two images being projected in front of them. The first was a map of central Iran and covered the mountainous area near to Isfahan. The second was an image taken by a drone just the day before.

The briefing officer gave them a moment more and then pointed with his handheld laser at the photograph. "As you can see, there is nothing visible. The Iranians have hidden it well from the American satellites, but when I show you the infrared version ..." he clicked a button and the picture switched to the green shades of an infrared image "... you can see here that we have a heat spot. Not a big one, so again the Iranians have built well. However, we have analysed the traffic patterns in the area and big trucks go up this road that leads to nothing. We have never seen the trucks past this point and we are now sure that this is the facility for processing the uranium ore."

Aasim raised his hand. "A question. If the ship carrying the ore is being dealt with, then why do we need to attack this facility? It will be heavily guarded and if we go in we may never come out again."

He could see his men nodding in the dim light and the briefing officer smiled down at them. "A fair question. If that ship is stopped there are other sources of the ore, maybe from North Korea, and it would just mean a delay. If the facility is destroyed then it would cause Iran a major problem. With the US monitoring satellites overhead, rebuilding a facility of this type would be impossible without detection. This one must have been built before that close monitoring began. It seems the Iranians have been planning for the long term."

"And if we fail?"

"If you fail we may have to use an airstrike. That would be obvious and even if successful would cause huge problems for Israel. You need to make it look like an industrial accident to the investigators. An unfortunate occurrence that they cannot blame on us or the Americans. Shall I continue with the briefing?"

Aasim leaned back in his chair and waited. The briefing was thorough and detailed, as it always was for Israeli Special Forces missions. He made no notes, relying instead on his remarkable memory. His team would be scribbling in their notebooks, but even those would be destroyed before the mission started.

The briefing ended and the officer on the small raised platform turned up the lights. Aasim looked around at his men. Although he knew them all, they were not his usual team. They were good, every one of them, but he felt more comfortable with his own people that he had trained with again and again.

"Further questions?"

Aasim stood and looked at this team before turning back to the briefing officer. "I mean no offence to anyone in the room, but why these people? Why not my own team or one of the teams that these soldiers come from?"

There was a murmuring from around him; they had been asking themselves the same question. All would have been happier with the people they knew better than their own families.

The briefing officer looked around the room at the eight men. "Another fair question. Reaching this deep into Iran there is a real possibility that one or more of you may be captured. If so you will almost certainly be tortured. Despite your training, you will break at some point and we want to delay that as much as we can. All of you are first generation Russian Jews, so that when you are swearing and cursing under torture it will probably be in your first language. If they believe you are Russians we hope they will stop and consult higher authority before they harm the soldiers of their allies."

There was a silence in the room. It was cold, but it made sense and these soldiers of a beleaguered nation knew the risks involved in operating outside their borders. They expected no mercy if captured and would give none in return.

"If there are no further questions we will start walking through the mission in ten minutes. You will be issued your equipment later and you will practice with that in the morning. There will also be a detailed briefing from our technical experts that you will definitely need."

Chapter 60

The two Typhoon fighter jets released their brakes and powered along the runway at RAF Mount Pleasant. As they lifted off they climbed rapidly above the Falkland Islands and turned onto a south-westerly heading. Although they were going to exit the two-hundred-mile exclusion zone around the islands they would be careful to stay outside Argentine airspace.

Behind them on the ground, radar operators were scanning for any sign of response from the South American mainland, as Argentinean Air Force fighters could be expected to respond in case of an incursion into their territory.

Once settled on to their patrol path, the two aircraft moved apart to allow a wider search corridor to be monitored. This was the ninth day that these search patrols had been staged with two aircraft taking off in the morning and two in the afternoon. Despite the occasional amusement of teasing the Argentinean Air Force in their outclassed Skyhawks, the pilots were getting bored.

With both the Forward Looking Infra-Red and the electronically scanning air to surface radar sensors engaged, the two pilots scanned the frigid waters as far as Tierra del Fuego. An hour out of Mount Pleasant both aircraft identified a surface target heading towards them across the Southern Ocean, just where the signal from Ivan's satellite phone had predicted it might be, before the battery ran down.

The flight leader left his wingman at altitude to watch for any interference from unfriendly aircraft while he took his own aircraft down for a visual identification. With his cameras rolling, he passed over the cargo ship and then climbed away, making a rapid rolling turn to pass across it a second time before both aircraft turned for home.

Neither aircraft transmitted a contact report. Maintaining radio silence about their target until they landed was part of the briefing they had been given and the results of the camera pass would be available within minutes of their arrival back at base. Maybe this time it would not be a false alarm.

Behind them Han stood at the bridge window watching the two aircraft disappear into the misted distance. He was still tired from the voyage through the Drake Passage. A force seven headwind had battered the ship all the way through and the size of the waves swamping the bow of the ship had been terrifying to the Chinese gangster. Despite the reassurance from the ship's captain, he had been convinced that they would founder at any second. Now, out into the wider ocean, the sea had eased, but the ship was still pounding into large waves.

Han turned to the captain. "What were those aircraft here for?"

The captain shrugged. "It is to be expected in this area. The British do not trust the Argentineans, after the sneak invasion of the Falkland Islands back in the eighties, and the Argentineans object to the British being in control on the islands they call

'Las Malvinas'. So there is military activity all the time. We are of no concern to them, but they come and have a look anyway."

"You are sure of this?"

The captain irritated Han by shrugging again. "Why would they care about a rusty old tramp steamer like this one? As long as we stay outside their military exclusion zone they will give us no trouble."

"Do we stay outside the zone?"

The captain nodded. "I have the extent of the exclusion zone plotted into my instruments and we will pass by the southern edge. Once we are past it, we turn a little to the north and head for the Cape of Good Hope at the foot of Africa. Then across the Indian Ocean and home. Do not worry, Mr Han, the British will not bother us; we will be there on time and with our cargo intact."

Chapter 61

Lieutenant Commander Susan Platt was still puzzling over her orders as her ship, HMS *Humber*, passed through the narrows of Port Stanley Sound in the Falkland Islands. The River Class Patrol Ship turned to the east as soon as it was into Blanco Bay. She continued heading east past the Port Stanley airport until she was clear of Cape Pembroke, then she altered her course to the south-east at her maximum speed of twenty-five knots.

Thankfully the seas had calmed after the force seven gales of the day before or pounding through the waves at this speed would have been extremely uncomfortable in the small vessel. Susan read her orders again as she stood in the compact bridge, allowing her first lieutenant to control their progress. In the orders, transmitted directly from Joint Head Quarters at Northwood, she was told to proceed away from Port Stanley and to head towards the south-east corner of the two-hundred-mile exclusion zone. Once there she was to await further instructions. Radio silence was to be maintained.

It made no sense to her. Any incursion from the Argentineans would most likely come from the west, towards the South American mainland. In fact, she had been due to head out that way on a routine patrol the next day. Having to drag her crew out of the Globe Tavern, just as they were about to start celebrating the Chief's birthday, had caused considerable grumbling, especially as most of the crew had to leave their unfinished first beer behind. Still, as the crew had told her many times before, 'if you can't take a joke you shouldn't have joined'.

Two hundred and forty-three miles to the north-east, HMS *Tenacious* was powering south at her maximum speed. The engineering officer had been as good as his word and the progress since Ascension Island had been impressive. Commander McGee checked his watch for the third time, then gave the order to take the boat to a depth of ten meters below the surface. At this depth they would be able to receive the daily update from the Falkland Islands on the Very Low Frequency antenna without having to surface and give away their position.

They were in position five minutes before the transmission was due to arrive and at this depth they could just feel the effect of the waves on the hull. McGee waited, standing close behind his communications officer and his staff. The message arrived in a burst transmission that only took a second or two to be received and recorded.

"Have we got it?" McGee asked.

"Yes, sir, message received and recorded. I'll have it printed out for you in about two minutes."

McGee turned away towards his first officer. "Right, take her down, John. Maintain course and speed."

The printed message was handed to him marked for his attention alone. He took the small piece of paper and walked to his private cabin where he kept the code book that was for skippers of submarines only. He sat at the small desk and smoothed the paper out before he dialled the combination and pulled the code book out of the wall safe. The message was short and to the point. It relayed the Typhoon's sighting report and gave the course and speed of the target ship. The last line gave him some comfort about what he was going to do. It told him that HMS *Humber* was moving to the correct position.

He sighed and destroyed the message. Standing up, he put the code book back in the safe and closed the door. He spun the Manifoil Mk 4 combination lock to seal it shut. Very soon he would follow HMS *Conqueror*'s example and become only the second nuclear-powered submarine ever to sink a ship. He was not looking forward to it one little bit.

He walked aft to the navigation station and checked their position. Together with the navigator, he plotted the course and speed of the target ship and compared it to the track of his own boat. He checked his watch. His Spearfish torpedoes had a range of 48 kilometers so he should be in firing range in two hours just after the target appeared from behind East Falkland.

Chapter 62

Aasim Kraskov came awake as soon as the loadmaster touched him on the shoulder. He knew that meant they had crossed into Iranian airspace and now they would find out if their bluff would work. In a secure hangar, back in Israel, the C130 Hercules transport aircraft had been repainted into civilian colours and now they were masquerading as a SAFAIR relief flight, taking supplies to an area that had been devastated by an earthquake.

As a humanitarian flight, the Iranian air traffic control officers had given them clearance to overfly the country, but only on a very tightly controlled course. The plan was for them to have radio problems and to drift away from that planned course to the drop zone. Success depended on how quickly the controllers became alarmed and called in the air force interceptors.

Aasim stood up from his red canvas seat and walked down the narrow aisle, wakening the other seven members of his team as he went. He stopped in the rear end of the cargo bay by one of the pallets of relief supplies. He began to check his equipment. From the helmet on his head to the boots on his feet and including the folding assault rifle across his chest, everything he had was Russian military issue. Even the coins in his pocket, which he and all the others had been given back in Tel Aviv, were Russian.

The first of his men walked up behind him and started to check over the unfamiliar Russian parachute. This was to be a High Altitude Low

Opening drop, so the parachute had to work first time; there was no time for a reserve chute to deploy if there was a problem. The loadmaster walked to the start of the sloping rear cargo door and signalled the eight men to form into their two lines of four each side.

They waited as calmly as they were able. A night HALO drop was dangerous, but all of them were prepared, as much as they could be. Going down this fast from such a high altitude limited the amount of equipment they could take with them, so their supplies of extra ammunition and explosives were limited. They would have to be used sparingly.

Above the door a small red light came on and they braced themselves for the rapid exit they would need to stay together. The light began to flash dimly and Aasim whispered a quiet prayer. The door controls whined as the two large hatches in the rear of the aircraft powered open in opposite directions and they stood staring into the roaring wind and the night. The green light came on and the eight men ran at the ramp and flung themselves into the dark, each one hoping that the aircrew had delivered them to the right place. All of them adopted the free-fall position to control the drop and began to concentrate on the radio altimeters strapped to their chests. As they dropped they heard the Iranian interceptors scream past above them heading for the C130 delivery aircraft.

Aasim risked a look upwards and saw that the two fighters had their landing spotlights on, illuminating the lumbering cargo aircraft. There was nothing he could do to help them and he just hoped that his team had not been seen exiting the ramp. He checked his altimeter and then looked around. The thin sliver of the new moon gave very little light and he could only see two of his people dropping with him.

The ground below him was coming upwards at an alarming speed and, despite his intensive training, the nerves began to kick in. His altimeter pinged to warn him to be ready and he looked down again to watch the dial unwind. At the proper height he pulled the ripcord and felt the canopy deploy from the pack on his back. As it deployed the massive deceleration slammed the breath from his body. He had time for one shaky breath before he had to bend his knees and roll himself into the landing on the hard earth. He rolled and came back up on to his feet, grabbing the lines of his parachute and hauling them towards him before the black nylon canopy could be picked up by the breeze and drag him, possibly causing an injury.

With the parachute canopy collapsed and shoved roughly into the pack again, he illuminated the tiny dim light he carried. One by one his men came out of the dark and added their canopies to his to make a pile. Five, six, where was the seventh? He looked around, fearful that something had gone wrong. He was forced to smile as his last man came out of the night swearing quietly in Russian.

"What happened?"

"I dropped in a wadi. Nearly broke my bloody leg."

"OK to take a little walk now?"

"No problem."

As his men buried the parachute packs, Aasim drew the mini satellite navigation unit out of his pocket and switched it on. He waited until it had located the satellites and fixed their position. He called up the preplanned destination and waypoints and waited again while the small machine made its calculations.

"Not bad, not bad at all. If our pilots make it back we may have to buy them a beer or two. We are just eight miles from our target for tonight. We should be in our lay-up position in around about three hours. Follow me."

He could have told them to be quiet and he could have told them to keep a sharp lookout, but with the men of the Sayeret that would just have been insulting. As he walked he unfolded the stock of his AK-74S assault rifle and clicked it into place. Tomorrow night would see whether this plan had any chance of success.

Chapter 63

"Target acquired, sir."

"Range and bearing?"

"Forty-one kilometers on a bearing of one eight seven degrees. Single screw, speed approximately fifteen knots."

McGee turned back to the plot table and watched as the information he had been given was marked off. The target ship was almost exactly where it had been predicted, based on the information from the Typhoon air patrol.

"Anything else in the area?"

"Twin screws heading south-east from East Falkland at twenty-five knots."

McGee smiled to himself. The Prime Minister had kept his word. This might not be quite as bad as it could have been.

"Very well. Come to course one seven five degrees and prepare to fire."

"One seven five degrees, aye, sir," the helmsman repeated as he turned the wheel.

"Are we ready, John?"

"Torpedo loaded in number one tube and bow doors open, sir."

"Well, gentlemen, since the Ministry of Defence has bought us this nice radio-controlled target to play with it would be a shame to disappoint them. Fire one!"

The vibration of the heavy, wire-guided Spearfish torpedo leaving the tube was felt throughout the boat. "How long to impact?"

"Sixteen minutes, sir."

"Very well. Time for a coffee while we wait, I think, gentlemen," McGee said to his control room officers with a smile.

On cue, a steward brought a tray of coffee mugs to the small group around the plotting table. McGee took his and made a conscious effort to appear calm. The thought of sinking an unarmed merchant ship, without warning, did not sit well with him and the story about a moving target was pretty thin. He sipped the brew and waited.

"Eight minutes, sir."

McGee nodded. "Thank you, Number one."

They all looked towards the torpedo guidance station where the operator was controlling the weapon through the wire guidance system. "Terminal guidance sonar has acquired the target."

McGee closed his eyes and hoped that the River Class Patrol Ship from the Falklands would get there in time to pick up the crew of the doomed freighter. Then he hoped that there was nobody else in the area where the three hundred kilogram warhead would explode in just a few seconds.

Chapter 64

From their position in the small wadi, in the shadow of a large boulder, they could not see the processing plant. They could see the road that ran up the valley and they could see the trucks, which turned off that road and vanished under some form of camouflage. Whoever had hidden this facility had known his business.

The walk across the barren hills and water-scored valleys last night had been punishing, but nothing they weren't used to after training in the deserts of Israel. By dawn they had reached their layup position and mounted their own small camouflage nets, to give them a little shade and to let them observe their target.

Throughout the day they had taken turns to watch the trucks come and go, but they had not seen a single security patrol. That could only mean that they had positions under the covering camouflage and were determined not to be seen by drones or satellites. At the end of the day they had seen a military staff car leave followed by a security escort truck. That confirmed the Iranian army was involved.

Aasim felt one of the team crawl up beside him in the observation point; he rolled a little to one side to make room. "Hey, Cachi, how did it go?"

"Good. I went about a kilometer that way," he said, pointing. "There are a few wadis that run towards the facility. The second one could fit our needs. It doesn't run directly towards the plant, so we would not be seen approaching, then at the bottom there is a narrow watercourse that runs a long way down the hillside."

"Deep enough?"

"Deep enough if we crawl."

"Sounds good. Any alternatives if that one turns out to be a problem?"

Cachi eased his position and moved a sharp pebble way from his groin. "There is another one, not as good, but it might make a good exit route or a good place for a diversion if we decide to have one."

"Maybe, but I would prefer this to be silent until all hell breaks loose. With luck the demolition will be enough diversion for us to get out of there. Now get one of the others to come and relieve me and you and I can run through the plan again."

Cachi nodded and slid backwards down the slight slope that hid them from any guards in the valley. Aasim waited until he was relieved before he too slid down into the dip they were hiding in. He crawled under the camouflage sheet, grateful for the shade from the towering rock behind them.

"Has Maccus come back yet?"

"Over here Aasim, just getting some water."

Aasim waited with his second-in-command until the third man crawled over and joined them. "Well?"

"Well, my friends, let me tell you, I think all our birthdays have come at once."

"Tell me."

"Set back about four hundred meters from the cliff edge is a cooling vent. It is hidden beneath an overhanging boulder a lot like this one," Maccus said, slapping the rock they were shaded by. "Any warm air coming out will be dispersed by the shape of the rocks, so the drones and their infrared sensors won't see it."

"Is it any use to us?"

"I think it may be. The shaft is just wide enough for a man and the slope down to the facility is fairly shallow. My guess is they have used an existing underground watercourse to save some effort in the building."

"Did you go down it?"

"I did. About one hundred meters down it there is a panelled hatch that closes when the air is not blowing through it. It is held in place with a series of heavy screws in the surrounding flange. I tried them and they have not been in place long enough to get rusted in. They are now all loosened. I can have it fully opened in about fifteen minutes once I get down there again."

Aasim sat back against the boulder behind him. "So, two points of entry. The gods of war are with us, it seems. And sitting here a secondary plan has come to me if the first one does not do enough damage."

Chapter 65

Colton sighed heavily. "Major Wilson, I have lost count of the number of times I have asked you this. You told Agent Chen Pam that you thought you knew what was going on in that mining facility. Now I'll ask you again, what do you know that we don't?"

Jim looked up from the bare table to the exasperated man sitting opposite him. "And I have lost count of the number of times I have answered you. I have no idea what you are talking about."

"Are you saying that Chen is a liar?"

Jim looked to the corner of the room where the lovely dark-haired woman sat watching the interrogation. He could see from her expression that she was regretting the slip of the tongue that had nearly made her break her promise to him.

Jim sighed and leaned forward across the table. "No, I'm not saying that at all. You have to remember we were all in a heightened state of tension. She may have misheard me at some point."

The FBI Deputy Director sat back in his chair and looked up at the ceiling, then down at Jim again. "I can keep you in this room for a damned long time unless you start to cooperate."

Jim gave him a small smile. "Actually, no, you can't. This is Canada and the Canadians are being very generous in allowing you to interview me. At some point they will either have to charge me with something or let me go. Your anti-terror laws don't apply here."

Colton stood up abruptly and his chair tipped and slid back across the bare tiled floor. He looked down at Jim for a moment and then strode to the door and left the room. Chen stood quietly and walked across to the fallen chair. She stood it up and moved it back to the table where she sat down gracefully.

"Jim, I'm sorry I made a mistake and let it slip that you knew something. I have kept my promise to not pass on the details. But we have let you speak to the British Consul, so why will you not tell Colton what he needs to know?"

"Is this what they call grumpy cop then rather beautiful cop? It's a nice technique, if I was able to tell you anything, but I'm afraid you are going to have to keep your promise and maintain the line that I do not know any more than you do. In fact since you were there longer you should be the one sitting on this side of the table. You need to trust me a little longer. I swear it's worth it."

Chen looked down at her hands, then back up at Jim. "If Colton finds out I am holding out on him my career is over and I'm probably looking at jail time."

Jim paused. "Chen, I don't want to be melodramatic, but I swear to you on my daughter's life that it is important enough for you to risk that. I've got the problem being handled and I will stand up in court and tell them you knew no more than you have told Colton."

She nodded and smiled. "I said I trusted you and I will keep my promise."

****

Colton walked into the next interview room and sat down next to Special Agent Mason. Across the table Geordie sat and watched them both.

"Has he told you anything?" Colton asked.

"Nothing much, sir. Just that he and the big guy came to rescue their friend. Claims he knows nothing more."

"And you believe him?"

Mason shrugged. "Not sure either way, sir."

Colton turned to Geordie and stared at him for a moment or two. "Are you seriously telling me that Wilson did not tell you what he knows about this Chinese operation?"

"That's about the size of it. Must be a throwback to when he was an officer and I served under him. Maybe that's why he didn't tell me. What do you think?"

"I think you're a damned liar."

Geordie shrugged. "Well, you're entitled to an opinion, but I still know nothing."

Colton rocked back in his chair, then picked up the thin file in front of him. He read through it slowly then looked up at the calm black man in front of him.

"Geordie Peters. That name rings a bell somewhere. Should I know you?"

"I don't know. I suppose it depends on your hobbies. Do you watch a lot of porn?"

Colton grunted and was about to lose his temper when Mason coughed to gain his attention. "Sir, you remember the story about the British soldier who pulled that stunt with a bulldozer in Afghanistan? It was in all the papers and on the

TV news a while back. Well, that's him," he said, pointing at the now smiling Geordie.

Without another word Colton stood and left the room, struggling to keep his fiery temper under control. He strode back to the interview room where Jim Wilson waited and grabbed the door handle. The door crashed back on its hinges and Colton walked back in. Chen stood and vacated the chair by the table. As Colton sat down she calmly closed the door and returned to her seat in the corner.

"Well, it seems you didn't even tell your men what you knew. They can't answer the question either, so that leaves it down to you."

"So Ivan and Geordie don't know anything either, do they? Same as me then, isn't it? Now, Mr Colton, when do you think this exercise in futility will end?"

Colton seethed and his face turned an even deeper shade of red as he struggled to contain his temper. "I ask the questions and I'm going to ask you again, what more do you know about the purpose of that mining?"

Jim sat back in his chair and folded his arms. He was trying to think of a suitable response when there was a light tap on the door. Chen stood up and opened it to find another of Colton's agents standing there.

"Sir, there's a phone call for you and it's urgent."

"Take a message and I'll call them back."

"I don't think I can do that, sir. The call is from the White House."

"The what? Who in the White House?"

"The President's personal assistant is on the line and as soon as she gets you she will put you through to the President himself."

Colton's face paled rapidly. "Are you serious?"

"I wouldn't joke about a thing like this, sir. Could you come? They did say it was urgent."

Colton stood and walked out of the room without a word. He followed his agent into a side office where the receiver of the telephone lay on the blotter in the middle of the desk. He cleared his throat and picked it up.

"Deputy Director Colton."

"Ah, good morning, Deputy Director. I'm putting you through to President Baines now, sir."

There was a pause and then the voice, familiar through a thousand interviews and broadcasts, came on the line. "Am I speaking to Deputy Director Colton of the FBI?"

"Yes, Mr President, how can I help you?"

"Well, it seems you are holding a Major Wilson, late of the British Army, in custody. Is that correct?"

"It is, Mr President. You see, sir, he seems to know something that we need to know and he is being difficult about …"

"I'm sure he is. He is a very determined man, as I know from personal experience."

"You know him, Mr President?"

"I do, and I have to tell you that the United States owes that man, and his two soldiers, an enormous debt of gratitude for something they did for us a little while ago. So tell me, have you got his two men there as well?"

Colton was stunned. "Yes, Mr President, they're all here, but how did you know?"

"Good. Now you are going to release them right now and then you are going to use that FBI Gulfstream aircraft you borrowed to get them to Seattle. I will be landing at Boeing Field tomorrow morning in Air Force One and I want to speak to them before I get off the aircraft. Is that clear? Oh, and to answer your question, when an FBI Deputy Director suddenly leaves the country Homeland Security take notice and ask questions."

"Yes, Mr President, your instructions are clear, but officially they are in the custody of the RCMP."

"Mr Colton, I don't really care what you have to do, but make it happen and now. Oh and another thing, for the big Welshman, Ivan Thomas, tell him I'll be bringing him some of those chocolate cookies he likes so much."

Chapter 66

The bunk Han was lying on seemed to rear up and he was thrown across the cabin by the force of the blast below the ship. He struck the steel wall of the small room and slid down to the bare steel floor in a daze. The sound of screaming klaxons brought him to his senses and he realised that the room was tilting to one side. Before he could get to his feet the tilt increased and the stout bags of gold he had stored there began to slide out from under his bunk away from the wall where the door was.

He struggled to his feet and lurched rather than walked to the porthole. Through it he found he was looking down at the sea where the sea should not be. He heard screaming and shouting from on deck and then the howling klaxons stopped, leaving the ominous sound of groaning metal. He fought his way to the door and wrenched the handle down. The heavy metal plate swung towards him hard and he had to jump to one side to avoid being hit. He looked back at the gold bags sliding across the room then climbed out into the passageway and staggered along the heaving, shuddering deck to the outer door.

Smoke was billowing along the corridor causing him to cough and making it difficult to see where he was going. The outer door to the deck was swinging on its hinges as he got there. Left open by other fleeing men, no doubt. He forced his way out onto the tilting deck and looked forward. He struggled to comprehend what he was seeing. The stern of the ship was rising from the water and as he looked down he could see that the bow was rearing upwards. The ship was burning and breaking in half even as he watched.

He turned and used the safety rail to climb up the increasing slope to the stern of the ship, where he knew the two orange lifeboats were stored in their launching racks. As he reached the aft deck he could see that panicked men were scrambling into the two lifeboats and he moved as fast as he could to join them. He made it to the first boat just before the outer door was slammed and locked shut. He fought through the mass of heaving bodies to a seat and buckled himself in. The rest of the men eventually did the same and the senior man aboard from the ship's crew operated the release lever.

Nothing happened. The expected drop into the water and the violent landing didn't happen. The boat stayed firmly on its launching rack, shuddering as the ship beneath them died. Han looked through the small round window next to him. Through the thickening smoke, he could see that the other lifeboat was in the same position. The stern of the ship had reared up so much that the launch ramps were almost horizontal, so the boats could not drop free.

There was a scream of tortured metal from behind them as the ship finally broke in two. The stern fell towards the water and the two lifeboats were ejected from their ramps at high speed. The impact with the water was more violent than the boats had been designed for and two of the security harnesses ripped out of their mountings, flinging two men into the forward bulkhead where they slid to the deck, leaving trails of blood behind them, and lay still, with massive head injuries. The huge wave generated by the stern half of the ship as it fell hit the lifeboat and spun it upside down and over twice. Then the boat settled and automatically righted itself.

The men inside were bruised and battered, but most were alive and the boat was afloat. Han turned slowly round to look at the ship's officer behind him.

"Did we send a distress call?"

The man shook his head slowly. "No, there was no time. The power systems failed just after the explosion. It is not a problem. There is a distress beacon on each lifeboat and they operate as soon as we hit the water."

"How far are we from rescue?"

The officer slowly and gently rubbed his forehead to see where the bleeding was coming from. "It depends if there are any ships nearby. If not then the nearest help is on the Falkland Islands. We must just wait; there is nothing else to do."

Chapter 67

Jim, Ivan and Geordie stood in front of the Boeing Museum of Flight, flanked by armed and watchful FBI agents, and watched the pale blue and silver Boeing 747 sweep in for a graceful landing on Boeing Field, just south of Seattle. Air Force One taxied around and came to a halt with its nose pointing at the museum in the space that had been cleared for it. A convoy of black Chevrolet Suburbans with smoked-glass windows pulled up along the road between the three men and the aircraft, with the President's armoured limousine in the middle of them.

The Presidential security detail fanned out rapidly and took up position to cover the area. At each end of the road Seattle Police cruisers had blocked any approach by the public. There was a long pause as the steps were moved up to the aircraft and the forward door opened. A young woman came out and stood on the top of the aircraft stairs looking around. She saw the small group by the museum and tripped lightly down the stairs. She walked through the surrounding security detail and Geordie could not help but notice how gracefully she moved.

"Are you Major Wilson and his friends?"

"I'm Wilson."

"And I'm Geordie, bonny lass. Who might you be?"

She smiled at the handsome black man. "I'm Josie. I'm one of the President's personal assistants. Would you all follow me, please?"

She turned and walked back towards the big blue aircraft. Jim and his two companions started after her as did the FBI detail. She stopped and turned back.

"Is one of you Deputy Director Colton?"

"That's me," Colton said.

"You don't need to come with us, sir. The President will be seeing these fine gentlemen alone and the security detail has everything else covered."

Colton was about to protest, but thought better of it and allowed the four people to walk away from him. He watched them mount the stairs and vanish inside Air Force One. Inside, Josie led them to a door and knocked before opening it and ushering them in. As they entered, President Randolph Baines stood up from his desk and held his hand out.

"Welcome, gentlemen. Thank you for coming to see me. Have a seat."

The three men took the seats on the opposite side of the desk that the President had pointed to.

"Now then, since we are back in Seattle, the home of decent coffee, can I offer you one? Doesn't matter, they are on the way anyhow."

There was a knock at the door and a steward brought in the tray of coffee mugs with the Presidential seal on them. There was also a small plate of chocolate cookies.

"Ivan, help yourself to the cookies. During your adventures I guess you have been a bit deprived lately."

Ivan gave the smiling President a sheepish grin and gave in to his one and only vice. He took a bite and the smile creased his craggy face.

"Your chef hasn't forgotten how to make them, sir."

"She wouldn't dare. She was quite excited when I asked her to make a batch for her number one fan."

President Baines leaned back in his large leather chair and looked at the three men opposite him. "I think you have a story for me. Would you like to start telling it?" He looked at his watch. "I've got about an hour before my first appointment. We left early so I would have time for you three."

Jim looked at his two companions. "Shall I start?" They nodded over their coffee mugs. "Well, sir, it all started in a small café near to the cabin in British Columbia that I now live in with Megan. You remember Megan?"

"I make a point of remembering beautiful young women who help the United States as much as she did. Go on."

Jim told the story of his kidnapping and subsequent escape, then Ivan and Geordie told their parts in all that had gone on. The President was silent, absorbing it all.

"That fits with the briefing I've had, but your way of telling it is far more interesting. Now, Geordie, I've read the transcript of your interview.

Did you really ask the Deputy Director of the FBI if he watches porn?"

Geordie managed to grin and look sheepish at the same time. "Sorry, sir, I just couldn't resist it."

President Baines smiled back at him. "Well, it certainly brightened my day when I read that, but you might want to be careful of that in future. Deputy Director Colton is not a forgiving person. Anyway, Jim, tell me what happened to Mr Van der Merwe?"

"He is in RCMP custody facing a number of charges. I suspect he will be staying in Canada quite a while longer than he anticipated."

President Baines nodded. "You remember I told you I used to be a District Attorney in Seattle before I got into mainstream politics? Well, those skills don't leave you, it seems. So what are you holding back and not telling me? Maybe the same question Deputy Director Colton has been asking you for days? Time for you to come clean, Major Wilson."

Jim put his coffee mug down very carefully and looked across at the President. He knew from his previous dealings with him that this was a rare man, a scrupulously honest politician and an honourable person.

"Err, this is a little difficult, Mr President. If what I suspect goes public you may be forced into actions you might wish to avoid. Additionally, I may have to expose some actions that others would not want you to know about. I'm a little bit stuck here."

"My guess would be that you need to clear the decks before you tell me that last part of the story. Would that be correct?" Jim nodded. "So in the communications room there is a secure phone waiting for you and your Prime Minister is waiting on the other end of the line by now."

"How did you know he would be the one?"

"The FBI allowed you to go to the British consulate in Vancouver to use their secure phone. We couldn't hear what was said, obviously, but we could track where the call was placed to. So unless you have a girlfriend in Downing Street, I guess you were speaking to Phillip Morton. Josie is waiting outside to take you up there."

Jim rose and left the room to find Josie right where she should be. She walked him forward and up the staircase to the upper deck communications suite where he found the phone waiting for him.

"Well, gentlemen, while Major Wilson is having his chat would you like the ten cents tour of the aircraft? It's quite impressive. One of Boeing's finest pieces of work and built here in my home city. There's another of my people outside who will take you round while I speak to some local dignitaries."

Josie brought Jim back to the President's office and knocked on the door. Jim was surprised to find his friends not there.

"I thought it might be easier for you to tell just me your story, so I've sent the guys on a tour round the aircraft. Is that OK with you?"

"Thank you, sir. Very thoughtful. I would have had to ask them to leave the room anyway."

"And?"

"And the Prime Minster has agreed to let me brief you on what I found out and what he has done about it. He has also agreed to me telling you the reasoning behind it."

"Perfect. Go ahead."

"Firstly, sir, I don't want you to feel insulted that we didn't tell you up front. We were trying hard to stop you being painted into a corner by the actions of others. Our primary intention was to stop another war in the Middle East."

"Major, after the debacle of Iraq and Afghanistan that's a damned good intention, but now let's hear your story."

Chapter 68

Lieutenant Commander Susan Platt stood on the bridge of HMS *Humber* and waited. The engines were idling and turning the twin screws just enough to keep them head to the waves, in the position they had been ordered to. There had still been no indication of why they had been ordered to patrol here, in this quiet corner of the Falkland Islands exclusion zone.

She scanned the empty horizon again, knowing that the lookouts or the radar would have alerted her to anything heading towards them, but it was something to do as they idled the day away. The dull roar of the explosion came as a shock. The column of smoke from over the horizon a few moments later gave them a direction.

"What the hell was that?" Platt asked. to nobody in particular.

The bridge crew shrugged or shook their heads. She thought for a moment, then gave the order.

"Half ahead both. Helm, take us towards that column of smoke."

The helmsman acknowledged and turned the ship, as the screws bit into the frigid water of the South Atlantic. The ship picked up speed quickly, as she was designed to, and they ploughed towards the strange smoke at a steady twelve knots.

The lookouts scanned ahead, but whatever was generating the smoke was below the horizon and invisible to them. With radio silence in force Susan could not call for any confirmation, but the radio operator scanned for any distress calls. There was nothing at first as they drove forward to investigate.

"Skipper. Radio distress beacons activated dead ahead."

"How many?"

"Two. No voice communication."

"Very well. Helm, full ahead both. Ring for rescue stations, rig the recovery nets."

The small vessel surged ahead with all the thirty-five crew moving swiftly and effectively to their stations. In ten minutes everything was ready for a rescue, just as they had practiced a hundred times. As the vessel reached her maximum speed of twenty-five knots the masts on the superstructure of the stricken cargo ship came into view. Minutes later they could see the burning aft end of the ship. Of the bow there was no sign. It was already on its final plunge to the bottom of the ocean.

The starboard lookout whistled softly. "To quote Batman, 'Holy Shit!' What the hell could have caused that?."

Susan felt the same. "Thank you, lookout. Just reports will do fine from now on. It's a good question, though. Yeoman, raise the Falklands. Tell them what we are seeing here and give our position. Tell them we are recovering casualties and get them to put the hospital on standby."

"Skipper, two enclosed lifeboats in the water aft of the ship. Both seem to be the right way up, but not under power."

"Acknowledged. Helm, take us towards them, but stay clear of the ship. We don't want to get caught in any further explosions. I wonder what cargo she was carrying to do that."

HMS *Humber* swung wide and came in alongside the first orange lifeboat. Two crewmen leapt across onto the roof of the boat and opened the hatch. They looked inside to find the battered and injured crew. Lines were thrown from the deck of the *Humber* and secured to the cleats mounted fore and aft on the orange boat. Strong arms pulled the lifeboat alongside and the task of getting the casualties aboard began.

Some of the people in the lifeboat could make their own way out and up the rescue net on to the *Humber*'s deck. They were taken below as quickly as possible. The injured took longer and were handled as gently as possible to avoid jarring broken legs and arms. One man was dead and he was left to the last, but he, too, was handled gently and with respect. Once the lifeboat was empty one of *Humber*'s crew made a final check inside and then let loose the mooring lines before leaping back to his own ship.

The *Humber* eased forward away from the empty lifeboat that spun in her wake. The patrol ship turned and headed slowly towards the second lifeboat that was now drifting further away from the sinking freighter. As they came alongside, the same two men leapt across the gap and secured the mooring lines in the practiced ballet of rescue. As they opened the hatch Han was standing there waiting to be the first out of the carnage within.

His hair was tousled and he had a nasty gash running from his forehead down to his jawline. His arrogance was still intact and he shrugged off the helping hands as he climbed out of the orange boat and stepped across the gap onto the Royal Navy ship.

The walking wounded were helped across and the more severely wounded were lifted out on stretchers, and then passed across to the waiting hands on the *Humber*. Three men were dead inside the boat. The two who had been flung from the stern into the forward bulkhead had their skulls fractured and their necks broken. The old captain of the cargo ship sat in his seat with his mouth hanging open. The stress of the sinking had been too much for him and his heart had given up. The dead were passed across and taken around to the aft deck to await their arrival in Port Stanley.

Susan Platt walked across to the microphone stowed on the rear bulkhead of the bridge and spoke into it. "Gun crews close up. Gunnery Officer to the bridge."

The Lieutenant Gunnery Officer was there in less than two minutes. "Guns, I want those two lifeboats sunk. We can't leave them out here causing a raft of false sightings. Anyway, it will give your crews a little bit of extra target practice. How do you feel about the 30mm for one of them and the 20mm for the other?"

The Lieutenant smiled broadly. "Delighted to oblige, ma'am," he said before dashing off the bridge to brief his crews.

Susan returned to her favourite spot by the bridge windscreen to watch the firing practice just as Han walked onto the bridge. "Who is in charge here?"

The skipper turned around and looked at the newcomer. "That would be me. How can I help you?"

"It is essential I am taken ashore immediately. Why are you delaying?"

"We are about to sink these two lifeboats and then we will decide what course of action to take. I will call for a helicopter to meet us from the Falkland Islands and those with the worst injuries will be airlifted off first. If there is room you can go with them."

Han bristled with indignation. "Unacceptable. I require you to bring the helicopter for me immediately. These others can wait. I will also require passage to the mainland to be arranged for me."

Susan controlled her irritation. "I'm afraid I'm not running a travel agency and I've told you already what we are going to do."

"And I have told you that is unacceptable. I insist …"

Susan held up a hand to stop the flow of words. "Chief, will you escort this gentleman off my bridge and take him down to the medic to be checked over?"

The Chief Petty Officer grinned and took Han by the elbow. "Certainly, ma'am. Now, sir, if you would like to accompany me down to the main deck we'll get that wound dressed."

"Take your hand off me, you peasant."

"Now, sir, that's not very gentlemanly, is it?" the Chief said as he tightened his grip on Han's elbow. "You don't want to be here making a fuss when people are trying to work, now do you? Let's go and try ever so hard not to slip down those nasty steps, shall we?"

Susan smiled at her Chief. Not bad for someone whose birthday party she had ruined. She turned back to the microphone.

"Commence firing when ready."

The two guns made short work of the lifeboats and as they sank the bridge crew turned to watch the stern half of the freighter sink beneath the hungry waves. The smoke cleared rapidly in the breeze and the small amounts of debris would soon be dispersed. The skipper shrugged and gave the order to make all speed for Port Stanley.

Chapter 69

Major Arash Okhovat checked himself in the mirror before he left his office. As usual, his uniform was immaculate, with knife-edged creases in all the right places and everything that should shine was gleaming. He adjusted his cap and smoothed his moustache before pulling on his leather gloves and picking up his brown leather riding crop. As the security officer for this base he was determined that everything should be at top standard if he was ever to win his way back into a fighting regiment. Even at two o'clock in the morning there was no chance of him allowing his security staff to become slack and complacent.

He opened the door and marched out into the corridor with the riding crop slapping against his leg. It would be a useful test to see if his video surveillance team were on their toes. If he surprised them in the surveillance room they would suffer for it. He diverted away from the direct route and went to inspect one of the perimeter stations. As he reached it the man inside spun round, slammed to attention and saluted. Okhovat inspected him silently as the man stood rigid in front of him. He was pleased to find that the soldier was properly dressed and showing the required deference to an officer of his rank. He insisted on that at all times. He grunted and turned away before walking onwards along his intended route.

He walked along the elevated walkway above the rows of centrifuges. The last one had been installed and tested a week ago. All they needed now was the shipment of raw material they had been promised. Once that arrived, this would become the most important facility in Iran and he would be noticed again. He slowed his pace as he approached the door of the surveillance room. He did not want his tread on the metal walkway to alert them.

As he reached the door he gripped the handle and slammed it open. The four men inside sprang to their feet and spun around to face him. They all went rigidly to the prescribed position of attention and the Corporal in charge saluted him and reported everything correct. Okhovat paced slowly to the Corporal and inspected him from top to toe without saying a word. He moved on to the next man and then the next. After inspecting the fourth man he turned and walked behind them to inspect their uniforms from the back.

With all of them staring fixedly ahead and not watching their screens, none of them saw the shadow slip into the main computer room two floors below. Cachi slipped around the edge of the room, trying to avoid being picked up by any more surveillance cameras. The one covering the door had been unavoidable and he could not believe his luck when the alarms stayed silent. He avoided the banks of mainframe computers and moved to the back of the space before opening the door to the circuit control room.

Once inside, he checked for any other cameras and then turned on the lights. The wiring looms came out of conduits mounted in the wall and led to circuit control panels. It could have been a nightmare, but the builders had installed neat labels in Farsi on every switch and junction. Most of the Israeli Special Forces were trained and fluent in both Arabic and Farsi and this team was no different. Cachi read the labels and then found the main circuit diagram mounted on the wall. He smiled and shook his head slightly when he found the main breaker switch. This would never have been allowed in an Israeli installation, but here every circuit led to a single large switch. He checked the diagram again and it was true, every single circuit in the plant would shut down if just this one switch was disabled. Foolish – and it would help a lot.

He checked around the floor and as he expected there were pieces of discarded cables lying about in odd corners. It seemed electricians were the same the world over. He selected a piece of reasonably thick copper cable and stripped the insulation from it. Then he went back to the main circuit breaker switch and examined it carefully. This would work. A piece of copper conductor dropped across the contacts would short out the switch and would look like shoddy workmanship to any investigator. He made a silent apology to the electrician who would be blamed, and dropped the copper wire into place.

There was an almighty flash and a stench of burning as the lights flickered and went out. He opened the door to the circuit room and looked into the computer hall. The lights that had been on the front of the grey computer cabinets were gone and the small red light on top of the surveillance camera was out as well. He smiled as he lifted the small VHF radio to his lips.

"Objective One achieved. I say again, Objective One achieved."

He paused and waited for the double click that came as Aasim thumbed his transmit button twice. The rest of the team would now be on the move down the ventilation pipe that Maccus had found, and he had his next objective to reach before the security force could assemble. As he left the computer room and entered the centrifuge space he could hear confused shouting from the walkway above him. It sounded like some officer blaming everyone else for what had happened and demanding that they fix it immediately. He had served with officers like that before, until he volunteered for the Special Forces.

The crash of boots along the metal walkways meant he could walk without fearing they would hear him and the emergency lighting over the fire doors left the middle of this large space in comfortable darkness. He started to work his way along the line of centrifuges. The research team had done their work well. As he opened the small access hatch on the side of each machine he found the wiring to be exactly as they had predicted. It was the work of less than a minute to cross-connect the wires so that, when they were started, it would burn out the drive system in seconds.

Throughout the facility, in each of the large centrifuge rooms the rest of the team were carrying out the same sabotage. Each machine was left turned on so that as soon as the power was restored, the centrifuges would start and the drive system on each and every one would burn out. With just a little bit of luck the power outage would be blamed and Israeli involvement would not be suspected. Far better than planting explosives and putting the Iranians on guard should they ever need to revisit this facility.

Cachi ducked down behind the last machine as two of the security guards from the surveillance team clattered in through the door, waving flashlights, and stumbled across towards the circuit control room. He waited until they were out of sight and then walked calmly out of the centrifuge room towards the fire exit at the rear. With the circuits dead he could open the door without fear of triggering an alarm and he slipped out into the warm night air.

With his night vision goggles pulled down over his eyes he could see the rest of the team leaving the site and skirting around the sentries who had been given none of these useful devices. Relying on infrared cameras linked to a central system and a set of powerful searchlights, run through a central power system, had been a mistake that any competent security officer should have picked up and corrected.

Chapter 70

Geordie cursed under his breath as the steering wheel wrenched in his hands again. The track up to Kelly's cabin really was a bit much for the pickup truck they had hired at the airport. A Jeep or a Land Rover would have been much better, but none were available so they had to make do. The cabin heaved into view as they crested a small rise and then Geordie slid the vehicle to a stop in the clear area in front of the cabin.

Kelly's dented old red pickup was parked off to one side, so they knew she was around somewhere, unless she was out in the forest photographing wildlife. Jim was the first out of the truck and heading for the cabin to see Megan and the baby for the first time in far too long. The door opened and a black and white blur streaked towards him as Bracken ran to greet him. The dog wriggled around his legs, whimpering and barking with excitement, and then rolled onto his back to let Jim tickle his belly.

Once he felt he had greeted Jim sufficiently the dog ran to Geordie and Ivan and dashed backwards and forwards between them in an orgy of excitement. Jim stood up and watched the dog fondly for a moment and then turned towards the cabin. Megan was standing on the porch with the baby in her arms. For a second or two Jim stopped and just looked at her: she really was remarkably beautiful with dark almond eyes and her hair flowing down over her shoulders.

Geordie walked past Jim and took the baby from Megan's arms. "Hey, bonny lass, I reckon you'll need both arms to say hello to the boss, eh?" He looked down at the gurgling baby. "Hello, sweet cheeks. Remember your old Uncle Geordie?"

Megan gave Geordie a smile that would melt a lawyer's heart and ran down the steps to Jim. She flung herself into his arms and hung on tight. He gently kissed the top of her head and stroked her back.

"Are you two all right? How've you been managing up here?"

Megan brushed her hair off her face as she eased back and took Jim's hand. "Come on into the cabin. Kelly's waiting in there with her new dogs and you'll have to be introduced to them if you don't want to get bitten."

Jim and Megan walked up the steps hand in hand until they reached Geordie. Jim held his arms out and Geordie passed the baby over. He looked down at his daughter and the tears welled in his eyes for a moment as he thought of the danger she had been in. He had held it together until now, but the worry about the two most important people in his life had been intense.

They went in and sat down, after Kelly had told her two dogs that Jim was one of the good guys. Megan went into the kitchen as Ivan walked in trailed by Bracken. She reappeared with a pot of her signature strong coffee and poured them all a mug.

"By hell, I've missed your coffee," Jim told her.

She smiled. "Is that all you've missed?"

He smiled back. "We'll talk about that later. So now, have you had any troubles up here?"

Kelly looked up from tickling her dog's ears. "You could say that. Bracken saved Daniela's life when we were attacked and Megan blew a creep off my porch with a Winchester. Apart from that it's been pretty quiet, just baking and a bit of quilting like us ladies do."

Jim's mouth had dropped open a little. "We thought you would be safe up here once these two had got you away from our cabin."

Megan nodded at Kelly. "We were safe, weren't we? Three dogs and two women who know how to look after themselves. The attackers didn't know what hit them."

Jim looked at Kelly. "So I owe you again? One of these days you'll have to let me pay back."

She grinned at him. "I'll think of something one of these days. Now have you three eaten? We were just deciding what to cook."

Geordie stood up from the bench by the rough wood table. "How about you let me cook, so you lot can catch up properly? How do you fancy a proper curry?"

****

The cabin was silent as Megan finally managed to settle Daniela in her crib. The excitement had been too much for her to go to sleep easily. Jim turned back the covers as Megan walked over to the big bed and climbed in beside him. He put an arm round her shoulders and pulled her close. He kissed her gently and then more firmly as he cupped her perfect breast with his spare hand.

"Now then, we were going to discuss what else I had missed while I was away."

She smiled up at him. "Instead of telling me, why don't you just show me?"

"Now that is one of your better ideas," he said as he slid his hand across the smooth warm skin of her stomach.

He felt her hand slide up his leg and take hold of him. "My, you really have missed me, haven't you?"

Chapter 71

As the dawn broke over the rugged mountains, the Israeli Special Forces team was back in their layup position keeping over watch on the hidden facility below them. They saw the yellow panel van come barrelling up the road and then swerve under the camouflage sheets. The squeal of overtaxed brakes could be heard even up here on the hill.

Down below, the electrical repair team that had been summoned from Isfahan climbed out of the van to be met by a worried sergeant of the guard. "Every electrical system is out; even the security cameras are down. Major Okhovat is going to burst a blood vessel if you don't get them fixed before the base commander gets back here."

The electricians picked up their tools and carried them briskly into the interior of the darkened building. Their first port of call was the main circuit control room and their flashlights showed them the burned-out main breaker almost immediately. They were still staring at the half melted switch when the security officer stormed into the room behind them.

"What is the problem? Why are the lights not back on?"

The older workman tuned around and spoke in a quiet respectful voice. "It is not so simple, Honoured Major. The main switch has melted and fused the contacts. We will have to take it out and fit another one."

"Why has this happened? What has caused this?" Okhovat said, striding to the breaker that the electrician had pointed to.

The Major took one of the flashlights and examined the main breaker for himself. The half melted piece of copper across the contacts was obvious even to him.

He spun to face the electrician nearest to him. "Explain this! How has this got here?"

The electrician looked at the offending piece of metal and paled. "I cannot explain this, sir. It was not here when we installed it."

Major Okhovat felt the flush coming to his face as his temper boiled within him, and then it exploded into an uncontrollable outburst, like the ones that had got him thrown out of his regiment and sent to this backwater. The riding crop whistled in the air and struck the cringing workman across the face, ripping his cheek open and causing blood to fall across his overalls.

"This is incompetence or sabotage and you are to blame!" the security officer screamed. "If it is not fixed immediately I will have you shot before the morning is out."

The workman cradled his damaged face and stepped back. "Honoured Major, it cannot be done in so short a time. There are checks to be made before we can turn the system back on and finding a replacement and fitting it will take time."

Okhovat bristled and gripped the crop so tightly that he could feel the pain in his hand. "If you value your lives, you have one hour. No excuses. The general will be here shortly and these systems will be functional for his arrival."

With that the security officer pushed both men out of the way and stamped out of the room. He had his scapegoats, the blame would not fall to him, but now he would instil fear in his security teams. They must not be given time to think.

*****

Up on the hillside Aasim and his men were oblivious to the drama being played out inside the building they had attacked. They were in high spirits. Even for an Israeli Special Forces team this had worked remarkably well. Not a man had been seen and not a shot had been fired. If their sabotage worked then this would add to the legend of the *Sayeret*.

While he was off watch Aasim sat with his second-in-command, Cachi, and rested in the shade of the big boulder. He was distracted and worried.

Cachi nudged him. "Tell me."

"Tell you what?"

"Tell me what is making you chew your bottom lip and draw circles in the sand."

Aasim smiled. "I have been thinking that, even if every centrifuge down there is ruined, the facility will still be there and can be repaired. Then all they need to find is another source of uranium ore and the threat is back again."

"True, but our mission is complete. We will have bought some time."

"Maybe, but if we could damage the building itself then it would become visible to the American satellites and our cousins across the ocean could make sure it never works again."

Cachi nodded. "When the centrifuges blow there is a real chance they will cause a fire and then your worries go away. Is that not enough?"

Aasim paused and then shook his head. "I think I want more certainty than that. We did not use any explosive last night, so how much C4 do we have?"

*****

In the circuit room the panicking electricians worked feverishly to install the replacement breaker. They had been lucky; there was a replacement available in the store sheds. It was left over from when the installation drawings had been simplified to save time. They finished wiring it in as the hour ran out and Major Okhovat reappeared with a rifle-armed security team behind him.

"Is it done? If not, my men are here to carry out your execution."

The older, injured workman stood up from his toolbox where he had been tidying things away. "Honoured Major, the damaged breaker has been replaced, but you must let us carry out the safety checks before we turn it on again."

The security officer sneered at the cringing man before him. "Sergeant, if these men do not turn on the system in ten seconds you will take them outside and shoot them. Is that clear?"

"Yes, sir!" The sergeant turned to his firing squad. "On my command, take these men outside."

Okhovat gave a small smile as he turned back to the two terrified workmen. "Ten, nine, eight …"

The younger man took two steps to the main breaker and, gripping the lever, he slammed it closed. The lights flickered on and they heard the computers go into their start-up routines in the next room. Then they heard the ominous sound of the mass of centrifuges powering up.

"What is that? Sergeant, go and find out. Move!"

Chapter 72

The staff at the hospital in Port Stanley worked calmly and effectively, treating the casualties from the sunken cargo ship. Extra medics from RAF Mount Pleasant had been flown in to support them. Most of the injuries were from impact with solid objects like steel bulkheads or the seats in the dropped lifeboats. Two of the engineers had severe burns from where a steam pipe had ruptured and scalded them, but none of the injuries were life threatening, now that they had reached medical care.

Han had been the last to leave HMS *Humber* as he held back to speak to the skipper. All of the conscious casualties had been intensely grateful and had thanked the crew as they were carried ashore. Susan Platt expected that Han was about to do the same, since he seemed to have some authority over the crew and passengers.

"What have you done about organising a flight for me out of this dirty island?"

She was a little taken aback and not a little irritated. "Not a damned thing. As I told you, Mr Han, I am not your personal travel agent. Once you get ashore the civilian authorities will no doubt be pleased to help you. Goodbye and have a safe trip."

"Just a moment. I need the exact position of the ship when it went down. I have a cargo that needs to be recovered."

Susan suppressed a laugh. "Well, good luck with that. The average depth of the Atlantic is about 11,000 feet and the currents could have moved the ship quite a distance on her way down."

She turned away from him and opened up the log. She noted the coordinates that had been recorded during the rescue and tore off the top page of the note pad. She walked across to Han and handed him the sheet of paper.

"There you go, Mr Han. I'm sure someone will loan you a scuba tank for your little swim. I'm told sea bathing is very good for the skin, but you might want to cover up that cut on your face."

"You are insolent!"

"And you, sir, are rude and ungrateful. Now get the hell off my ship before I have you kicked off."

Three days later Han was flown out of the Falkland Islands on a Royal Air Force C130 Hercules cargo aircraft bound for Ascension Island and then on to the United Kingdom, on one of the scheduled supply runs. Those who were fit to leave hospital flew with him and were grateful to do so. Han complained bitterly that a better aircraft should have been found for him, but since the Air Force and the civilian authorities were sick of him by now, nobody listened.

The aircraft was met on arrival at RAF Brize Norton, in Oxfordshire, by two investigators from the British Maritime and Coast Guard Agency, an official from the Chinese Embassy and an agent from Lloyds of London. The crewmen and passengers were interviewed to try and establish what had caused the loss of the ship. After two days of interviews there was no clear reason established. The cargo of iron ore that the crew claimed to have been carrying would not cause an explosion and there had been no collision. The violence of the explosion could only have been caused by some form of explosives. Terrorism seemed unlikely and the four-man team agreed that the most likely cause was a drifting sea mine, but where it might have come from was impossible to tell

Once the interviews were completed, Han left the RAF base as quickly as he was able and vanished from official view. His contacts in the Chinese community in London organised the flight he needed to leave the country, and within a couple of days he was gone.

Chapter 73

The gleaming staff car with the two motorcycle outriders and the following jeep of bodyguards crested the last rise before the processing facility. The car was carrying Brigadier General Danush Hemmati to the base he commanded. He lay back in the luxurious rear seat and watched through the windscreen over his driver's shoulder. The camouflage was a marvel and he always enjoyed trying to find a flaw in it to twist the tail of that pig Okhovat.

Today he sat up abruptly. There was smoke rising from three, maybe four places and staining the clear blue sky. A fire? In his base? What the hell had that fool of a security officer done now? Hemmati sat forward and slapped the lieutenant in the passenger seat on the shoulder.

"Radio the base. Find out what the hell is going on. What has caused those columns of smoke? I need to know and if you get hold of Okhovat find out why I have not been called."

The lieutenant tried to raise the base without success, not knowing that every man had been called to fight the multiple fires in the centrifuge halls. The staff car swung up to the first gate under the camouflage and slid to a halt.

"Why have we stopped?"

The driver turned around in his seat. "The gate is shut, my General, and there is no guard there to open it."

The General pushed his door open. "Both of you with me! No wait! Lieutenant, go and bring the bodyguards forward. Driver, man the gate!"

The bodyguards were already leaping from their vehicle and double timing forward with their weapons at the ready. They pushed the security gate open and Hemmati led the way towards the main building. He paused as he came across the bodies of two workmen by the pockmarked white wall, with their tools scattered across the ground beside them. He walked forward rapidly to the fire exit door and wrenched it open.

Inside, chaos reigned. Around a third of the centrifuges were burning and the fire was spreading from them to the fabric of the building. Security men ran here and there, making ineffectual attempts to control the fire, while Major Okhovat stood in the middle of the devastation screaming confusing orders and lashing out at any man that came within range of his riding crop.

Under pressure Hemmati became cold and calm, one of the reasons he was destined for promotion in the near future. He turned to the Lieutenant who stood beside him.

"Get back to the car and get on the radio. Contact headquarters and get as many men here as they can round up. I want them here immediately. Tell them to commandeer helicopters, use trucks, anything they need. Contact the fire brigades in Isfahan and get them moving out here now. Take no excuses and get me the names of anyone who delays."

The young Lieutenant saluted and ran as fast as he was able back to the staff car by the gate. Within thirty minutes, his frantic calls for help had trucks and helicopters on the move from a range of barracks in the area. Protests from air traffic control had been silenced and orders given that nobody was to delay the influx of troops to fight the fire.

*****

The mass of confused radio signals was music to the ears of the crew flying the MI-17 helicopter. They had been prepositioned on Basrah airfield just across the Iranian border in Iraq. With the aircraft painted in the colours of the Iraqi army they had gone unnoticed as they parked within the British Special Forces compound in the corner of the air base. With the dawn they had stripped the markings off and exposed the Iranian ones beneath. Now, with the massive extra internal fuel tanks in the passenger area, they were flying at their maximum airspeed of one hundred and fifty knots towards the stricken base.

The two pilots and the air crewman were all Israeli and if this went wrong they knew they were all dead men, but their Special Forces team needed a way home and, with all the confusion, they had a good chance of flying in and out undetected. As they got closer to the processing facility they could see helicopters circling and approaching from a number of directions. They could also see that the camouflage over the base was well alight and smoke was filling the valley and causing a massive column into the sky.

They detected the radio locator beacon from their team and swooped in for a landing on the ridge above the base. Their wheels had hardly touched the ground when eight men seemed to rise up out of the earth and run towards them. The crewman slid back the side door and the eight men piled in and strapped themselves into the seats. Before the door could be shut they had lifted off again and turned back towards the nearest border.

Aasim leaned forward and gripped the crewman's arm to stop him closing the sliding door. He grinned and held up the small black detonator box. Then he pressed the button and watched as the charges they had left behind them exploded.

The massive boulder shook, and then slowly toppled forwards. It hit the top of the slope and its own momentum helped it to roll over. Gravity took control and rolled it again until the huge mass of solid rock was bouncing and rolling down the hillside, gaining speed as it went. As the helicopter turned and dipped down into a wide wadi they lost sight of the boulder, but they were confident it was on course.

Behind them, the rolling boulder flattened a hidden security post. It hurt nobody there as the guard was inside the building fighting a losing battle with the fire. Hitting the post at such speed bounced the massive rock into the air and sent it flying across the perimeter road. It landed on the roof of the facility and caved it in. It passed through the surveillance control room and wiped out every screen in there. It passed on through the metal walkways and down onto the centrifuge floor. Here it met flesh and blood. Men were crushed or ripped apart by the power of the rock monster that landed among them. It careered onwards, uncaring, and smashed through a wall into the next centrifuge hall. More men died screaming in here as well, before the boulder eventually came to rest.

The thick cloud of dust and rock fragments doused much of the fire in the first two centrifuge halls. The Lieutenant from the staff car returned to find his general sitting against a ruined centrifuge with his legs a bloody pulp. He had died with his command. He held an automatic pistol in his hand and the Lieutenant turned around to find Major Okhovat lying spreadeagled on the concrete floor with a bullet wound in his forehead. His bloodstained riding crop lay beside him. The Lieutenant kicked the leather crop across the room and returned to the radio to make his report on the accident to higher authority.

The MI-17 helicopter continued on course towards its planned destination. The Special Forces team would be dropped onto an Israeli Dolphin class submarine at the head of the Persian Gulf before the aircraft returned to Basrah airfield and resumed its earlier markings. That way there was less chance of awkward questions being raised if the eight men were seen.

Chapter 74

President Randolph Baines walked into the briefing room of the White House for his regular intelligence update. Previous presidents had found these tedious and avoided them whenever they could. Baines, on the other hand, was fascinated by the way situations developed and enjoyed them immensely.

"Good morning, gentlemen, and what exciting things do you have for me this morning?"

The briefers all stood as he entered the room flanked by his National Security Advisor. "Good morning, Mr President."

"Let's not stand on ceremony, please. I have a busy day planned for me and I would hate to be late for my meeting with the Boy Scouts of America in the Rose Garden."

"Well, sir, most of the situations are much the same as your last briefing with just a few small developments. However, we do have one interesting thing that the satellites have picked up in Iran."

Baines leaned forward and rested his elbows on the highly polished table. "Go on."

"Early this morning we detected a heat source in the mountains not far from Isfahan. You can see the position here on the map. The heat source developed and grew into what we are pretty certain is a major fire. We have seen numerous helicopters heading towards it from all over the place and there were what looked like fire trucks on the road."

The President smiled slightly to himself. "So why is a fire in Iran of interest to us?"

The briefing officer pressed his control and a new slide appeared on the large screen. "This is the image of the same area taken two days ago. As you can see, there is nothing there. So we have to ask ourselves just what is burning? We have discounted a fuel dump as there have been no secondary explosions that we might expect as the fire ignited storage tanks."

"So what do your expensive satellites and highly paid analysts tell you is there?"

"We are unable to tell at the moment, sir. Once the fire is under control and the massive cloud of smoke clears we may be able to make an educated guess."

"Anything else you can tell me about it?"

The briefer nodded and pressed his control again. He pointed to a helicopter flying along a wadi.

"This seems to be an anomaly as well. As I said, there are numerous helicopters flying to the site of the fire. Our best estimate is that they are bringing in personnel to fight the fire. You can see they are parked up here on this flat piece of ground. However, this aircraft is flying away from the area at high speed and seems to be flying very low and using the shape of the earth to hide itself."

The President nodded to himself in the darkened briefing theatre. Major Wilson had been right and now he knew more than the CIA.

"All right then. Do we have assets on the ground in that area?"

"We have agents and their contacts in Isfahan, Mr President, but not nearer."

"Not a problem. All those people who have been flown in at high speed will be talking about their adventure in the next couple of days. Get your contacts to listen to them in the coffee shops and report back. In the meantime, why don't we just ask our Iranian friends what is going on out there?"

"Sir, that would expose the fact that we have satellites watching them."

"Son, the Iranians may be many things, but they're not stupid. They know fine well that we keep an eye on them. And while we are at it, why don't we send one of the nuclear observation teams we have in the country to take a look?"

"They would probably be refused permission, sir."

"And that in itself would tell us something, don't you think?"

Chapter 75

With Daniela back in her own bed, Megan came to the big table in the main room of the cabin by the waterway. She and the three men had spent most of the day clearing up the damage the Chinese guards had done when they found her and the baby gone. The smashed windows would have to wait for a couple of days, but Ivan had fitted neat wooden panels over them to keep out the wind.

Geordie came out of the kitchen balancing five plates on the big tray he had found. He laid the tray down on the table and handed the plates around.

"There you go, Kelly, my famous cottage pie. Made to my old mum's special recipe. Well, as near as I could get, in this country."

Kelly took the offered plate. "I'm sure it's still wonderful. Most of your cooking is, even if the curry is a bit fierce."

Geordie chuckled. "I have to make it that way or these two complain they can't taste it. There you go, Ivan, and one for you, boss. Here's yours, bonny lass."

He sat down and pulled his own plate towards him, then picked up his fork. Then he paused and put the fork down again before turning to Jim.

"Boss, you remember telling me you owed me one when we were up near the mine?"

Jim swallowed and put down his own fork. "Why am I nervous? Go on then, what do you need?"

"Well, I'm going to need Megan's permission as well for this one."

Megan smiled at Jim's discomfort. "Geordie, he told me you saved his life again, so whatever you need."

Geordie nodded at her. "Well, I'm getting married again and I would like you to give the bride away, if you will?"

Jim's eyes widened. "Janet? My ex-wife? Won't she mind?"

"It's her idea. She wants there to be no friction between us."

"I can't say no then, can I?"

Geordie smiled gratefully. "And I've got Ivan lined up to be the best man."

The Welshman gave one of his rare smiles. "Sounds like typecasting to me."

"Thanks, folks. Janet will really appreciate this," Geordie said.

He turned back to his plate and picked up his fork. As he was lifting it to his mouth the door to the cabin swung open to reveal Han standing there, cradling an MP5 sub-machine gun.

"Good evening, all of you. Please don't get up or I may be forced to fire."

He walked forward into the room with the weapon pointing at the group around the table. His eyes scanned them until they came to rest on Jim.

"I do not know these two men. I assume they were the ones who helped you to wreck my mining operation? And another lovely lady that I do not know either. A shame you involved yourself with these people."

Jim drew his legs back under him ready to leap if the opportunity arose. "What do you want, Han?"

"Why to fulfil a promise of course, Major Wilson. I promised you that if you did not do what I needed, your woman and your child would suffer. I keep my promises and now as a bonus these others who helped you can die as well. You, of course, will be last, so you can watch them suffer. Do not think I did not see you get ready to jump on me and I see your black friend has slipped a knife into his sleeve. Put it down on the table."

Geordie let the knife slip out of his sleeve onto the table while keeping his eyes firmly fixed on the man with the gun. Ivan slid his hands below the table ready to tip it over if he could only get Kelly to move back from the other side.

Han smiled as he waved the barrel of the MP5 slowly back and forth. "Who should be first? Always an interesting decision to make, don't you find?"

The roar of a gunshot filled the cabin and Han staggered forward before dropping to his knees and collapsing to the floor. The sub-machine gun fell from his grasp as he rolled over onto his back and lifted his head to look towards the door.

The man who stood there holding the large revolver bowed slightly. "My apologies for disturbing your meal. I hope the blood of this creature will not stain the wooden floor. It would be a shame to spoil such an attractive cabin. Please stay seated."

He walked forward with his gun covering the people at the table. "Be still. No harm will come to you. My business is with this one only."

He stopped by Han's feet and looked down at him with dark eyes. Han coughed up blood and struggled to speak.

"Why? What is this for?"

"Han, you have failed the brotherhood. More than that, you have stolen from us and failed an important customer. The Iranians have demanded their money back since you did not deliver the uranium ore, and we must pay. We also know that you found gold and kept it for yourself. Not a brotherly act. And worst of all, you killed a colleague when it seemed your little scheme would be discovered."

Han struggled to shake his head. "No, it is not true. These are the ones who have lied and stolen from the brotherhood. They should be the ones to die."

The newcomer looked down. "Even at the end you still lie and try to shift the blame. It is unworthy of a brother:"

The standing man lowered the weapon until it pointed down at Han. Then he fired two rapid shots into the wounded man's chest and a third into his head. He put the revolver back into the holster under his left armpit and bowed slightly to the stunned group at the table.

"Again, my apologies for disturbing your meal. I am afraid I will have to leave you to deal with the remains of this creature as I need to be far from here as soon as possible. I hope you understand. The brotherhood has no quarrel with you and you will not hear from us again."

With that he turned and walked out of the door and into the night. In the bedroom the noise had woken Daniela and she began to wail.

North Of Fifty Four – Factual Content

One of the reviewers of my first book commented on the anomaly of using US spellings and terminology in a book with British heroes. My previous publishers and I debated this point and we decided that we would use US standards. I hope my readers who are more used to the Queen's English will forgive me and I hope it did not affect your enjoyment.

As with all my books I try to be as factual as possible and this one is no exception. This chapter will give you the facts I have used, so that you can make a judgement about whether my story is credible.

ARA *General Belgrano* was a light cruiser in Argentine service from 1951 until 1982. Previously named USS *Phoenix*, she saw action in the Pacific theatre of World War II before being sold by the United States Navy to Argentina. The vessel was the second to have been named after the Argentine founding father Manuel Belgrano (1770–1820). The first vessel was a 7,069-ton armored cruiser completed in 1896.

After almost 31 years of service, she was sunk on 2 May 1982 during the Falklands War by the Royal Navy submarine *Conqueror* with the loss of 323 lives. Losses from *General Belgrano* totalled just over half of Argentine military deaths in the war. She is the only ship ever to have been sunk during military operations by a nuclear-powered submarine and the second sunk in action by any type of submarine since World War II. The sinking of *General Belgrano* was highly controversial in both the United Kingdom and Argentina at the time and remains so to this day. However, the Argentine Navy has historically held the view that the sinking was a legitimate act of war, a position that was asserted by the Argentine Navy before various courts in 1995.

For further details see https://en.wikipedia.org/wiki/ARA_General_Belgrano

HMS Conqueror was a Churchill-class nuclear-powered fleet submarine that served in the Royal Navy from 1971 to 1990. Conqueror was the third and last of her class, along with HMS Churchill and HMS Courageous, each manned by 103 officers and rates. The class was named after Winston Churchill who served as the British Prime Minister and First Lord of the Admiralty The main aim of these submarines was to counter the Soviet threat by spying on the USSR nuclear submarine movements at sea and shadowing and if necessary attacking Russian ships and submarines if the Cold War ever got hot. For further details see http://www.militaryfactory.com/ships/detail.asp?ship_id=HMS-Conqueror-S48

The Beaver is a single-engine, high-wing monoplane built by De Havilland of Canada from 1947 to 1967. When production ended, 1,657 had been built and hundreds of them are still flying today. It was designed to be a reliable bush aircraft and has proven to be exactly that. Many of the variants in use in Canada today are floatplanes due to the remarkable number of lakes and waterways that can be used as landing fields. Its outstanding short take-off and landing capabilities make it ideal for hauling cargo and passengers into and out of wilderness areas usually only accessible by foot or canoe. Wheeled versions were used in other parts of the world and various militaries used these for a range of tasks for many years. The engine is a large, reliable, nine cylinder Pratt and Whitney Wasp, although later versions have been given a turbine engine.

The village of Kitsault does exist and has an interesting history. It was originally established, at the head of the Alice Arm waterway, around 1918 when mining came to the valley and a railway was also built to access the silver in the area. The town of Kitsault itself was established around 1979 as home to the miners who were working a molybdenum mine and had around 1200 residents. Around 1982 the price of molybdenum crashed and the town was evacuated. In 2004 it was bought by an Indian/American businessman who is spending an appreciable amount of money to both buy and maintain the town. It has now been closed to the public. North of Kitsault there is a lake in the mountains with an almost ninety degree bend in it. This is Bowser Lake and is not as narrow as the fictional lake I describe.

I have tried to describe the mass of coastal islands and waterways on the coast of British Columbia, to be found north of Vancouver. This area is sparsely settled and really does have very few roads. The people there are hardy and self-sufficient, as they need to be. Many of the smaller settlements are still populated to a great extent by the original inhabitants of Canada, commonly known as First Nations or First Peoples, although they often refer to themselves by their various tribal names. They do tend to have two names, one for dealing with other Canadians and then their own tribal name. Of all the Canadian provinces, British Columbia has the largest concentration of these fascinating people, many of whom make their living in the logging industry or hunting and fishing in the rich waters off this coast.

In the coastal area, near Megan and Jim's cabin, where I have set part of my story, one of the major groups of native people is the Heiltsuk. Originally there were many of these people, who have lived in the area for at least 10,000 years, although recent archaeological evidence shows they may have been there for more than 13,000 years, probably the oldest settled community in the world. In 1793 they made contact with Europeans and more importantly with the diseases the Europeans carried. The population was killed in droves by these diseases, mainly smallpox, and by 1919 the population had been reduced to about 225 individuals. Happily, the population is now recovering. Interestingly and understandably, after their huge length of time living in the area, these people believe the land is theirs and that Europeans have stolen it from them. They are famous for using their considerable woodworking skills which are evident in the construction of oceangoing canoes called 'Qatuwas'. They oppose the excessive logging and mining that they believe is doing considerable damage to the forests and poisoning the ocean. They also object to the rampant overfishing of the waters that have supported them for millennia. Go to http://www.firstnations.de/fisheries/heiltsuk.htm for more information about these first Canadians.

The Gitanyow peoples are known collectively as the Gitanyow Nation. The Gitanyow Nation comprises two Pdeek (Clans), the Lax Gibuu (Wolf) and the Lax Ganeda (Frog/Raven), organized into eight Wilp (House Group). They live in British Columbia just below the start of Alaska. In common with others of the First Nations they oppose the damage being done to the environment by excessive logging and overfishing. For more information see http://www.gitanyowchiefs.com/about/vision/

Pitchblende is the ore that is mined and then processed to eventually become uranium. It is radioactive and certainly in the early days had a dreadful effect on those mining it. It is processed into yellowcake which, if properly refined, is somewhat less radioactive and can be handled more safely, although there are still serious risks of contamination. The process produces a considerable amount of toxic waste matter, including radium and that, coupled with the sulphuric acid used in the process, can cause a significant environmental impact. The runoff from the processing operation I have described in this story would indeed kill every living thing in the affected lake and the environment would take a long time to recover. Radium was discovered by the great Marie Curie and was also what eventually killed her. Yellowcake, when further refined, becomes uranium 238, which is fissionable and can eventually become the plutonium used in nuclear weapons.

The John Browning-designed Winchester Model 1894 is the most prevalent of the Winchester repeating rifles. The Model 1894 was first chambered for the .32-40 cartridge, and later, a variety of calibers such as .25-35 WCF, .30-30. Winchester was the first company to manufacture a civilian rifle chambered for the new smokeless propellants, and although delays prevented the .30.30 cartridge from appearing on the shelves until 1895, it remained the first commercially available smokeless powder round for the North American consumer market. Though initially it was too expensive for most shooters, the Model 1894 went on to become one of the best-selling hunting rifles of all time. It has the distinction of being the first sporting rifle to sell over one million units, ultimately selling over seven million before US production was discontinued in 2006. In the early 20th century, the rifle's designation was abbreviated to "Model 94". See http://www.winchesterguns.com/ or Wikipedia for more details.

The Remington Model 700 is a series of bolt-action rifles manufactured by the Remington Arms company. The Remington 700 comes in a large number of variants, with different stocks, barrel configurations, metal finishes and calibers. Both the US Army's M24 Sniper Weapon System and US Marine Corps' M40 sniper rifles are built from the Remington Model 700 rifle. For more detail see https://www.remington.com/rifles

The M1911 pistol is considered by many gun collectors and veterans to be the greatest self-loading pistol ever made and the grandfather of the modern handgun, which despite its age, is still used alongside modern pistols today. Designed by John Moses Browning in 1910 with patent dates going as far back as 1897, the .45 caliber pistol was adopted into the US military arsenal on February 14, 1911. For more information visit (www.imfdb.org). It has been superseded by a 9mm pistol, but is still used by some Special Forces operators who value the stopping power of the larger round.

The Chinese Type 56 is a Chinese 7.62×39mm assault rifle. It is an unlicensed variant of the Soviet-designed AK-47 and AKM assault rifles. Production started in 1956 at State Factory

66, and since then it has been produced by Norinco, who continue to produce the rifle primarily for export.

The Royal Engineers wear a cap badge with the motto "Honi Soit Qui Mal Y Pense". However, the badges they wear on the lapels of their dress uniform bears the word "Ubique". This word also appears on the badges of the Royal Artillery. The Engineers insist that theirs means "Everywhere" while the Artillery one means "All Over The Place". The Quick March of the Royal Engineers is entitled "Wings" and is a fine tune. There are video clips of this on YouTube if you are interested.

Six Trafalgar Class nuclear-powered attack submarines are in service with the Royal Navy. The submarines were built by Vickers Shipbuilding and Engineering Limited (VSEL), now known as BAE Systems Submarine Solutions. Trafalgar Class submarines were preceded by the Swiftsure Class and are being succeeded by Astute Class submarines.

The first submarine in the class, HMS *Trafalgar* (S107), was commissioned in May 1983. The remaining submarines are HMS *Turbulent* (S87), commissioned in April 1984, HMS *Tireless* (S88), commissioned in October 1985, HMS *Torbay* (S90), commissioned in February 1987, HMS *Trenchant* (S91), commissioned in January 1989, HMS *Talent* (S92), commissioned in May 1990, and HMS *Triumph* (S93), commissioned in October 1991.

In December 2009, the Royal Navy decommissioned HMS *Trafalgar*, the first submarine of the Trafalgar class. The HMS *Turbulent* was scheduled for decommissioning in 2011 but has remained active and was deployed to the Falkland Islands in February 2012.

The Trafalgar- Class submarine is armed with Raytheon Tomahawk Block IV land-attack cruise missiles (TLAM). A Tomahawk missile is fired from 533mm torpedo tubes. The Tomahawk missile has a range of up to 1,600km and a maximum speed of 550mph. It is equipped with a two-way satellite data link that allows the reprogramming of the missile according to varied battle conditions. HMS *Torbay* was the first Royal Navy submarine to be fitted with the Tomahawk missile in April 2008.

The Trafalgar Class also has homing torpedoes to attack submarines and surface vessels within a 65 km range. It is equipped with five 533mm torpedo tubes that are capable of firing Spearfish torpedoes and missiles. These tubes can carry a total of 30 torpedoes and missiles. The Spearfish from BAE Systems is a wire-guided heavyweight torpedo with an active / passive terminal homing sonar. It has a range of 65km at a speed of 60kt

The Trafalgar Class is equipped with the Thales Underwater Systems 2076 Stage 4 integrated passive / active search and attack sonar suite with bow, active intercept, flank and towed array sonars. A collision-avoidance radar is also fitted on the submarine.

In February 2010, Thales UK was awarded a contract by BAE Systems to upgrade three Trafalgar Class and three Astute Class submarines with the Sonar 2076 Stage 5 system. The new system will replace the 2076 Stage 4 system. http://www.naval-technology.com/projects/trafalgarclass

HMS *Tenacious* is not one of the names used for the Trafalgar class. The last HMS *Tenacious* was a T-class destroyer during World War II. After the war she was converted to a Type 16 Frigate to make her more suitable for use during the Cold War.

The River Class patrol ships can be used for anything from fire-fighting to disaster relief operations. There are 4 in all; HMS *Tyne*, HMS *Mersey* and HMS *Severn* and HMS *Clyde*. HMS *Clyde* operates around the Falkland Islands in the South Atlantic. *Tyne*, *Mersey* and *Severn* have a crew of about 45 sailors, working at least 275 days a year at sea enforcing British and European fisheries law. They have a top speed of twenty-five knots and a range of 5500 miles. Armament includes a single mounting carrying an Oerlikon 30mm gun, designed as a ship-protection system to defend Royal Navy frigates from various short range missiles, rockets, grenades and explosives. The gun is controlled from a remote operator console elsewhere on the ship. The ship also has GAM BO 20 mm Gun short range anti-aircraft gun in a simple hand-operated mounting carrying a single Oerlikon KAA200 automatic cannon. It can fire 1000 rounds a minute and has a range of 2000m. For more information see http://www.royalnavy.mod.uk/the-equipment/ships/patrol-and-mine-hunters/patrol-boats

Eight ships of the Royal Navy have borne the name of HMS *Humber*, although none is in service at the time of writing. The first was a fire ship built in 1690 and the last was a River class minesweeper built in 1984 and subsequently sold to the Brazilian Navy.

Today, enclosed lifeboats are the preferred lifeboats fitted on modern merchant ships because of their superior protection against the elements (especially heat, cold and rough seas). Some ships have freefall lifeboats, stored on a downward sloping slipway normally on stern of vessel. These freefall lifeboats drop into the water as a holdback device is released. Such lifeboats are considerably heavier as they are strongly constructed to survive the impact with water. Freefall lifeboats are used for their capability to launch nearly instantly and high reliability in any conditions, and since 2006 are required on bulk carriers that are in danger of sinking too rapidly for conventional lifeboats to be released. Seagoing oil rigs are also customarily equipped with this type of lifeboat.

Sayeret, or reconnaissance units in the Israeli Defence Forces (IDF), specialize in intelligence gathering and surveillance. In practice, these units also specialize in commando and other special forces roles, in addition to reconnaissance (the degree of specialization varies by units and current needs).

All combat brigades in the IDF have a unit with improved weaponry and training used for reconnaissance and Special Forces missions, trained to use advanced weapons and reconnaissance technology, as well as hand-to-hand combat. For more details see https://en.wikipedia.org/wiki/Israeli_Special_Forces_Units

The AK-74 or "Kalashnikov automatic rifle model 1974" is an assault rifle developed in the early 1970s by Russian designer Mikhail Kalashnikov as the replacement for the earlier AKM (itself a refined version of the AK-47). It uses a smaller 5.45×39mm cartridge, replacing the 7.62×39mm chambering of earlier Kalashnikov-pattern weapons

The AKS-74 S is a variant of the AK-74 equipped with a side-folding metal shoulder stock, designed primarily for use with air assault infantry and developed alongside the basic AK-74.

Safair is an aviation company based at Kempton Park in South Africa. Operator of one of the world's largest fleets of civil Lockheed L-100 Hercules cargo aircraft, a version of the military C-130 Hercules air transport. It also conducts aircraft chartering; leasing and sales; contract operations and leasing services; flight crew leasing and training; aircraft maintenance and modification; aviation safety and medical training; and operations support. For more details see https://en.wikipedia.org/wiki/Safair.

The *Dolphin 2*-class are the largest submarines to have been built in Germany since World War II. The *Dolphin*-class boats are the most expensive single vehicles in the IDF. The *Dolphin*-class replaced the aging Gal-class submarines, which had served in the Israeli navy since the late 1970s. Each *Dolphin*-class submarine is capable of carrying a combined total of up to 16 torpedoes and Submarine-Launched Cruise Missiles. The cruise missiles have a range of at least 1,500 km (930 miles) and are widely believed to be equipped with a 200-kilogram (440 lbs.) nuclear warhead containing up to 6 kilograms (13 lbs.) of plutonium. If true, this would provide Israel with an offshore nuclear second strike capability

One *Dolphin* was sent to the Red Sea for exercises, briefly docking in the naval base in Eilat in June 2009, which Israeli media interpreted as a warning to Iran.

Canadian Forces Base Esquimalt (CFB Esquimalt) is Canada's Pacific Coast naval base and home port to Maritime Forces Pacific and Joint Task Force Pacific Headquarters. The base occupies approximately 41 square kilometers (10,000 acres) at the southern tip of Vancouver Island on the Strait of Juan de Fuca, in the municipality of Esquimalt, British Columbia, adjacent to the western limit of the provincial capital, Victoria.

Northwood Headquarters is a military headquarters facility of the British Armed Forces in Eastbury, Hertfordshire, England, adjacent to the London suburb of Northwood. It is home to five military command and control functions. The Commander Operations remains with the current operations staff on the Northwood site. Among Commander Operations' responsibilities are command of Commander Task Force (CTF) 311 (UK attack submarines) and CTF 345 (UK nuclear missile submarines). For more detail see https://en.wikipedia.org/wiki/Northwood_Headquarters

The FBI does have executive jets available for use by senior personnel. There is at least one Gulfstream V in use. For more detail see http://www.gao.gov/assets/660/652387.pdf

The British Consulate General in Vancouver, Canada can be found at 1111 Melville Street, Suite 800.

The Beagle Channel is a strait in the Tierra del Fuego archipelago on the extreme southern tip of South America partly in Chile and partly in Argentina. The channel separates the larger main island of Isla Grande de Tierra del Fuego from various smaller islands. The channel's eastern area forms part of the border between Chile and Argentina and the western area is entirely within Chile. The Beagle Channel, the Straits of Magellan to the north, and the open-ocean Drake Passage to the south are the three navigable passages around South America between the Pacific and Atlantic

Oceans. However, most commercial shipping uses the open-ocean Drake Passage. The channel was named after the ship HMS *Beagle* during its first hydrographic survey of the coasts of the southern part of South America which lasted from 1826 to 1830. During that expedition, under the overall command of Commander Phillip Parker King, the *Beagle's* captain Pringle Stokes committed suicide and was replaced by Captain Robert FitzRoy. The ship continued the survey in the second voyage of the *Beagle* under the command of Captain FitzRoy, who took Charles Darwin along as a self-funding supernumerary, giving him opportunities as an amateur naturalist. For more details see https://en.wikipedia.org/wiki/Beagle_Channel

Interestingly, I found out during my research that originally Jewish people in Russia did not use surnames. These were imposed by the Jewish Surname Adoption Mandate — The Czar's Edict of 1835. The edict concerning Jews, issued on May 31, 1835, by Czar Nicholas I, defined the final state of the *Jewish Pale of Settlement*, and included the following provision regarding Jewish surnames: *"Every Jew, in addition to a first name given at a profession of faith or birth, must forever retain, without alteration, a known inherited or legally adopted surname or nickname."* For further details see http://www.surnamedna.com/?articles=history-adoption-and-regulation-of-jewish-surnames-in-the-russian-empire

RAF Mount Pleasant does exist and was built in the Falkland Islands to guard against further threats from Argentina after the 1982 war. Argentinians to this day believe that the islands they call Las Malvinas rightly belong to them. The islanders disagree.

Eurofighter Typhoon is arguably the world's most advanced multi-role combat aircraft providing simultaneously deployable Air-to-Air and Air-to-Surface capabilities. It is in service with 6 customers across 20 operational units and has been ordered by two more. The aircraft has demonstrated, and continues to demonstrate, high reliability across the globe in all climates. It has been combat proven during operations in Libya and other theatres. See https://www.eurofighter.com/

The Argentinean Air Force has some extremely brave and skilful pilots, as they demonstrated during the Falklands conflict. Unfortunately for them, they are using outdated aircraft that are no match for the Typhoons of the Royal Air Force. Their problem is perhaps best illustrated by a story of an exchange that is often seen on the internet and which is probably untrue.

Argentinian Air Defence: "Unknown aircraft, you are in Argentinean airspace. Identify yourself."

Aircraft: "This is a British aircraft and I am in Falkland Island airspace."

Air Defence: "You are in Argentinian airspace. If you do not depart our airspace

immediately I will be obliged to launch interceptor aircraft."
Aircraft: "This is a Royal Air Force Typhoon. Send them up, I'll wait."
Air Defence: (Silence)

Does High Altitude Low Opening (HALO) parachuting exist? It certainly does and it is dangerous. It was developed originally by Colonel John Stapp of the USAF. Only experienced parachutists, mainly those in the Special Forces, are trained in its use as a stealthy insertion technique. Should there be any kind of failure there is little or no time for a reserve chute to deploy.

The Mil Mi-17 is a Russian helicopter in production at two factories in Kazan and Ulan-Ude. It is known as the Mi-8M series in Russian service. It is a medium twin-turbine transport helicopter. There are also armed gunship versions. Mi-17s are operated by the Afghan Air Force and 45 are operated by the Iranian Air Force. In July 2010 two Mi-17 were flown by a mixed crew of United States Air Force and Afghan Air Force personnel in a 13-hour mission that rescued 2,080 civilians from flood waters. The US was reportedly considering adding the helicopter to the US military inventory for Special Forces use in order to obscure troop movements. The US has used some Mi-8s and Mi-17s for training, and has purchased units for allies in Iraq, Afghanistan and Pakistan. Maximum speed: 280 km/h (151 knots,

174 mph) Range: 800 km (431 nautical miles, 497 mi) (with main fuel tanks). With internal ferry tanks fitted the range can be considerably longer.

I hope these facts convince you that my story is a little more than just a flight of fancy and I hope you enjoyed reading it. I also hope you will consider reading my other books which are listed in the next few pages.

This book is the seventh in the Jim Wilson series and at the moment it is intended to be the last. But Jim, Ivan and Geordie have a remarkable talent for getting into trouble so they may put their lives on the line again. Who can tell?

If you have been kind enough to read this book, or any of the others in the series, an honest review on Amazon or Kindle would be very much appreciated.

For more information about my books please visit my website.
http://www.nigelseedauthor.com/

In this story the Prime Minister mentions the problem of PTSD (Post Traumatic Stress Disorder) which is a serious issue for many ex-forces personnel. A friend of mine, Tony McNally, served in the British Army as a Royal Artillery Gunner. At 19 years old he was sent to fight in the Falklands War as a Rapier missile operator where he shot down two enemy jet aircraft. After serving in Northern Ireland he left the forces and was diagnosed with PTSD. He was told to write down his thoughts and feelings, which led to Tony writing his new book 'Still Watching Men Burn', which he found therapeutic and helpful with his PTSD. He has now published his page-turning new book of trauma poetry and a short story about World War One titled 'Screaming In Silence'. For more detail see www.tonymcnally.co.uk An example of his poetry is below

PTSD
I'm happy and sad
Compassionate and bad
Can't sleep at night
Can't do anything right
I wanna be alone
But not on my own
I'm in love but I hate
I'm a burden on the state
I'm possessed by the war
I killed what for?
I see shrinks I see docs

Remember my arctic socks
I'm disloyal cause I'm ill
Is it right to kill
I can hide in a crowd
My face a grey shroud
I cry for no reason
My country shouts treason
All the pills and the booze
Make bad memories ooze
I was 19 in June
Under a bright crystal moon
I died that day
But I'm still here to say
For the brave and the free
My award PTSD.

© Tony McNally

Photograph "Courtesy of Grupo Bernabé" of Pontevedra.

Nigel Seed

Born in Morecambe, England, into a military family, Nigel Seed grew up hearing his father's tales of adventure during the Second World War which kindled his interest in military history and storytelling. He received a patchy education, as he and his family followed service postings from one base to another. Perhaps this and the need to constantly change schools contributed to his odd ability to link unconnected facts and events to weave his stories.

Nigel later joined the Army, serving with the Royal Electrical and Mechanical Engineers in many parts of the world. Upon leaving he joined the Ministry of Defence during which time he formed strong links with overseas armed forces, including the USAF, and cooperated with them, particularly in support of the AWACS aircraft.

He is married and lives in Spain; half way up a mountain with views across orange groves to the Mediterranean. The warmer weather helps him to cope with frostbite injuries he sustained in Canada, when taking part in the rescue effort for a downed helicopter on a frozen lake.

His books are inspired by places he has been to and true events he has either experienced or heard about on his travels. He makes a point of including family jokes and stories in his books to raise a secret smile or two. Family dogs make appearances in some of his stories.

Nigel's hobbies include sailing and when sailing in Baltic he first heard the legend of the hidden U-Boat base that formed the basis of his first book (V4 Vengeance) some thirty eight years later.

The Other Books by this author

Drummer's Call

Revenge of a Lone Wolf

Simon Drummer is on loan to a bio-warfare protection unit in the USA when the terror they fear becomes real. A brilliant Arabic bio-chemist is driven to bring an end to the suffering of his countrymen. He believes that the regime that oppresses them could not exist without the support of the US government and the weapons they furnish. He needs to bring the truth to the American people in a way that will grab their attention. So begins his journey to bring brutal death and understanding to the USA. And now Simon must help to find him and stop him.

The Minstrel Boy

A Future History

Billy Murphy minds his own business and sings his songs in the pubs around Belfast. Then the IRA decides that he can be useful to them in preparing to restart the armed struggle for Irish unity. He finds himself caught up in their plots and learns the truth about the Troubles that he had never been told. But there are others who watch and take revenge for past atrocities. Billy must be careful not to come under suspicion and find his own life at risk from the terrorist killers he is working for.

The Jim Wilson Series

V4 – Vengeance

Hitler's Last Vengeance Weapons Are Going To War

Major Jim Wilson, late of the Royal Engineers, has been obliged to leave the rapidly shrinking British Army. He needs a job but they are thin on the ground even for a highly capable Army Officer. Then he is offered the chance to go to Northern Germany to search for the last great secret of World War 2, a hidden U Boat base. Once he unravels the mystery he is asked to help to spirit two submarines away from under the noses of the German government, to be the central exhibits in a Russian museum. But then the betrayal begins and a seventy year old horror unfolds.

Golden Eights

The Search For Churchill's Lost Gold Begins Again

In 1940, with the British army in disarray after the evacuation from Dunkirk, invasion seemed a very real possibility. As a precaution, the Government decided to protect the national gold reserves by sending most of the bullion to Canada on fast ships that ran the gauntlet of the U boat fleets. But a lot of gold bars and other treasures were hidden in England. In the fog of war, this treasure was lost. Now, finally, a clue has emerged that might lead to the hiding place. The Government needs the gold back if the country is not to plunge into a huge financial crisis. Major Jim Wilson has been tasked to find it. He and his small team start the search, unaware that there is a traitor watching their every move and intent on acquiring the gold, at any cost.

Two Into One

A Prime Minister Acting Strangely and World Peace in the Balance

Following his return from Washington the Prime Minister's behaviour has changed. Based on his previous relationship with the PM, Major Jim Wilson is called in to investigate. What he finds is shocking and threatens the peace of the world. But now he must find a way to put things right and there is very little time to do it. His small team sets out on a dangerous quest that takes them from the hills of Cumbria to the Cayman Islands and Dubai, but others are watching and playing for high stakes.

160 Degrees East

A fight for survival and the need to right a terrible wrong.

Major Jim Wilson and his two men are summoned at short notice to Downing Street. The US Government has a problem and they have asked for help from Wilson and his small team. Reluctantly Jim agrees, but he is unaware of the deceit and betrayal awaiting him from people he thought of as friends. From the wild hills of Wales to the frozen shores of Russia and on to the mountains of British Columbia Jim and his men have to fight to survive, to complete their mission and to right a terrible wrong.

One More Time

A Nuclear Disaster Threatened By Criminals Must Be Prevented At All Costs

Jim and Ivan have retired from the Army and are making their way in civilian life when they are summoned back to the military by the new Prime Minister. Control of two hidden nuclear weapons has failed and they have been lost. Jim must find them before havoc is wreaked upon the world by whoever now controls them. It is soon apparent the problem is far bigger than originally envisaged, and there is a race against time to stop further weapons falling into the hands of an unscrupulous arms dealer and his beautiful daughter. The search moves from Zimbabwe to Belize and on to Norway and Spain, becoming ever more urgent and dangerous as the trail is followed.

Twelve Lives

A Threat to Millions But This Time It's Personal

During a highly classified mission for the British Government, Jim Wilson and his two companions make a dangerous enemy. A contract has been put on their lives and on those of their families. Jim moves the intended victims to safety and sets about trying to have the contract cancelled. However, his efforts to save his family uncover a horrendous plot to mount a nuclear terror attack on the United States and the race is on to save millions of lives.

North of Fifty Four

A Crime Must Be Committed To Prevent A War

Jim Wilson is forced to work for a Chinese criminal gang or his wife and child will be murdered. While he is away in the north of Canada, his wife manages to contact Ivan and Geordie for help. The two friends set out to save all three of them, but then the threat to many more people emerges and things become important enough to involve governments in committing a serious crime to prevent a new war in the Middle East.

Short Stories

Backpack 19

A Lost Backpack and a World of Possibilities.

An anonymous backpack lying by the side of the road. Who picks it up and what do they find inside? There are many possibilities and lives may be changed for the better or worse. Here are just nineteen of those stories.

The Michael McGuire Trilogy

No Road to Khartoum

From the filthy back streets of Dublin to the deserts of the Sudan to fight and die for the British Empire.

Found guilty of stealing bread to feed his starving family, Michael McGuire is offered the "Queen's Hard Bargain", go to prison or join the Army. He chooses the Army and, after training in Dublin Castle, his life is changed forever as he is selected to join the 'Gordon Relief Expedition' that is being sent south of Egypt to Khartoum, in the Sudan.

The Road to Ladysmith

Only just recovered from his wounds Captain McGuire must now sail south to the confusion and error of the Boer War.

After his return from the war in the Sudan, McGuire had expected to spend time recovering with his family. It was not to be, and his regiment is called urgently to South Africa to counter the threat from the Boers. Disparaged as mere farmers the Boers were to administer a savage lesson to the British Army.

The Bloody Road

Michael McGuire has left the army, but as the First World War breaks out his country calls him again.

At the start of the war the British expand their army rapidly, but there is a shortage of experienced officers and McGuire is needed. He is sent to Gallipoli in command of an Australian battalion that suffers badly in that debacle. He stays with them when their bloody road takes them to the mud and carnage of the western front.

If you have enjoyed this book a review on Amazon.com would be very welcome.

Please visit my website at www.nigelseedauthor.com for information about upcoming books.

Printed in Great Britain
by Amazon